NIGHT OFFICE

ASSET RESOURCE MANAGEMENT

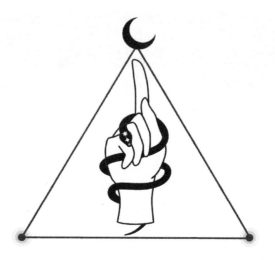

NIGHT OFFICE

THE COLD EMPTY

COMPILED BY **MARK TEPPO**

ASSET RESOURCE MANAGEMENT

APS–268/r　　　　　FOR INTERNAL USE ONLY

51325 Books

Produced in association with **51325 Books** and Firebird Creative, LLC (Clackamas, OR).

Yes, but can they whistle?

A Night Office publication
ARM – APS – 268/r
rev. 3/ ed. 10.2022

http://nightoffice.org

SCOPE: This Advanced Psychological Strategies assessment exercise is a training manual used by Night Office Asset Resource Management. The exercise requires the use of a Personal Therapeutic Construct, and all field operatives who undertake this APS must have completed at least 36 hours of PINEAL training in the creation of, management of, and dismissal of self-actualized therapeutic personalities.

This assessment tests the integrity of various nth-dimensional sub-structures of the psychological matrices, as well as the field operative's neural flexibility and capacity for mental peregrinations without suffering psychotic degradation. Results from this exercise will be tabulated into a Mental Acuity and Psychological Stability score, which will be recorded in the field operative's Life Integrity Existential Schematic.

Commentary in regards to the relative success or failure of any given end point within this exercise is provided to downplay any lasting mental, emotional, physical, or psychological scarring that may occur.

Night Office Asset Resource Management makes every effort to keep these training manuals in accordance with the most current policies, procedures, and practical applications of relevant esoteric knowledge, but Night Office Asset Resource Management offers no assurances that materials are truly up-to-date.

DISCLAIMER: This Advanced Psychologial Strategies assessment exercise is intended to faciliate a field operative's exploration of workplace hazards, mental health stressors, and other psychological complexities that may present themselves during the course of performing designated Night Office tasks. While Night Office Asset Resource Management has attempted to thoroughly address all possible scenarios and outcomes of these psychological assessment exercises, it is entirely likely that new stressors, hazards, and other causes for psychotic breaks may present themselves as a result of, or during the process of, or in the aftermath of completing this exercise. To the extend that local, state, and federal guidelines, mandates, and statutes regarding extra-terrestrial entities, cosmic fungi, and other non-Euclidean monstrosities even exist, Night Office Asset Resource Management makes no guarantee that procedures, policies, and practices as suggested in this assessment exercise make any effort whatsoever to follow these existing guidelines, mandates, and statutes. Nor does Night Office Asset Resource Management assume any responsibility—implied, implicit, or suggested to the contrary—for psychological, physical, and/or mental damage, grief, or distress a potential candidate may incur as a result of, or during the process of, or in the aftermath of completing this assessment exercise.

INSTRUCTIONS: This Night Office Asset Resource Management Advanced Psychological Strategies assessment exercise is a series of interwoven narrative choices that will test your mental acuity and psychological alacrity. At the end of each passage, the candidate will be provided with a variety of narrative options. It is up to them to decide which path is the correct path. Candidates should continue to explore the narrative branches until they reach an end point, whereupon you will be provided with a summary statement in regards to the assessment, as well as a Mental Acuity and Psychological Stability score.

Please refer to the Appendix upon completion of this assessment for further details about your MAPS score.

SHORT FORM ACKNOWLEDGMENT: The act of turning this page is a tacit acknowledgment on the part of the candidate that they are engaging in this psychological assessment exercise, and that they do so of their own volition.

Candidates further acknowledge that they are not being forced to undertake this assessment as a proxy agent for another individual, being, or entity that might have co-opted their intelligence.

Read & Understood: _____
[initials]

THE
WHITE
ROOM

START

It's a terrible cliché to wake up in a white room, but that's exactly where you are. Though to be fair, it's not really white. The privacy curtain hiding you from the rest of the room is eggshell or taupe—one of those colors. Maybe it's the lighting? The walls aren't much better. They remind you of unfinished industrial projects or temporary warehousing. *Field hospital*, a voice in your head says, which makes sense, given the privacy curtain, the unforgiving mattress, and the metal-frame of the bed. Oh, and the IV that's *drip-drip-dripping* something into your arm.

The bag is nearly empty, which means you've been here for awhile. *That's not good*, you think.

The room is cold. Not in that "someone cranked the thermostat down as a cost-cutting measure because that's how this place operates" sort of way, but in that "oh, this place hasn't seen the sun in a long time, and you will never get warm again" sort of way.

"Hello?" you call out.

There is no answer.

You've been here too long, the voice in your head says.

You struggle to remember what happened. *Butterflies . . . ?*

You're on your own, the voice snaps. *Ground yourself. Start with what you know.*

Right. Start with this room. This empty, boring room. That plastic curtain. These walls . . .

No, no. Something more concrete. The blankets. Yes, start with the blankets. Simple sensory data.

They're nice and heavy, these blankets. Whoever runs this place didn't skimp there, at least. You lift the blanket and check that you've got arms and legs. *Yes, two of each. Good.*

There's a bandage around your left arm. Something happened? *Yes, something happened*. Nothing else, though. No signs of staples or stitches. No burn marks or sigil markings (which would be bad news). Bruises on your thighs and on the inside of your arms, which isn't any worse than what you come home with after a serious night of sparring at the gym.

You check your head. Nothing feels out of place. No extra holes. You've got all your hair; your head hasn't been shaved in some strange esoteric pattern. Your mouth is dry, but that's no surprise, really. You have all your teeth.

There's no clear physical reason why you're in this bed. The injury to your forearm isn't that bad.

Mental check, the voice suggests. *Do you know who you are?*

Night Office field operative. Closer. You are part of a standard response team that was sent . . . where were you sent? It comes to you after a moment. *Ah, yes, Antarctica.* You were sent to investigate a non-responsive research station. You came with a guy named Argot and a guy named Sagalico. You're the second team, after . . .

What were their names? You just had them a minute ago. Bleeker? No, Brinkmann. That's right. Brinkmann, Peele, and Gull. They were the first team. Your team was supposed to finish whatever . . .

And that's when you realize why you're in the bed. You don't remember the mission parameters beyond the simplest facts. In fact, you don't remember anything about what happened after you got to the station. It's all

(a white rabbit in a snowstorm)

a blank.

What was that? For a moment, you felt like you were someone else, that you were *somewhere* else. It was a fleeting sensation, like someone whispering in your head, and when you heard their words, you remembered a different life. A different reality. A dream, but not a dream . . .

Well, whatever it is or was, at the very least, you've got short-term amnesia, which is totally an occupational hazard. The brain tries to forget things all the time. Usually it is terrible,

terrible things that no one should have to see the first time, much less remember later. You had a couple of sessions about this sort of thing during Orientation & Inoculation—the Night Office tries to give you some tools before it sends you out to fight monstrosities from non-Euclidean dimensions. These sessions taught you how to craft an imaginary friend, someone who could act as a therapist and as a mental anchor for when you're deep in the mind-bending muck of a mission.

That's the voice you hear in your head, in fact. Your imaginary pal is droning on right now, pretending to be a tenured psychology professor: *It's not that the human brain can't process the enormity of cosmic indifference; it's that a very tiny part of the brain thinks it is a special snowflake. This tiny blip of ego gets worked up when confronted with the rather vast scale of the universe.*

This sort of ad hoc therapy cuts down on the need for external psychological assistance. It's one thing to train people to fight unspeakable monsters and tentacled space jellies. It's another to train brain doctors to help those traumatized by their jobs. In this instance, head shrinking someone requires empathy and relevant experience, and if you've got that, you're more useful in the field than behind a desk.

At least, that's the argument Expenditures, Accounts & Recovery uses. *Budgets should be squeezed*, they like to say. *Don't make us squeeze too hard.*

So, yeah, take your licks, try not to lose your mind, and spend your discretionary income on alcohol to kill the brain cells where horrible memories are stored. Ah, short term memory purges.

Though, there are times—like now—when you wish you weren't so well trained at compartmentalization and purging.

Anyway, you've done a mental and physical situation report. Some good news; some bad news. Might as well figure out what to do next before your bladder wakes up. That bag of saline went somewhere . . .

You can throw off the covers, find some socks, and get on with things. Hopefully, contextual clues will bring back what's been locked away before, you know, you do something stupid.
Go to 1.

Or, you can be a little more cautious and stay in bed awhile. Muster some enthusiasm to rummage around the memory bins. But not too long. You don't want to tip over a container of really old memories.
Go to 2.

THE
MISSION

1

It's time for a reality check. Everything is a bit fuzzy (more on that in a second), but you know two things: you are a Closer for the Night Office, and your job is to stop all the eldritch horrors intent on enslaving the human race. Those two principles are enough; the rest starts coming back.

You're in the Antarctic. Your team came in to deal with . . . *something* . . . at an old research station retrofitted and upgraded by a company called Endoluvion. It was a Russian station once, wasn't it? Doesn't matter. Endoluvion renamed it MacReady Station. Some kind of homage or something. Little details like this are still slippery.

Anway, the station has modern amenities: LED TVs, an intra-station wireless network, and micro-fridges which are great for storing contraband alcohol. Why? Because the winters are really fucking long down here at the bottom of the world, and yes, drinking yourself to death is frowned upon, but a tipple or three can make those endless games of cribbage a little more bearable.

The station went dark during the coldest month, which wasn't unusual, as the storms that terrorize the plateau can play havoc with radio signals. However, when contact was restored, McMurdo didn't receive an "A-OK" from the Endoluvion team. The radio jockey picked up a garbled signal: childlike voices, repeating nursery rhymes in several different languages (one of which was supposedly extinct); ritual chanting; and some verbal glossalalia that got the wonks in Labyrinthian Observation & Byzantine Elucidation all worked up. The advisory from LOBE was brief: *Get a team down there ASAP.*

Asset Resource Management's response was surprising: they tasked two teams. They never send two teams.

You, an Opener named Argot, and a Guide named Sagalico were the second team. The first team was Brinkmann, Peele, and Gull. You were nearly twenty-four hours behind them; they were already on the ground at MacReady while your plane was still getting fueled up at O'Hare. Somewhere during the leg from Sao Paulo to Antarctica, the first team missed their check-in. Your mission parameters changed. You weren't doing a L & L—a Look & Listen—anymore, you were doing a Clear & Clense. *Shut it down*, the message from the home office read. *Seal the place forever.*

All eyes on you now. Close it.

You recall a bumpy landing, a sky burning with stars, and weather so cold it made the metal wings of the plane creak and pop. The three of you made it into the station and then—

That's where things get weird in your head. You were on a tight time-table. Get in, sweep the place, recover the other team (if possible), and get the hell out. You had a three hour window before your plane had to leave, but . . . well, you missed that window.

Instead of clearing and clensing, you ended up in a medical infirmary bed somewhere in Ice Station Despair—that's what Sagalico called it, didn't he?—and it's really, really quiet.

Where is everyone? Why are you all alone? What happened to the others?

So many questions. Your memory is a mess. It's like someone took the highlight reel from the last few days and cut it up into a thousand little strips of film. It's going to take some effort to piece it all back together.

First things first, though. How mobile are you? What happened to your arm? Are there any other injuries you need to address? Is the rest of your team still alive? Is the obelisk still in the lab—

What obelisk?

Fuck. There are holes in your memory. Not good.

Brinkmann. Brinkmann did something.

You grasp at that faint thought. Yes, Brinkmann. He was the other team's Opener. What did Brinkmann do?

You've been around long enough to know that Asset Resource Management gives the field team a great deal of lattitude. It doesn't really matter how you keep the Old Ones from erupting into this plane of existence. It only matters that you do.

Though, it'd be nice if Openers didn't interpret this blind eye from management as permission to be total assholes, but that's another story for another time. Maybe later.

But Brinkmann. What about Brinkmann? He probably poked something he shouldn't have. It likely ate him, along with a bunch of other poeple. The rest of his team? Well, it doesn't really matter. Your job is to Cleanse and Clear. Any and all obstacles. And you can't do that from an infirmary bed.

Time to get moving.

Pants would be a good start. Modern amenities notwithstanding, it's fucking cold in this station. And your kit. You should find your kit too. You'll need

(the knife)

your discipline stick.

Yeah, a part of you is still screaming about what happened before, isn't it? Things have definitely gone sideways. But there's no time to fuss about it. You'd getter get moving.

Go to 18.

Hang on a second. Why are you in this hospital bed? Why are you hearing voices in your head? Maybe you shouldn't go charging off without a little more thought on how you got here.

Go to 34.

2

SIX WEEKS EARLIER . . .

Hang on. That's excessive. Let's not go that far back.
Go to 3.

Seriously. That's going to take, like, forever. What about your bladder? What if someone is waiting for you on the other side of that privacy curtain with a knife, or a blowtorch, or a . . . a ham sandwich?

What? *A ham sandwich?* What the hell is that?

Oh, right. There was that conmmendation a year ago for . . . what was it? "Optimistic caution while confronting primordial darkness."

Management speak for: "You know, maybe we should think about this a bit before we go charging in . . ."

Fine. Let's "*ham sandwich*" this up for a bit.
Go to 5.

3

Statistically speaking, a Night Office field operative is going to lose their mind in the first three months of deployment. The grind is relentless, and it's easy to muck up a sigil when you've haven't slept for a week. Or stare too long into the Abyss. It can look so ... restful, can't it? And it's been so long since you've had a proper rest.

Anway, if you last a year, Asset Resource Management will—grudgingly—make a note in your Life Integrity Experience Schematic. Everyone calls is a "WK" marker—"Worth Keeping." On your second anniversary, you get another maker and you become eligible for special assignments.

Most field operatives remain part of the core trinity of the Asset Resources Management field deployment pool—that interlocking triumvirate of Opener + Closer + Guide. Special assignments—"out of town" jobs—are mythical unicorns. Rumor has it that if you surive one of these assignments, you get your own office. Somewhere above the thirteenth floor.

Field operatives are a cynical bunch, however, which is totally a job requirement, by the way. They think "out of town" means "dying in a horrible way that doesn't leave enough body parts behind to bother shipping them back home."

Aunt Clarice always said you shouldn't be so dour. *Think positively and the world will be positive in return*, she used to say. Boy, she didn't want to hear that parroted back at her when cancer moved into her spinal column, did she? Near the end, though, she did manage to find that joy again, Well, she was doped out of her mind most of the time, so it's not entirely the same thing, but it sort of is, you know?

Anyway, the point here is: you don't question a Night Office assignment. You know the risks. Fighting cosmic horrors is why you signed up. A special assignment is a chance to actually make a difference, and that's why you volunteered to serve, isn't it?

You know what? You read the briefing material. You saw the inflight documentary. You got this. You don't need a pep talk. Get to the point.

Besides, your bladder isn't going to wait much longer.

Go to 4.

Hang on. A special assignment? Maybe you should start at the very beginning. This isn't the same as dealing with an outbreak of Ffularian Fungal Fever at a truck stop. This is the big league.

Go to 5.

4

The Antarctic is one of the last unexplored places on this dingy marble. Sure, there were several attempts to survey that ice-covered continent, but most of these were cut short or ended poorly (c. f. Appsley-Cherry). During, between, and after the various large-scale military squabbles of the twentieth century, governments thought they could stash secret bases down in the cold empty, and several did, but many of those have gone dark. There are rumors about what happened to those stations, of course, and lot of that nonsense can be traced back to the Nathaniel Derby Pickman Foundation's original expedition.

The Pabodie-Lake expedition was ostensibly tasked with field-testing new core-sampling technologies developed by Professor Frank. H. Pabodie, but its not-so-secret mission was to verify what Pickman found. Officially, the expedition was lost, but unofficially, there are sealed files somewhere in the Night Office archies.

A dozen years later, Starkweather and Moore were supposed to vet the records of William Dyer and Mr. Danforth. What did those two see down there in the ice? That was all the Night Office wanted to know. Moore didn't make it back, and no one knows what happened to Starkweather after he returned.

The Cold War distracted everyone, and the Night Office had more pressing issues to address: the Belarus Event, for one; the Appalachian Curse, for another. The mystery of the ice was forgotten. Records were sealed and locked away.

Anyway, a week ago, Night Office radio sweepers intercepted SIGINT out of McMurdo. A radio jockey was hearing things on a wavelength that hadn't been used since the 1960s. Voices speaking Russian at first, then French, and then in a language none of the radio operators knew. Since they'd seen the movies and read the old stories—there isn't much to do during the winter in the Antarctic except keep up on pulp conspiracies—they wanted a second opinion.

LOBE gave them one. It didn't take the brains in Labyrinthian Observation & Byzantine Elucidation long to decode the skips and pops coming off the Antarctica Plateau. There was bad news and worse news. The bad: what the radio jockeys were hearing was a summoning invocation; the worse: the signal was a recorded loop, which meant either the ritual had been completed a long time ago, or it required sustained expression. Days. Weeks. Years. Of course, the most inaccessible place on the planet, where you are completely cut off from the rest of humanity for weeks—months, even—at a time, is a perfect location if you don't want to be interrupted for a spell.

While your floor was waiting for Asset Resource Management to allocate resures, someone set up a pool: *How long had the message been running?*

You put fifty bucks on sixty-eight years. You wanted seventy-four, but Harkness beat you to it.

Asset Resource Management put together two teams, and you were in the air before LOBE gave their opinion on how long the message had been runing. *Seventy years.*

Oh, well, it was only fifty bucks.

Naturally, the mission went to shit as soon as your team landed.

Right. Got it. Time to get to work.
Go to 1.

Wait. A seventy-year-old message? Summoning invocations? Cosmic horrors? Hold on. Did you really sign up for this?
Go to 9.

5

So, yes, six weeks ago . . . you got a color-coded envelope from Invoicing, Receiving & Itemizing Systems.

It was late in the week. You and a couple other Closers were playing for pocket change with a Coleman-Smith deck. You remember a bunch of folks prairie-dogging up from their cubicles when the guy from IRIS showed up with that fluorescent envelope. He wore hazmat gloves, which was overkill, but when he called out your name, you understood why he was wearing the gloves. You didn't want to touch that envelope either.

"Yeah, that's me," you admitted.

Inside the envelope was a single sheet of cream-colored Abbey Wove paper. It listed your name, your employee number, the name of the operation, and the location of the operation briefing: Azure Byzantine—one of the conference rooms on the thirteenth floor.

"Which one is Azure Byzantine?" you asked Tremayne, the Opener in the cubicle next to yours.

"It's the one opposite the fountain," he said.

"No, it's the one that looks out over the greenhouses," said another Opener.

"No, that's Vermillion Tessera," corrected someone else.

Everyone was super helpful, but you knew they were all secretly relieved their names hadn't been on the envelope.

Hazmat gloves. Radioactive color-coding. You were poison. They wanted you gone.

You didn't bother packing your desk. As per Night Office regulations, you didn't have anything of a personal nature in your cubicle. A good agent is a tidy agent.

The unmarked button in the elevator took you to the thirteenth floor. When you arrived, you checked the fire evacuation map near the stairwell. Ah, yes. Azure Byzantine was the small conference room on the far side of the floor, past the nook with the industrial shredder.

You remember pausing as you passed the nook, unable to stop yourself from admiring the hulking machine and its capacious maw. The machine could handle three inch binders—full ones!—without overheating or scattering paper snow everywhere. Imagine how much easier your job would be if you had one of these babies . . .

Anyway, past the shredder station you found a narrow door marked with a blue-framed mosaic. It was a baffling pattern that made your eyes slide away. *Azure Byzantine.*

You opened the door and entered the room.

The lights flickered on. The room was empty. No table. No chairs. No white board. The walls hadn't even been painted.

Hang on. Isn't this where you started? The only thing missing is the hospital bed. A strange feeling washes over you. It's not déjà vu. It's more like . . .

Go to 6.

This wasn't what happened. You must have made a wrong turn. Except, this is your memory. How can you make a wrong turn in your own head?

Go to 7.

This is some kind of practical joke, isn't it? Like one of those pranks that Beecher is always pulling.

Go to 8.

6

One of the reoccurring issues with this job is the nightmares. You are warned during Orientation & Inoculation. Your active brain will forget most of them, the instructors tell you, but your body won't be as forgiving. There's a seminar on coping skills where you learned some useful techniques. But, in the end, all this denial and compartmentalization leads to déjà vu at inopportune times.

For the moment, let's assume PINEAL properly vetted your Introspective Summary and Isolated Schematization when you were first hired. While they noted your \potential for manipulating the way, you opted out on the PALM—ISS—33/r form. The Way wasn't for you.

That meant *Alpha* or *Omega*, and you chose the latter. The agent of endings. A Closer. One who stands before the full spectrum of cosmic futility and say, "Not today, tentacled things."

You're strong and stable. As much as the mind devourers try to convince you there's an underside to a Möbius Loop, you know there isn't. But that doesn't stop them from trying.

Which is to say there are certain conditions that trigger deep brain twitches. Cute puppies. Intercom paging policies at grocery stores. White rooms. These things can make you stumble. Make you look twice. Make you think—

Have you fallen into the Dark Labyrinth? The Old Man's voice is strong and loud. *Surely you paid attention during that session?*

—something isn't right.

Yes, you think. *I was paying attention.*

Reality gets slippery on the job. That's why the Night Office teaches you about self-assessments. How to invent and interact with Personal Therapeutic Constructs (see *Beyond the Walls of Sanity* [*APS—481/q*] for more information).

You know how to build mental memory palaces that allow you to find yourself. You have personality matrix maps that remind you of who you are. That's the whole point of your Life Integrity Experience Schematic. *Some* paperwork will save your life.

Anyway, what were you doing?

(don't forget about the knife)

Oh, right. You were in bed, resting. A bout of rheumatoid fever, was it? Or some virulent strain of whatever is going around this year . . .

No. There was a mission briefing. You learned about the thing in the ice. Then you got on an airplane. O'Hare to São Paulo. São Paulo to Troll, the Norwegian station on Antarctica. From Troll to . . . wherever. When you landed, there was a storm. And an obelisk.

(where did you put the knife?)

The obelisk is important . . .

This is wrong. Maybe you should try again.
Return to the WHITE ROOM.

This is wrong. Maybe you should untie the knots.
Go to 10.

7

Follow your back-trail. That's what they told you to do when you got lost. Follow the thread. It's an old trick, but hey, it works.

And so, you left that empty room and returned to the elevator. The map. Yes. You checked the map again. Azure Byzantine was right where it was supposed to be: past the shredder station, between the break room and that other room—the one with that strange sequence of letters and numbers. *GR* . . .

You retraced your steps. The shredding station and the machine that would devour all the documentation in the world if you and an army queued up to feed it. Then, yes, there was the break room, and it was as dismal as the one on your floor. Burnt popcorn smell and all.

The memory is stronger now, anchored by the pscyhosomatic response from your belly. You aren't hungry, but there's something about that popcorn smell that makes you feel . . . alive. Yes. That's it. You are definitely alive.

Ah, and then the door again. The sign next to it says "Azure Byzantine."

How did you miss this the first time? Oh well, some quirk of memory perhaps. It doesn't matter. You found your way back.
Go to 15.

What about the other door? The one marked—what was it? Oh, go look. This is your memory. The one marked *GR3122*?
Go to 17.

8

Is someone playing a joke? Is this a trick of your own psyche? Have you lost your way already?

You know about memory palaces—mental constructs that ground you. The space jellies like to get in your head and mess with things. If you've got a strong palace, they can't rewire you. That's why empty rooms seem suspicious; your brain might be trying to reorient itself and you've caught it during a reboot.

As you consider this

(void)

emptiness, a shiver passes through the floor. Or maybe it passes through you. It's hard to tell. It feels like—

No, that shiver was inside you. You were experiencing a case of the hiccups. You weren't in control for a second. Everything turned inside out and then inverted back again. Yes, a meeting room. Back at the office and—

(looking forward now)

The door slams open behind you, and someone rushes into the room. They dump an armload of paperwork and a laptop on the table.

(this is the Way, isn't it?)

The individual turns around and makes a noise that reminds you of the feral cat that lives behind the place where you drop off your dry cleaning. "Bastet," he says.

He's shorter than you, and his hair is curly in that "I don't know how to tame this mane" sort of way and not a "this is practiced sexy" sort of way. His jacket—which is some ungodly cross between a faux-leather windbreaker and a casual sports coat—is too large on his frame. He's wearing owlish black-rimmed eyeglasses and he's got more than a hint of eyeliner.

"Where did you come from?" he demands.

"I was here before you arrived," you say. "Back when this room was empty."

"What? Empty? What do you mean?"

You point at the table. "That wasn't here a moment ago."

He wrinkles his nose, like he discovered a dead rat in his sock drawer. "It wasn't? Oh, that's not good."

"No, I don't suppose it is," you say. You're being polite because you don't really understand what he's talking about.

"Are you . . . are you here for a briefing?" he asks.

"I suppose I am," you say. "Look. How about we start over—"

"Not like that!" He puts up his hands, a genuine look of fright on his face. "What are you trying to do?"

"I'm—I'm trying to figure out what—what are you talking about?"

"Recursion loops," he snaps.

"Wait. What kind of loops?"

"The infinite kind. The kind where you don't realize how fucked you are until you're walking into your own asshole,"

"Do you do that often?" you ask.

"Do what?"

"Walk into yourself."

"You don't—" He sighs loudly. "This is off-beam," he says.

You don't have any idea what is really going on, though that isn't new. No one ever tells you everything.

Go to 11.

Off-beam?

It's not a term you are familiar with, though you get the idea from context. It's more than his lingo, though, it's everything: his clothing, his manner of speaking, his hair style. It's *familiar*, but it's not the *same*. Everything is *off*, all right . . .

Go to 13.

9

It's too late to have second thoughts about this now. But, okay, let's recap the series of bad decisions that brought you here.

First, there was the incident at Camp Harrowroot, when that jackass Hughie Daryrimple tried to drown you. Well, he *said* it was an accident. The raft flipped, sending a lot of kids into the murky water. Some were dog-paddling madly with no regard for anyone else in the water; some were trying to hang on to the raft. You weren't panicking like the rest, but neither was Hughie. He was trying to shove your head under the water, and when you fought back, he kicked you in the chest. The little bastard was grinning the whole time too. Sure, you took care of things a few years later, but at the time, you were a bit hysterical about it all, weren't you?

Then, during your last year in school, Alice McTaggart wanted you to ruin Sally Nesth's prom experience. Sally's date, Ralph Gunderson, had publicly dumped Alice not a week earlier. Alice wanted revenge, and yes, from an adolescent perspective, such drama was entirely understandable, but Alice wanted more. You pretended not to understand what she was talking about, but then she had to whisper: "I know what you did to Hughie Daryrimple."

Okay, okay. Maybe we shouldn't dwell on the past.
Go to 1.

Oh, *that* Hughie Daryrimple. It's starting to come back to you now, isn't it?
Go to 12.

10

What knots? There aren't any knots. You're in a meeting. No, you're in a hospital bed. No, you're in a plane. There's a storm. The meeting was cancelled. There is no mission. You didn't hurt those people. No. No. Something's in here with you. Here? Where are you? You were in a hospital bed. No. That's not you. That's—

(*Untie the knots. That's what you have to do first. Untie—*)

There are no knots. This isn't the way it—

There is only one side to the Möbius Loop. You run in one direction and you end up back at the beginning. You run the other way and you end up here again.

Where is here?

(*Untie the knots. You'll see. Take off the blindfold.*)

There is no blindfold. There are no knots.

You're in a bed. This is a recursion nightmare. This is slippage. Sagalico warned you about these. You can find your way back. You can—

(*How can you untie the knots if your hands are tied?*)

There's only one side to the Loop.

(*How far can you run?*)

Start at the beginning. Don't falter. Untie the knots.
Go to 25.

11

"No one ever tells me anything," you say.

The individual spreads his hands and offers you a mock bow. "Welcome to the Night Office."

It would be funnier if it weren't so true.

"Okay, well, I'm Pip," he says. "I'm, ah, well, since I worked up the presentation, that—um—makes me the resident expert—"

The hair on the back of your neck stand up. You turn toward the door, your hands drifting into the First Charm of Warding. A growling noise rises outside the room, and the door swells inward, like something is leaning against it. Then, as quickly as it comes, the pressure recedes.

"Did you—?"

"It's Thursday," Pip says. "There will be two more. We're waiting for the second one."

"Waiting for what?"

"The bend back," Pip says. "The hole in the recursion."

"Why?"

Pip sighs. He blinks several times, all big eye behind those owlish glasses. "You really don't know, do you?"

You figure this is probably not the time to lie. "No," you say.
Go to 14.

If there was ever a time to lie, this is probably it. "Of course I do," you say. "You should get on with what you're supposed to be briefing me about."
Go to 19.

12

In retrospect, helping Alice McTaggart get revenge on Ralph Gunderson may not have been the best idea. Alice freaked out about what you did and told her parents. She also confessed to Ralph, who told *his* parents (which was surprising, given the location of the boils you had magicked on him). Both sets of parents called your "step-dad," who lost his temper with your "mom." (Technically, your aunt, but let's not complicate things more, shall we?) So much shouting ensued; your aunt's favorite chair got smashed; the police showed up. Somewhere in there, Burt got physical with Clarice.

Oh, the whole block felt the temperature drop twenty degrees right after that.

Anyway, the police apologized for the mix-up; Alice's and Ralph's parents were told to mind their own goddamned business—"Get your son to the Emergency Room already, for Christ's sake!"; and Burt . . . well, Burt wasn't around after that and no one really missed him, did they?

You, on the other hand, finally got some attention from your aunt, didn't you?

Since you're clearly got the touch, you might as well learn to do the arts correctly, was all Clarice said. One of those teachable moments, wasn't it? It was better to guide you toward self-determination and compassion rather then let you traipse along the dark paths without a fucking clue as what you were doing. Sympathetic magic is tricky, and Clarice was impressed you hadn't killed anyone.

And, technically, Hughie Daryrimple had a psychotic break. It wasn't your fault that the hideously expensive (and insanely aggressive) therapeutic efforts of the doctors at the Applewood Institute didn't produce the results his family had been hoping for. And it wasn't your fault that the door to the roof was unlocked that afternoon. You weren't even there when he jumped the balustrade and fell to his death. In fact, your name only showed up once in the vistor logs. Five years prior.

Which was—yes, yes—around the time that you were attending that community college nearby. But let's not dwell on that. Their records are sealed, anyway. Best to leave it all alone.

Beyond the petty larceny, solicitation, and wanton disregard for personal property, there's a history of skipping along dark paths and peering into the strange gaps between this world and the next. It's not a surprise that you caught the attention of the Night Office.

Clarice warned you, though, didn't she? *They'll use you up,* she said. *They want to stop the Ineffable, and they don't care how many have to die. Just as long as it isn't them.*

They'll give me a home, you argued. *They'll give me purpose.*

Staring into the Abyss isn't purpose, dear lamb, it's just unnecessary sacrifice.

But you had signed up anyway. Maybe it had been a final act of defiance. A final demonstration that you weren't going to live under her wing and her constant side-eye for your whole life. That you wanted something better than what she could offer.

In hindsight, however, she was right. Pity you never got a chance to tell her.

Wow. This is off-track. How about we get back to the briefing?
Go to 7.

Rummaging about with your skeletons isn't going to help. You'd better get back to the mission.
Go to 34.

13

"I'm sorry," you say. "I must have stumbled into the wrong meeting." Before the analyst can stop you, you leave the room.

When you close the door, it clicks shut. You can see the sound waves as they ripple through the walls. You feel it in your head too, and you put out a hand to steady yourself. You haven't felt vertigo this bad since that night when you and Dahlia MacKenzie shared an entire bottle of that black label mescal she brought back from Oaxaca.

(Worth it though, wasn't it?)

The sign on the wall changes. The colors spin. The letters rearrange themselves. The carpet changes to tile and then back to carpet again (though it is a different color this time). The lights flicker. Some of them spark and go out. Eventually, the ripples pass and everything stabilizes.

Except your gut. That's still tight, because you know you're not in Kansas anymore.

Not that you were before, either. It's just a saying, a cultural reference you and another field operative share, which ties you two together. Grounding reality is easier when you're not doing it alone.

The Old Ones exert a strong pull on consensual reality, one of your instructors once told your class. *They don't exist, per se, but they cast a presence across multiple dimensions. The stronger their influence, the greater the possibility that reality will fray and become something else. It may seem like your world, but there will be differences. These differences can kill you.*

Everything can kill you, one of the other trainees had whispered to you. *Why should this be any different?*

Cubicle farms are the same everywhere however. It doesn't matter which reality you are in.

You glance into one of the cubicles, half-expecting to see a space jelly in a plastic tub with a headset, selling *Cephalopod Quarterly* subscriptions to cold-blooded New England pensioners.

Across the floor, the elevator dings.

You suddenly wonder who else might be in this empty office building. You duck into one of the empty cubicles as the elevator arrives. You listen intently, trying to hear any sort of noise. The HVAC system hums in the background. Something is breathing loudly—oh, that's you.

Slowly, you peek up over the edge of the cubicle wall. The area near the elevators is empty. While you hold your breath, the elevator doors close.

Whew. False alarm. Now you're just spooking yourself. This isn't helping. You need to get back to that meeting. That's what you came here for, isn't it?

Go to 15.

Great. Now you're jumping at shadows.
Go to 40.

14

The analyst sucks in a lot of air, and you wonder if there's going to be any left for you. He holds it in for a second, and then lets it out again. It's such a moment of high drama that you wonder if this is all some manner of practical joke. Did Perkins put this guy up to this? Is Chandler still mad at you? Is that ass Murphy still nursing a grudge about that game of shuffleboard?

"Do you remember Harrow?" he asks.

You're confused by his question. You remember a summer camp called Harrowroot, but there wasn't anyone named 'Harrow' there. "Who?" you ask.

He frowns. "That's what I was afraid of," he mutters. He opens his laptop. The camera eye scans his retina, and the computer unlocks. The screen shivers and transforms into a blue and purple desktop.

You can't help but stare at the background.

All Night Office computers have the same background, as mandated by System Knowledge Information Management. Firstly, a consistent background reduces visual stress; and secondly, it's a reminder that SKIN controls everything. On your computer—the one you left in your cubicle—the desktop background is black and mauve. Not blue and purple. And the sigil in the upper righthand corner of his screen isn't the Second Ward of Protective Camouflage.

"What is that?" you ask, pointing at the screen.

"What?"

"That sigil."

"That's—" He adjust his glasses and swallows. "That's Acheron's Sigil of Compassionate Correlation."

"Acheron's what?" You've never heard of a sigil like this. Nor anyone named Acheron.

"Oh, shit." His shoulders slump. "You're not from this index."

"What's an index?" you ask, even though you don't want to know. You're letting this world drag you in. You're letting it become the dominant reality.

Something is definitely bent out of true. It might be you. It might be one of Them. You can't be sure, and the only way to find out is to go deeper. Right?

Go to 16.

You know who *you are*, you say to yourself. *You know* where *you are. This is all bullshit.*

Go to 20.

15

You open the door, expecting the same empty room as before, but it's not. Now it looks like your standard corporate meeting room. A long table. Chairs. A laptop attached to a projector. A white screen where a mind-numbing presentation will be displayed.

There are two people in the room. They've clearly been waiting for you. The first, an ex-military looking fellow with a high-and-tight haircut and a steely-eyed squint, gives you a quick once over. The sort of look that says "Risk Assessed and Quantified."

You don't measure up well in his estimation. Whatever. You're used to this sort of thuggish dismissal.

The other person is an innocuous looking fellow, wearing soft leather gloves and a very British-looking overcoat. He's the sort High-and-Tight eats for breakfast. But when this guy gives you the full weight of your gaze, those "serial killer thriller" warning bells that served you well during second semester at university start clanging in your head.

"You're late," High-and-Tight says. He's been fussing with his messenger bag. The man does not like waiting.

"These rooms are hard to track down sometimes," you say.

Gloves-and-Overcoat offers you a smile, but you're not fooled. This one is a predator.

This is your team. You're the Closer. High-and-Tight is the Opener. The other guy is the Guide—the one who can see into the Way. Neither of them strike you as solid team players, which is—unfortunately—pretty standard for Night Office field teams.

You nod toward the screen on the wall, where the reassuringly colored logo of the Night Office is slowly bouncing around. "We waiting for anyone else?" you ask.

High-and-Tight shakes his head. "I'm Argot," he says. He points at the other guy. "This is Sagalico."

"You going to be looking ahead?" you ask Gloves-and-Overcoat.

"What do you think?" he asks.

There's that smile again. This day has already gotten under your skin, and he's not helping.

You return your attention to Argot.

"Why don't we get on with the briefing?" you say.
Go to 21.

"I don't like him," you say.
Go to 24.

16

"It doesn't matter if I don't know what an index is," you say to Pip. "It doesn't matter if our chronologic matrices have valid checksums, or whatever terminology you use in your 'index.' We're out of phase. That's all that we can count on, right? And that means we still have time, doesn't it?"

"Yes, yes." He starts nodding. "If we were in sync, then nothing has happened yet. We can't fluctuate before the Occlusion anyway, and afterward—well, there's no point in worrying about things if the Occlusion is in play."

You want to ask about the Occlusion, but you're already getting a sense that this trip down memory lane has odd pathways that veer off in interesting directions. What is that they say about time? It doesn't exist until we think about it, and when we do think about it, it refuses to behave.

Or maybe that was something your aunt said about you after that incident at the museum?

Either way, it's best to not get hung up on *what* you know and *when* you know it. Your brain will figure it all out. If it doesn't, then there's no point in getting caught up about it, is there?

This is a terrible conclusion, part of your brain notes, and you don't disagree with it, but what else can you do? They actually talked about this during training. *Reality will get weird. The best way to deal with it is to not fight it. It still behaves according to rules; however, these rules may be arcane and abstruse to the human intellect. Not much that can be done about that. Hold on to your sense of self and ride it out.*

Which is easy for some deck-bound academic to say. It's a little more complicated when you're in the field.

"Get on with it," you say. "You were talking about holes and recursions, right? What do I need to know?"

"Right," Pip says, snapping back to his presentation. "So, ah, yes. Yes. Look, there's an expedition that went to the Antarctic a while back. A follow-up of a follow-up. You may have read about the first team. The Pickman Foundation expedition? No? How about Pabodie-Lake?"

You shrug. There's a lot of archival material you haven't read. Everyone's in the same boat here. So many incident reports to examine, so little time.

"Right, after Pabodie-Lake, Starkweather and Moore tried to figure out what happened in the ice. Starkweather made it back—a few years late, mind you—but his brain was no better than a pan full of scrambled eggs. They stuck him in a padded cell, hoping that he might come back enough to give a report."

"Did he?"

"Eventually. Kinda." Pip shrugs. "He was not *there* for a long time, but during full moons, he seemed to come back. And when he could see the moon, he talked. Non-stop. Most of it was nonsense—even by Night Office standards—but twice during these talkative periods, he was lucid for approximately forty-seven seconds."

"And what did he say during those forty-seven seconds?"

"He said that Moore betrayed them. That the Russians had opened the crypt. That we had to find the key. And that we should, under no circumstances, approach the spire."

"That's what you consider to be not 'nonsense'?"

Pip rolls his eyes. "Oh, it gets weirder. Each time he was coherent, he spoke in a different language."

"What? Seriously?"

"Seriously. Most of them were dead languages, too."

"Wow. That's weird. Even by Night Office standards."

"A team of head doctors think there are close to eighteen distinct personalities in his head. He's not possessed—that was considered—but most of the languages he uses haven't been spoken by native speakers for hundreds of years."

"So they're all invented personalities? How is that possible?"

"There are two theories," Pip says. "The first is that he's tapped some sort of memetic layer of consciousness where all this . . . this linguistic intelligence is still resident. The second is that he picked up these personality indexes during recursion loops."

"Ah," you say. "Back to the loops, then."

"Yeah," he says. "The loops."

You feel a headache coming on.
Go to 23.

"Have we had this conversation before?" you ask.
Go to 28.

17

You stop before the door marked GR3122. This isn't Azure Byzantine. Are you sure you want to do this?

Of course you do. Why else would you have let this slip into your memory?

You go into the room before you can overthink that question.

It's a small room, well-lit by wall sconces. A claw-footed cast-iron stove murmers contentedly in the corner. Bookcases line two of the walls, and opposite the door, there is a large tapestry. It depicts the know world, though there are some unfamiliar shapes along the edges. Uncharted islands. Forgotten atolls. Fictional archipelagos.

There's a man sitting in a plush wingback chair near the stove. He looks up from the book he's been reading as you enter the room, and his weather-beaten and bearded face creases with a broad smile. He's wearing a double-breasted suit that is too big for him (which is saying something because this guy looks like he's decidedly more than two meters in height). You notice that the left leg of his trousers hangs limply. He's missing his left foot.

"Hallo," he says cheerfully. "It's nice to see you."

His accent is urbane. Neither British nor Scandinavian. Some-where in-between. As if he comes from one of those uncharted islands on the map hanging behind him.

"Hi," you say. "I'm not sure if I'm in the right place."

"And what place is that?" he replies.

You show him the radiation-banded envelope you got a half hour ago from the Mail Clerk. "I'm supposed to be here for a briefing," you say.

He nods and smiles. "Ah, yes. But this time, you wanted some useful information instead of what"—he waves a hand toward the door behind you—"those people want you to know."

"This time?"

"You're recursing," he says in a way that suggests you should know what he's talking about. "You don't want to make the same mistake you made last time, so you're imagining a different history; you're making a different version of the past so you can change the future."

"Is that what I'm doing?"

"Theoretically, I suppose you are."

"But I'm a Closer," you say. "I don't change things. I seal them shut."

"Those actions are not as different as you say," he says. "Neither is Opening."

"That's what I did, isn't it?" You have a dim recollection of a white room, of rabbits, and something that shouldn't be where it is.

He peers at you. "You're trying to remember, aren't you?"

"I . . . I guess so."

"What do you remember?"

You glance down at the envelope you've been carrying around. It's thicker than you remember, and when you open it, you find a handful of briefing documents. "There's a research station in Antarctica," you say. "It's gone dark, which isn't unusual for winter down there, but it's also started broadcasting a beacon. Part of that signal is in a language no one has heard since . . ." You shuffle through the pages. "Not since Starkweather came back." You spot a footnote. "Who's Oresti?"

"Pedro Oresti? Ah, a marvelous scholar. Very inquisitive."

"He's not part of the Night Office."

"Nor am I," the old man says. "Not now, at least."

"But you used to be."

He inclines his head a little, as if that is all he is going to be say on that matter. "We should be talking about what you did," he says.

"What did I—"

But then you remember everything. The miserable landing at MacReady Station. The silence in the base. The empty hallways.

The bodies. The room in the ice. The hollowness at the center of it all. The whiteness. And in that whiteness . . .

He leans forward, his gaze sharp. "Do you know how I lost my foot?" he asks. "I cut it off before the rot could spread. You don't think flesh can go bad in the cold, but it can. And like all infections, you have to cut that out before it kills everything."

"Is that what I'm supposed to do?"

"Isn't that what a Closer does?"

You offer him a pained smile. Now he's sounding like one of your instructors, answering a question with another question.

"Why me?" you ask, sticking with the format.

"It was your turn," he says, sitting back in the chair. A shadow curls up in the hollow of his right eye. "There's no reason to it. Your name came up on the rotation. It was random."

"The universe isn't random."

He shrugs. "Then it wasn't chance. It was planned. That makes you the perfect tool."

"A tool cannot act on its own," you point out. "A tool must be guided by a conscious hand."

"Indeed. So whose tool are you?"

You suspend this memory, causing the old man's expression to freeze. You're somewhat surprised that you can stop this because while you know you are remembering what happened before you got to the station, this encounter doesn't feel like a memory. It feels more like something that you are actively participating in, as if you've stumbled into a different movie.

That thought reminds you of something else. Something from a previous . . . no, not a previous *life*. More like a previous *iteration*?

It's all very confusing.

Go to 27.

"I'm not a slave," you say. "I am my own person."

"Ah, free will," he says. "Always an entertaining choice."

He returns his attention to the book on his lap, and you realize this briefing is over.

Not that it was much of a meeting, but whatever. Welcome to the Night Office, where you're never told the true story about what is going on.

You snap off an ironic salute. When you leave the briefing room, the lights in the hall flicker and . . .

Go to 46.

"I work for the Night Office," you say.

"Very good," he says. "Devotion to duty is admirable." He points to the door behind you. "Off you go then. Finish this."

Your face heats up a bit with his casual dismissal, but what are going to do? Argue with him some more?

No point in that. With a sigh, you turn and head for the door.

Go to 144.

18

You find a pair of orange overalls in the locker outside the infirmary room where you've been sequestered. They aren't that flattering, but it's better than running around the station in your next-to-nothings. Clogs are easy to find—everyone wears clogs. And you snag a lab coat from Dr. Nakamura's office.

You check her computer and discover that it is password locked. You check under the blotter and don't find a useful sticky note. It looks like she's actually respecting IT's baseline security protocol. Annoying for you, of course, but good for her.

Her computer does show the current date and time, which gives you pause. You had a three-hour window to finish the mission before the plane took off. The pilot told Argot that the time limit wasn't negotiable if they were going to get back to Troll Station. Otherwise, they were going to be stuck at MacReady for awhile. Argot hadn't been pleased with the time window, but a countdown timer always focuses the mind.

Not that it matters now. That conversation happened yesterday, according to the floating clock on the doctor's computer screen. The plane is gone. You're on your own.

You've got to find a way to talk to someone out there. Let the Night Office know what is going on.

Go to 46.

It's no good to go charging into a situation you don't understand. That's how field operatives get turned into mindless slaves of fungi from another dimension. *Be prepared* is the motto—well, it's not the Night Office's motto, but whatever. It still applicable.

Go to 48.

19

He thrusts the stack of paperwork at you. "Here," Pip says. "You need to read and sign all of this." And while you try to make sense of what he has handed you, he fusses with his laptop.

The paperwork looks like a standard mission agreement contract, though the pages are all out of order. As you sort them, you discover a few pages are missing, which probably isn't a big deal as it is nothing more than boilerplate which you can't line out anyway.

Pip launches the presentation he was talking about. He skips through the first few slides, which appear to be filled with the standard sort of introductory text that make sure everyone in the room is up to date with the latest acronyms. It's all stuff you've just hand-waved Pip past, and now you're having second thoughts about doing so.

"Right," he says. He spins the laptop around so you can see it better. "Okay, so here's the problem."

You look at the screen. "Is it supposed to be a white rabbit in a snowstorm?" you ask.

"What?" He peers over the edge of the screen. "No, that's not—goddamn these machines. We're so overdue for new hardware. These things take forever." He picks up the laptop and shakes it, as if that might goose its processing power. The screen blurs to white noise and then resolves.

All you see is an image of a white room. An empty room. Like this room before Pip came in. You half expect him to walk into the frame.

No, that's not it. The shadows are wrong. This is the infirmary ward at MacReady Station, where you wake up. After . . .

And then you see it. Right in the center of the screen.

The obelisk.

This is so confusing. How could you have gotten so lost? Are you doing this right?

Go to 10.

That's it. That's the key.

No, wait. This is happening out of sequence.

It doesn't matter. All paths lead to the same conclusion. The same ending.

Find the key.

Go to 22.

20

"Murphy put you up to this, didn't he?"

"Who's Murphy?" A look of confusion starts across Pip's face. Before it gets halfway, it takes on a sickly sheen of terror.

"Okay, fine, whatever," you say. You put up your hands and back away.

"Wait!" Pip's heading for full-on panic. "You're making a mistake."

"No," you say. "My mistake was thinking this was a real special op." You look around the room one last time. "This? This isn't even a broom closet. It's just unused space."

He yells at you to stop, but you open the door anyway.

And there's nothing out there but darkness, and in that darkness, something hisses.

Pip is screaming behind you—words you don't understand—and you try to shut the door.

But it's too late. The overhead lights burn out, and the only source of illumination left is coming from Pip's laptop. But when a heavy tentacle knocks the computer aside, that light goes out.

Now it's dark everywhere. And cold. Really cold.

You can't close what you can't see. What you can't find.

Something grabs your hand. It could be Pip, but when whatever it is gives you a light squeeze—a friendly, reassuring squeeze—you know it isn't Pip.

IT'S TOO BAD THIS WASN'T A COOPERATIVE EXERCISE.

MAPS SCORE: 26

21

Argot hits a key on the laptop, and the screen saver disappears. You're looking at a topographical map of Antarctica. There are several locations marked.

Argot points to one of the markers. "We're headed for a place called MacReady Station," he says. "It's on the Antarctic Plateau, about sixty kilometers from the Pole of Inaccessibility. It used to be a Russian station, back in the 1960s. They were drilling for water or minerals or somthing."

"Did they find anything?" you ask.

Argot lifts his shoulders. "The station went dark during the '80s," he says. "Budget cuts, probably. Nothing in the record indicating otherwise. It was sealed up and abandoned. Until a few years ago when an independent organization acquired it from the Russian government. A company called Endoluvion. Based in Luxembourg. They do cell therapy research. Genomic sequencing. Growing arms out of the backs of rats. Shit like that."

"Shit like that," you echo.

"Why there?" Sagalico asks. His voice is soft. He's the sort of guy who refuses to raise his voice at a party, making everyone come closer in order to hear what he has to say. He likes everyone's quiet nervousness when they're forced into a stranger's personal space. "Why not somewhere more hospitable?"

"More hospitable locations means easier access," Argot says. "Easier for goverments and international regulators to drop in for a visit."

"Yes, yes," Sagalico murmurs. "All that documentation. All those watchers."

"Why are we going there?" you ask, trying not to think about what's going on in Sagalico's head.

"Why do you think?" Argot says. "Someone found something they shouldn't have. Someone licked a rock they shouldn't have. Someone had sex with something they—"

"They shouldn't have," you finish for him. "Yeah, yeah. I get that. But you don't need the Night Office for that."

Argot flicks to another slide. Line graphs of meteorologial data. "It's the middle of winter, which means it's dark all the time, and the weather is really shit," Argot says. "Many of the stations on Antarctica are only staffed during the summer months, when it gets up to minus twenty C and the wind is only fifteen knots or so. Those that are staffed year-round only keep a minimum number of people on-site during winter to make sure the station doesn't completely freeze out. It's not unusual for a station to go dark for a week at a time, what with the weather and the wind and whatever else the atmosphere is throwing up down there at the bottom of the world."

The next slide is a recent satellite map of Antarctica. "This is MacReady Station," Argot says, pointing to a blue dot on a map filled with swirling cloud formations. "It's got housing for thirty—maybe thirty-six, during summer—but that number drops to less than a dozen during winter. About a month ago, the last plane came out of MacReady, and everything was fine."

He clicks to the next slide, which looks exactly the same as the last slide, except the central portion of the continent is completely white. "This was taken a week ago," he says. "A massive storm moved in. Winds broke all kinds of records as they scoured the plateau. A lot of stations went dark.

"This happend once before, nearly thirty years ago. The Russians thought they lost one of their stations. There was a lot of chatter about it, and they couldn't get a plane out there until early spring."

"What did they find?"

He shakes his head. "Officially, the station sustained enough structural damage that they decided to abandon it. Wasn't worth trying to patch it up."

"Unofficially?"

"There weren't any survivors."

"Natural causes?"

"There's nothing natural about that plateau," Sagalico says. There's an echo in his voice which tells you he's looking into the Way.

"Okay, so MacReady goes dark, but it's winter and that happens. I assume Standard Operating Procedure is to wait out the winter before panicking." You glance at both men and then look at the slide again. "But it's only been a week, so what happened?"

Argot clicks to the next slide. It's a partial transcript from a radio shack. "A week ago, someone at McMurdo picked up a signal. Some kind of recorded message, almost like a beacon. It's in Russian, French, Italian, and . . . well, then it gets a little garbled."

You've been scanning the transcript as he's been talking and, yes, you see Russian, French, Italian, and . . . some text you can't fathom. "What's that?" you ask.

"We're not sure," Argot says, "But LOBE got all excited. They said it's not from this 'index'—whatever that means—and it's something—"

"It's from the Voerdamnikenari," Sagalico says.

You and Argot stare at the Guide. After a minute, Argot clears his throat. "You want to expand on that a little bit?" he asks.

"Yes," you say. "Please tell us more."
Go to 38.

Indexes. Something—someone—called the Voerdamnikenari. This is a lot to take in. Maybe too much. Are you sure this is helping you figure out what is going on?
Go to 40.

22

"Why am I thinking about a key?"

Pip is nervous about your question. He plays around with the presentation slides. Like he's looking for an answer. One that isn't there.

(waiting for you)

"Uh, there's nothing here about any sort of cryptographic blockchain," he says.

"Not that sort of key," you say.

He lets out a big sigh and stops flicking slides.

"I'm not cleared for this sort of thing," he whines.

"Neither am I," you admit. "But I'm in deep. I need your help."

You point at the slide on his screen. It looks like an empty slide, but that's not entirely true. There are hints of—

(a rabbit in a snowstorm)

—unseen objects on the screen.

"There's a key for that thing," you say, referring to something neither of you can see. "It can be unlocked. I have to stop it. I have to find a way."

He looks at the screen and frowns. "That's—that's not supposed to be there," he says. He reaches for the space bar, intending to advance the presentation.

"Wait," you say. "Not yet."

He fidgets with his glasses. "Now?"

You tilt your head. The screen hasn't changed. "I'm not sure," you admit. "But I think this is important."

"It's an empty slide," he says.

You shake your head. "It's not empty. It's just . . . white. But there are—something's there. Can't you . . . *feel* it?"

He rubs his fingers on the table. "It might be an occlusion."

"A what?"

"There's a condition that mountaineers call 'snow blindness.' You get dazzled by sunlight reflecting off snow, and your optic nerves shut down. Your ability to process visual information is compromised. It's not blindness, per se."

"So what I am experiencing is an . . . occlusion?"

"Maybe."

"And does this have something to do with *loops* and *indexes*?"

"I don't know. This is all above my pay grade." Pip sighs. "Okay, yeah. Maybe your brain is interpreting data on a subliminal level, and that is bifurcating your id. Maybe that's causing you to slip . . . out of phase, I guess."

"And that's how I move between indexes?"

Pip grimaces. "This is all very theoretical," he says.

"Welcome to the Night Office," you say.

He offers you a rueful smile.

"Okay, so this is all very theoretical and probably impossible, but let's call it a working theory."

"Sure," he says. After a moment of silence, he continues. "What do we do next?"

You tap the space bar on his keyboard and the slide show exits. "That was the last slide," you say.

"Yeah," he starts. "I wasn't finished with that last slide and—"

"No. It's not empty. There's something there."

"Fine. Whatever." He holds up his hands. "What do you want me to do?"

"Rearrange the deck," you say, indicating the computer. "Put this slide somewhere else. Don't tell me where. And let's run it again."

Go to 30.

"Run the slideshow again. I want to see what happens when I know what I'm looking for."

"Or not looking for," he says.

Go to 33.

23

You pinch your nose to fight off the headache blooming between your eyes. "Tell me what a loop is."

"Right, so you know Acheron's Correlation to—wait, never mind. Of course you don't. It's, uh, look, I don't know how much your index has quantified about all this—"

"Let's assume we've—I've—quantified nothing."

"Yeah, okay. That makes it—" Pip sighs. "Okay, in a nutshell: a loop is a construct of Kantian philosophy, Möbius mechanics, and Einsteinian relativistic subjective perception. There are hints in the record left by Pabodie and Lake, but it wasn't until Starkweather came back that we were able to formulate a working theory. A decade after that, Bargleflee realized one of the languages that Starkweather was babbling during his moon phase matched a script used in the Codex Acheroni. Bargleflee mapped Starkweather's glossolalia to a correspondence chart, which gave us a cipher key for the Codex. That's how we cracked the Fourteen Calls."

"Of course," you say, even though none of this was making any sense. Pip favors you with a smile that says he understands your confusion, but it can't be helped.

"The Calls allowed us to make contact with . . . well, allies, of a sort. The Old Ones destroyed their civilization a couple millennia ago—somewhere in Andromeda, I think. The survivors kept fighting the Old Ones as best they could. Kind of like us, but you know, they've been doing it for thousands of years."

"Enemies of my enemies are my friends sort of thing?"

"Exactly. We're not exactly ants to them, relatively speaking, we're more like cats."

"Cats are pretty intelligent," you point out.

"True," he admits, "But they're still cats."

"So, after rescuing Starkweather and figuring out what he's talking about *and* deciphering this old manuscript you've got lying around *and* invoking some esoteric summoning rituals *and* making contact with an alien intelligence, you figure out how time travel works. Am I following this correctly?"

"Sort of." He offers you an apologetic shrug. "Actually, they told us. Well, I mean, we had part of the theory worked out, but once we started talking to the Voerdamnikenari—"

"The who?"

"The Voerdamnikenari. The civilization that answered the Calls."

"Oh, right. Sorry."

"Anyway, it's sort of like that thing NASA did with the gold disk they sent out with all those probes. Math is the closest thing to a universal language in the universe, and if any civilization ever found our probes, they'd see that we weren't entirely uneducated. When the Voerdamnikenari realized we were scratching at the edge of the Recursion Theory, they decided we were worth talking to. We were pretty smart, for cats."

"I see. Nice of them to share."

He nods politely as he takes off his glasses and cleans them with the bottom of his shirt. "But you know how Management is. They have trust issues. And so they told a team to verify the insights we'd been given. Just to be sure they had told us everything."

You see the reticence in his earlier description now. "Ah, the scare quotes around 'allies.' They left out something important."

"They did," he says. "Invoking a Recursion draws Their attention."

"It's a trap, in other words."

He grimaces. "Basically."

"And Starkweather tripped over it, didn't he?"

"It wasn't Starkweather, but yeah, there was an Invocation, and it's like a beacon to the Old Ones. If we can't figure out how to collapse the Void Firmament, we're going to be overrun."

You laugh. You can't help yourself. "So, it's business as usual, then," you say.

He blinks at you for several moments, a startled expression fixed on his face. "Yeah," he says eventually. "Sort of. It's just the stakes are—"

"The stakes are higher," you finish for him. "They always are. It wouldn't be a Night Office assignment, otherwise."

He frowns and fusses with his laptop. Eventually, he closes it and tucks it under his arm. You realize you've offended him with your offhanded dismissal of the situation.

While it galls you to have to suck up to this guy, you should make nice. He does, after all, seem to have operational intelligence that you need to know.

"Look, I'm sorry. I was a bit of a jerk about that," you say. "I could really use some help here. Can you tell me a little more about these time loops?"

Go to 26.

It's not your job to play nice. It's your job to Close. If you're not properly informed, you're dead. So, yes, while you may have been a bit curt, you really do need to know what is going on. If everyone lives, you can apologize. If everyone dies, well, it doesn't really matter, does it?

"You said we were waiting for something," you say. "Maybe we should finish this briefing while there's still time."

Go to 33.

24

"I don't like you either," Sagalico sneers.

Argot slaps the table. It's a meaty sort of sound. A *I am in Charge Here* sort of sound. You suspect he likes letting folks know he's in charge.

"You're field ops, for crying out loud," he snaps. "You're supposed to not like each other. That's part of the regulations, ever since—"

He doesn't finish, and for a brief instant, you see a flash of something on his face that might be actual emotion, but he's a professional and he doesn't let his guard slip too much. "I need you two to be on edge," he says. "We've already lost one team and—"

"Wait," you interrupt. "We're not the first team?"

Argot fixes you with his steely stare. "No, we're not," he says.

'What happened to the first team?" you ask.

"That's one of the other mission parameters," he says. "Finding Brinkmann, Peele, and Gull."

"How long have they been . . . " You struggle with the last word. Night Office field operatives don't go "missing." They either come back or they don't. The world is saved, or it isn't. It's very black and white out there in the field. *Not knowing* is uncharted territory, and the Night Office does not like uncharted territory.

"They were supposed reach MacReady seventy-two hours ago," Argot says. "There have been two breaks in the weather since then. During those breaks, McMurdo picked up the beacon, but no other transmissions."

And since the world hasn't ended, the Night Office is sending in a second team.

"Can I get on with the briefing?" Argot asks, looking at you.

"Fine," you say. "Get on with it."

When Argot looks at him, Sagalico shrugs as if your opinion doesn't make a bit of difference to him.

Go to 21.

You're about to tell him to get on with it, but you notice Sagalico is humming quietly. He's staring at you, but he's not seeing you.

Go to 29.

25

Are you sure about these knots? They might not be—oh, those knots. No, wait. You're late to a meeting. You just need to—no, you've been briefed. You were supposed to kill everyone. No. No. Who told you that? Was it him?

(turning round and round and round)

Untie the knots. That's what have to do. Untie—

There is only one way through this loop. You run and run and *run run run* until you come to the beginning again, where you will realize you haven't moved at all.

(so many knots)

This is a recursion. This is slippage. Someone warned you about this. You can't go forward. You can only travel in a circle.

There is only one side to this story.

Stop. Start. Untie the knots.
Go to 43.

26

Pip shuffles his feet for a minute, and the look on his face suggests that he's having an internal conversation about you. You don't interfere. It's best if people come to their own conclusions about you—right or wrong, good or bad. That way you're not responsible for what happens next.

Pip's face softens. He starts to open the laptop again, but then changes his mind. "Okay, let's talk about time loops," he says. "I don't know how much your index has learned—" He stops, thinks about what he has just said and his expression tightens. "You don't know anything," he says slowly. "That's why you're here. Your index is still in flux."

"You're going to have to make more sense," you remind him.

"Okay, yeah. Yeah. So, here's the thing. Once you make the Calls—and this is really deep in the Way, okay? Like, quantum levels deep. The Calls create vibrations that cause bifurcation. Splitting. Multiplication. This is how you get indexed. As each index comes into phase with others, it gets locked in. It's no longer in flux. However, it's now part of this quantum state of multi-indexed existence. Time loops are when objects move across indices, but do so in a non-linear way."

He reads your expression, and indicates that you should hold out your hands. "Here. Put 'em flat. With a little space between them."

He sets his laptop down and puts his right hand above your left hand. "Say we have three indexes. Like this," he says. "They're all the same time stream. They're all moving in parallel to each other. Now"—he touches the back of his right hand with the index finger of his left hand, and then lifts it off—"an object is ejected from this index. It can't persist outside of this stack, and so it comes back as soon as it can."

He loops his finger down and touches it to the side of your left hand. "It makes contact again, but it's not in the same location—temporally—as it was in its original index. This second index rejects it"—his finger drifts away from your hand—"and so it must find another point where it can inject itself into an index."

He loops his finger back up to his hand, but touches the underside of his thumb instead of the back of his hand. "Right index now, but wrong position."

You nod, understanding his simple explanation. "That's the loop you're talking about," you say. "When something keeps coming back, trying to find its right place."

"Yes," he says. "It tends to work recursively, working backward until it finds its original location." He pauses for a second, and his tongue flickers against his lips. He's deciding whether to tell you something, and you can only imagine what sort of bad news it is.

It doesn't matter, really. They never tell you everything. It's always bad news, anyway.

"Each time this object touches an index, it can interact with that index," he says.

"This is how you can change the future," you say. "Or the past."

"Yes." He pauses. "Theoretically."

"Of course," you say. "It's always theoretical until someone survives the mission, isn't it?"

He looks at you. "You have to survive the mission," he says earnestly. "Because you're the one who—"

He doesn't finish. For an instant, you see a flash of light on the wall behind him. His shadow is shaped like a geometric solid. A rectangle with a triangular top.

The obelisk.

"I'm the one who brings them here, aren't I?"

He doesn't want to tell you, and you can't blame him, really. "Don't worry about it," you say. "It's not me. I'm a Closer. I'm not an Opener. It can't be me."

He puts his hand down. "I hope so," he says. "I really do."

The hair on the back of your neck starts to rise. The air in the tiny room crews thick and fetid. Pip's face blotches and he gulps in the heavy air. "It's coming," he says. "The recursion wave."

"Sounds like my ride," you say. You turn and head for the door to the room.

"Good luck," he says. "I hope—I hope I don't see you again. No offense."

You stop and look back at him. "None taken."

Wait for the wave to breach the door. The pressure builds. You feel a a sympathetic pressure building in your skull. You want it to go away. You want this—all of this—to be done.

Go to 144.

That wave is coming, regardless of whether you've got the door open or closed. You take a moment to calm yourself, even though you don't even know if yo have that sort of time. And then, you open the door.

Go to 236.

27

While the old man remains frozen, you glance at the briefing papers again. There are more of them than you remember.

(Did you read them all before?)

You snap your fingers, letting this *memory* continue.

The old man coughs, as if he has been holding his breath this entire time. "Whose tool are you?" he repeats, reminding you where you were in the discussion.

The back portion of the briefing papers looks like a typewritten manuscript. Like it is some sort of adventure novel.

"Maybe I'm not the protagonist I think I am," you say.

The old man chuckles. You look at the book in his lap again. It has the same title as the manuscript you're holding.

"I should read this," you say.

He sniffs. "Perhaps."

He really isn't going to tell you.

Okay, take a deep breath. Time to decide.

Read the manuscript.
Go to 36.

You're only going deeper into your own psychotic break. You know you're in the infirmary. You know things have gone to shit. You don't have much time. Get up. Get back to the mission.
Go to 58.

28

"Have we had this conversation before?" you ask.

"Maybe," he says.

"That's not very helpful," you point out.

He offers you an apologetic shrug. "Memory is relative," he says. "The loops create—well, our brains aren't built for it, really. Not like the Voerdamnikenari. They're—"

"Who?"

"The Voerdamnikenari."

"Are they a German splinter group?"

"No, they're an alien intelligence." He wrinkles his nose. "You don't know about the Voerdamnikenari."

"I must have missed that briefing."

"What about Antonito Bargleflee? The Codex Acheroni? The Fourteen Calls?"

You just keep shaking your head.

"Oh boy," he says. He looks like he is about to cry. "I don't know what to do," he admits. "You're not ready. There isn't time. I can't possible tell you everything you need to know before . . ."

As if on cue, the growling noises come back. The door starts to bend inward again. The analyst makes a noise like a frightened mouse. "No, no, no, no—" he starts to moan.

You snap your fingers, cutting him off. "It's Thursday," you remind him. "You said this was going to happen twice, and that the second one was going to be the important one."

You focus your desire and snap your fingers again. It's not a full Act of Will, but you've been Closing long enough that even a little effort like this has power. The door, which looks like a balloon filled with too much water, stops swelling. Something groans; it might be the analyst or it might be the door. It's hard to tell.

"Focus," you say. The door quivers for a second. Pip gulps in air. You hold your fingers ready for one more snap.

And then the pressure behind the door starts to recede.

You turn an index finger toward Pip. "Talk," you say. "I need to be ready."

"Right, right," he says. "Okay, so, uh, Starkweather came back—"

"Skip over that," you say. "What was it you said a minute ago about a Codex? And some Calls. What are those?"

"The Fourteen Calls," he says. "That's how we made contact with the Voerdamnikenari." Seeing your expression, he hurries on. "They're an intelligence who were scattered by the Old Ones a couple—I don't know, millennia?—a long long time ago. They're one of those entities who are drifting through time and space. We made contact through the Calls, which are . . . well, they're noisy. You can't really direct them. It's more like shouting through a megaphone than calling someone on the phone, you know?"

"The Voerdamnikenari aren't the only ones who heard us yelling," you say.

He nods. "Yeah, basically. We did an Invocation. They answered. And . . . and we suspect the Void Firmament got breached along the way which means . . ."

"They're coming," you finish for him.

He smiles weakly. "Yeah, they are."

"Awesome," you say with a hint of sarcasm. "Anything else that I might need to know before I have to go save the world?"
Go to 33.

"Great," you say without much enthusiasm. "I love this job."
Go to 35.

29

Sagalico is looking into the Way.

"What are you—" you start. Even though you're in Night Office HQ, you're in an unsecured and unsanctified room. Looking into the Way is dangerous. Things can look back. "He's not here," you say to Argot. "This isn't protocol."

"What . . . what have you—" Sagalico snaps back to the briefing room. "You did—"

Argot's no fool. He reacts quickly, reaching for his messenger bag.

Argot is going for a weapon, but you've not exactly unarmed here. Close his bag while his hands are still in it.

Go to 37.

Sagalico has obviously seen something that spooked him. But the Way isn't fixed. Not completely. You can still talk your way out of whatever he thinks you're going to do.

Go to 39.

30

Pip fiddles with his laptop. "Okay," he says. "I've rearranged the slideshow. Are you ready?"

"No," you answer honestly. "But let's do it anyway."

He nods and starts the presentation.

You stare at the screen. His slideshow makes more sense this time. It's not your—what did he call it?—it's not your index, but it is close enough. You can see the through-line on what you don't know.

Acheron's Correlation. Starkweather's madness. The multiplicity of languages that came out his head. Bargleflee's charts and the corresponding scripts in the Codex Acheroni.

The slides stutter. Script crawls of its own volition. You don't understand what the symbols mean, but you know what they do. You know what they call.

The Fourteen Calls.

And then, quite unexpectedly, the next slide is white. Completely—no, not completely. It's like a snowstorm, and you're trying to spot something

(a rabbit!)

white in it.

It's right there, isn't it? Right in front of you.

Reach out and touch what you know is there.
Go to 144.

Stay unfocused. Don't try to find something that doesn't exist. It's not even a memory. It's more like a—
Go to 254.

31

You execute the print command for the software package, and for a moment, you think the print file has gone into the void, but a light flickers on the printer and it starts making noise. Pages begin spewing into the tray.

You glance over your shoulder as the printer chatters. Do you have time to wait around for this drivel? It's not like there is going to be a test on whatever the hell it is that Morgan was writing.

You never know, the Old Man whispers.

You nod in agreement. "You never know," you say to the room.

The printer finishes the job. You grab the stack of pages and head for the door.

It's a really bad idea to get lost in some shitty spy caper manuscript while you wander through an abandoned research station that is undoubtedly overrun with space jellies, but . . .
Go to 36.

Read it later. There are more important things to do first.
Go to 106.

32

You type the nonsense password and hit RETURN. The computer screen goes blank, leaving you wondering if the password worked or not. As you're waiting, you hear a bleating noise coming from the back of the room. You look over your shoulder.

Something is crawling out of the shadow at the back of the room. It might have been a goat once upon a time, but it's more like a tangled mass of grass clippings and thorny roses now. Still has the horns, though. The grassy goat monster has more than a dozen stubby legs, and with each passing second, the bones in its legs get firmer. Its hooves get harder, and soon, you can hear a *clop-clop-clop* noise as those legs rattle against the floor.

You swear the horns are getting longer too.

The computer beeps, startling you. You glance at it, barely taking a moment to register that the password prompt has come back, and then you hear the *clop-clop-clop* speed up.

You dive out of the way as the grassy goat charges at you. It slams into the desk, its horns spearing the computer monitor. A shower of sparks erupts from the shattered monitor, and as you scramble for the door, the grassy goat whips its head from side to side.

The cables attached to the monitor snap, and the panel flies off the horns. It hits you in the back of the legs, knocking you off-balance. You stumble against the door of the room, pushing it fully closed.

You can't open the door while you're leaning on it. You need to move.

You roll off the door, fumbling for the handle.

The grassy goat hears your panic, and it charges, its horns lowered. You try to dodge, and you're partially successful. One of the horns goes into the door panel, and the other one goes into your leg.

Not only can you not open the door now, but you've got the horn of a dead and reformed goat monster in your leg. Who knows what sort of eldritch parasites and non-Euclidian micro-organisms have been injected into your bloodstream.

THE WORST WAY TO DIE HERE WOULD BE FROM THE ALIEN TOXINS IN YOUR BLOOD THAT ARE GOING TO EAT YOU FROM THE INSIDE. THANKFULLY, THE GRASSY GOAT WILL DISEMBOWEL YOU BEFORE THAT CAN HAPPEN. SMALL FAVORS.

MAPS SCORE: 41

33

Pip fiddles with his laptop and resets the presentation. "Okay, here we go."

A series of pictures flicker across the screen of his laptop. You're not in your—what did he call it?—your *index*, but it is close enough that you can follow what you're seeing on the computer screen. Acheron's Correlation. Starkweather's madness. The multiplicity of languages that came out of his head. Bargleflee's charts and the corresponding scripts in the Codex Acheroni.

Then, the slides stutter and move sideways. The script starts to crawl of its own volition. You don't understand what the symbols mean, but you know what they do. You know what they call.

The Fourteen Calls.

The slides get darker, as if a film has been placed over the laptop screen. You see things you don't want to remember. Things which haven't happened, but which you remember doing. You see a flicker of white—like a finger of bone. You see blood—lots of blood.

You see something so alien your mind blanks it out. A Voer-damnikenari.

More script that moves with insane intelligence.

The last slide is white. Completely white. And it's so sudden—so shocking—that you are thrown out of yourself.

You are thrown out time entirely.

Everything multiplies, as if you are seeing a dozen—no, more than that—*hundreds* of possibilities. Each one is a path that you can take. Some of them are paths you have taken already, even though you don't remember doing so.

Your identity fragments.

You have to choose a path, and you have to do so quickly. Before your mind tries to integrate all of these possible futures (and their pasts) into your psyche. Quick! Make a choice!

The index right in front of you.
Go to 61.

That *one*. Over *there*.
Go to 134.

No, not that one. *This* one. The one near your left hand.
Go to 166.

34

One of the physical trainers had a favorite saying he liked to offer at the end of a session: *Sure you look like shit, but always make sure the other guy looks worse.*

You make a mental note to track down the doctor's report when you get out of bed. Maybe that'll help jog your memory as to how you ended up in this infirmary bed.

What do you remember?

You close your eyes and practice deep meditation techniques, letting your mind empty. Unkink your chakras. There's a knot in your back like someone strapped a hot rock to your lumbar region. You try to wiggle away from it, but you can't get away from something under your skin. Remember Detroit three years ago? That knot of scar tissue isn't going away.

You weren't alone on this mission. You were part of a team. And there was a second team too. You had been called in because someone heard something that had made the listeners in Labyrinthian Observation and Byzantine Elucidation get all tingly. Something about a portal? No, not quite. A shoggoth city? No, definitely not that. Something else. Something *alien*.

Of course, when you talk about something alien in a room full of people who have been steeping in the lore of the Old Ones for their entire professional lives, you're talking about some really weird shit.

Or, as the joke goes around the Night Office: "Thursday."

As in: *"How was your day today, honey?"*

"Oh, you know. Non-Euclidian ziggurats. Space jelly constructs. Gates into infinite dimensions. Usual Thursday stuff."

"That's nice, dear. The Watkins invited us to their lake house."

"Is their aunt going to be there? God, it's so embarrassing when she drinks."

Joking about the job makes it seem normal, which is how you keep your sanity, right? It's okay to laugh at the senselessness of what you do. It's even okay to be a little terrified. But you learned a long time ago that freaking out isn't very efficient.

Efficiency matters. Obsessive-compulsive attention to detail might be humanity's saving grace, after all.

Anyway, you lay there for a minute, recalling that time when you and some of the others took over a hospital wing and convinced Harcourt he had been in a terrible car accident. It had taken him four hours to realize it was all a charade, and about six weeks before everyone stopped looking over their shoulder for his retribution. Could this be one of those practical jokes?

You lift the edge of the bandage on your left forearm. The wound is real. Some of the flesh is necrotic. Something took a bite out of you. Something that wasn't human.

Fantastic. Probably not a practical joke.

You yank out the shunt for the drip, and when the monitoring station starts beeping, you find its off-switch.

It gets quiet and you listen carefully.

All you hear is a distant moan that is the wind howling outside the station.

Where the fuck is everyone?

"You have to go look," you mutter to yourself. "That's the only way. You have to go look."

You're stiff in a way that suggests you've been doing strenuous exercise. There are more field dressings on your legs, and your calves and shins are discolored with bruises.

You're a mess. Better find some clothes.
Go to 18.

Your gear should be around here somewhere. Pants would be great, but what you really want is your discipline stick.
Go to 45.

35

The feeling comes on again. That tickle in the back of your throat. The hairs on your neck rising. Your intestines start to writhe.

"Open the door," you tell Pip. He flinches and shakes his head. "Do it now," you tell him, "before it comes back. That will give you a chance to get out of the way."

He shudders. His eyes are ping-ponging all over the place.

"I'm the Closer," you remind him. "I don't open doors."

"Oh, right. Right." He mimes slapping himself on the side of the head. He goes to the door, and as he reaches for the knob, a tiny sizzle of current meets him halfway. He yelps, but shows more backbone than you thought he posses, and doesn't stop. He pulls the door open and—

It's just a cubicle farm. There doesn't seem to be anyone at any of the desks. In fact, it looks like the floor hasn't been occupied yet. None of the desks you can see have anything on them.

You realize the carpet is the wrong color. There's a sign on the far wall. It's written in a script you don't know.

"Is this . . . ?"

He shakes his head. "It's not my index."

The growling noise starts, and you imagine it is coming from the throat of a great beast rushing toward you. You don't see anything, but you can feel its approach. The air darkens. Several of the panel lights in the ceiling flicker and go out. The cubicle walls start to waver, as if the individual molecules are starting to disassociate.

Pip is standing in the doorway.

"Get out of the way," you snarl as you step forward.

And then you see *it*.

You shove Pip aside.

Brace for impact. You're goign to get bounced somewhere. And it will likely be somewhere you don't expect.

You hope you've remembered enough about the mission to stay alive . . .

Go to 63.

Try to stay loose and flexible. It's going through you, and you're going to catch a ride. Be the reed, not the stone.

Go to 169.

36

You start reading the printed manuscript. It's a book called *The Albatross Legacy*, and it appears to be written by someone named Morgan.

PROLOGUE - VIENNA, 1986

Adrian Barstow knew the pair shadowing him were working for DIABOLIK. He was supposed to meet his contact with AMBER at the Rose Vault, the bar in the basement of the Grand Meridian Hotel, but he couldn't show up with these hired killers on his trail. He had to shake them, or kill them. He could do the latter readily enough as he was proficient in sixteen different martial traditions, as well as the darker arts known to a second-stage initiate of the Green Hand—the secret society that had taken him in as an orphan. But killing them would only tell DIABOLIK that he knew that they knew that he didn't want them to know what he was doing in Vienna, and he didn't want to send that message to the hidden masters of the nefarious crime syndicate that sought to destroy democracy in Europe. No, he had to find a way to confuse his shadows.

Barstow mingled with the crowd entranced by the lights of the Riesendrad, a 65-meter Ferris wheel that stood at the entrance of the Prater amusement park. Faces were awash with pinks and yellows and oranges as the wheel slowly made its clockwise rotation. As above, so below, Barstow thought. He made the ritual warding gesture as a woman's shriek—half in terror, half in feigned delight— drifted down from the top of the Ferris wheel. He stood by an old pillar and checked his back trail. There, he thought, spotting two faces that didn't reflect the lights from the wheel.

He left the square, heading north by northeast. He walked past the wax museum, where the lurid light of the front display would bifurcate the echo of his passing. One version of him would remain in front of the museum, striking a pose in front of a wax figure of a recent pop star, as if he was entranced by her pouting image. The other—the flesh and blood version—ducked down a nearby alley and walked swiftly to the recessed door of The Hallowed Stacks, an antiquarian bookstore known for its labyrinthian stacks. As well as a few secret exits . . .

Admit it. You're a little intrigued.
Go to 41.

Yes, but you're kind of in a hurry. Skip ahead.
Go to 101.

37

You don't have a lot of time. You have a quick Ward. It's useful for Closing Ziploc bags that don't seal well or doors that stick in humid weather. You can do it without thinking.

Argot's bag seals up around his hand. He can't get his gun out. It won't take him long to override your magic with his own, but at least you won't be dealing with both him and Sagalico at the same time.

The Guide is reaching under his coat for a weapon, and you decide old school is the best school. You body-check him against the wall. His eyes are glazed and a sheen of sweat is making his forehead shine. How deep is he? He bares his teeth—the sort of grimace you're more accustomed to seeing on the possessed than on a teammate—and you wish you had your discipline stick.

It's a piece of hand-tooled hardwood with a rough grip and a thickened tip. Looks innocent enough, but it's weighted in a way that its purpose is clear when you pick it up. It's been polished with your sweat many times, and it carries a little charge when you're in the mood. It gets people's attention, especially when they get smacked with it. A tap from your discipline stick would bring Sagalico back from the Way.

But you didn't bring it to this briefing, and so you have to resort to an open-handed slap instead. It creates a connection between the two of you, but what other choice do you have?

The world shifts as you smack him. He grunts, feeling the contact but not feeling it. He keeps struggling to get his gun out. You've got his arm pinned so that's not going to happen.

"Snap out of it," you snarl at him. "You're pulling us in."

There's a technical term for the Way, but no one ever uses it. It's that place outside of time and space, where the Old Ones swim. You can see the past and the future from there, and to some extent—by virtue of being an observer—you can influence the possibilities of a certain future.

It's a dangerous place to go, and a lot of Guide training is spent teaching them how NOT to look. Inference goes a long way, and it gives you some wiggle room. No one wants to be the idiot who stares an apocalyptic ending into existence.

But if you lean too hard into the Way, it starts to bend the rest of your reality—your index, to use a technical term. Teams have been lost because their Guide got caught. Everyone else got pulled in as they struggled to get out. Psychic quicksand, as it were.

Heat flares behind you. Argot has gotten his hand out of his bag. You smack Sagalico again. You probably won't get another chance. "Don't lock us in," you snap. "Look away."

Sagalico's eyes flutter, and somewhere, massive fields of butterflies fall out of the sky.

Something metallic and cold presses against the back of your head. "Let go of him," Argot says.

Sagalico shivers, his teeth clacking. He's not out of it yet. You're going to have to make a quick decision here. Who do you trust more? The man with the gun to the back of your head or the one who is losing his mind to a future that might not happen?

Trust is hard, isn't it?
Go to 44.

Will Argot shoot you? Only one way to find out.
Go to 49.

38

Sagalico pales as he comes back to you and Argot. "This is all—" he starts. "I'm not sure how much of what I've Seen is true."

"Noted," says Argot. "Get on with it, though."

"The expedition in '51. Starkweather's. They were supposed to verify what Pabodie and Lake thought they say in 1938. He—uh—there's someone else on that expedition. Someone who wasn't part of the Night Office." Sagalico shakes his head. "I don't know who this person was. Or why they were there. But they're important."

"Starkweather was the only one who came back," Argot says. "They never found the rest of the team."

"Yes, yes," Sagalico says. His eyes glaze over as he wanders into the Way again. You glance at Argot, who is flexing his fingers on his gun. He's not liking this either.

"The Calls," Sagalico mutters. "He showed them the Calls."

"Who did?" you snap.

"Starkweather. Starkweather showed us the way. He opened the Calls."

The way he is emphasizing that word is making you nervous. No one has messed around with Calls for a long time. Not since that English astrologer found a way to talk to . . . angels.

"The Voerdamnikenari answered," Sagalico says. "They're an old race. Not as old as . . ."

His mouth works but no name comes out. We all know better than to speak their names out loud.

"They were scattered eons ago," Sagalico says. "Wandering ever since. Hoping and waiting for another race to contact them."

"Through these Calls," Argo says.

"Yes, through the Calls," Sagalico echoes.

"Is that what happened in the Antarctic?" you ask.

"No," Sagalico says. "Yes."

You trade looks with Argot. The downside of the Way is that sometimes a simple answer is the hardest to get.

"They turned on a beacon," Sagalico said. "They are coming for the Invocation, which will open the Void Firmament."

"That doesn't sound good," you say.

"No," Argot snarls. "It doesn't."

Sagalico sags against one of the chairs. His face is slick with sweat. "We're too late," he whispers.

Go to 40.

39

Argot pulls a gun out of his bag, and he points it at you.

You hold still, letting him know you're not about to do something rash.

Sagalico is shaking his head, and his gaze is unfocused. "That's not—" He frowns.

He's tracking a possible future in the Way. The Way is where the Old Ones swim, and it's some nth-dimensional slip that compresses all of the galaxies into a single point that defies all reality—or some such nonsense like that. What Guides know—and use the Way for—is that you can see the past and glimpse the future from the Way. You're an observer, though, and the act of observing can influence. Look too closely, and you've just locked in the future you've been peeking at. Most of what the Night Office teaches you about the Way is how NOT to look. No one wants to be that idiot who gazes into the Abyss so hard that they create it.

Anyway, Sagalico has obviously gotten tangled in a thread of a possible future, and he's tugging on it.

What is he doing? You're not supposed to invoke the way in the Night Office. You shouldn't be calling attention to this location in this way.

Argot's thinking along the same lines as you. "What are you doing, Sagalico?" he demands. His question doesn't shift the barrel of his gun from pointing at you.

"Is that a . . . ? A recursion loop? How did this happen?"

Your stomach does a flip. *A recursion loop?* Talk about theoretical Way nonsense.

Sagalico's eyes come back into focus. "We're on a loopback," he says flatly. He points a gloved hand at you. "You did something."

"I don't know what you're talking about," you say.

"You've been here already. You're trying to create an inversion."

"A what?"

Argot moves around the table so that he can keep his gun pointed at both of you. "An inversion is when a timeline is canceled because of a specific event, or the lack of a specific event."

"Theoretically speaking," you point out. "We wouldn't even notice."

"Or we'd cease to exist."

"Yes, but once you start down that path, everything is relative. Everything gets split—over and over again. There's an infinite number of timelines." You glare at Argot. "You've sat in the same training," you say. "This is speculative. It can't be observed. We can't know because we're all relatively objective."

"Indexes," Sagalico says. "They call them 'indexes.'"

"Who calls what 'indexes'?"

"The other timeline. The one who sent you."

"Sent me? What the hell are you talking about?"

Sagalico looks at Argot. "This isn't our Closer. She's a permutation—a possible configuration from another index."

Argot cocks the hammer back on his gun. "So what do we do about her?"

You keep your hands in plain sight. This can't get any more out of hand.

Go to 42.

Sagalico's lost his mind. You need to take matters into your own hands.

Go to 54.

40

This is all back story, you know. Things went badly when you, Argot, and Sagalico arrived. The other team . . . the other team had been compromised. You were, too. That's why your memories are all fucked up.

Straighten them out. Find your way through.

Endoluvion found an artificat in the ice. They turned it on, and it started broadcasting across time and space. *Hey, there's intelligent life on this blue marble. Come and see!*

Or maybe the Voerdamnikenari sold you out, offering you as a sacrifice. When an Old One wakes, it doesn't care what it eats. It only wants to assuage its eternal hunger and go back to sleep. The Voerdamnikenari don't want to be next on the menu.

Someone touched the obelisk in the ice. They want you to think you did it, but you know that's not true. You're a Closer. You don't touch alien artifacts. You seal them away so no one can use them. Ever. And you're good at your job.

Enough of this laying about. Time to save the world.

Yes, but let's be careful about how we go running toward this disaster.

Go to 18.

Right. MacReady Station. Things are terrible. You need to get your gear. It's got to be somewhere in this station.

Go to 80.

41

Barstow ducked through the narrow panel. He was no longer skulking through a stone-lined passage that dated back several hundred years. He was standing in a back hall of a rustic, but well-polished, establishment. His eyes adjusted to the moody atmosphere provided by recessed lighting in the ceiling. A piano player was noodling through a mid-century Jazz standard in the open room ahead of him. Behind him, through a pair of hanging doors, he heard the metallic buzz of a kitchen staff.

A young woman in black carrying a tray of small plates made to squeeze by him, and he muttered a smooth apology as he pressed himself against the wall. He caught a brief glimpse of her face—narrow eyes, thin lips, gleam of some kind of metal jewelry in her nose—as she passed.

He followed her into the main lounge of the Rose Vault, where he quickly took stock of the room. The piano was on a raised stage, and floodlights provided most of the illumination in the room. Tiny pots with flickering lights marked the tables, and they offered enough light for Barstow to make out vague shapes. Bodies, but no features.

Opposite the stage, there was a curved bar, a burnished wave of pale wood. Shelves behind it were stocked with a deep selection of fine malts and rarified spirits. The glow of the wood and the bottles revealed the faces of those who sat at the bar, and Barstow scanned them for the face of his contact. He spotted her at the end, and he threaded his way through the maze of tables to her side.

"I admire magnanimous and busty evangelists who

redact," he said when she looked at him. It was a nonsensical phrase, but it included the proper mnemonic.

"Yes, but can they whistle?" She replied. She put her lips together—soft and velvety and so very cherry red—and whistled the opening notes of "Augurs of Spring" from Igor Stravinsky's classic Rites of Spring.

Morgan has a certain pulpy flair, don't they? It certainly pulls you right along.

Go to 51.

This isn't moving quickly enough. Skip ahead in the manuscript.

Go to 101.

42

"We should talk this through," you say. "There's no need to do anything rash."

Argot doesn't lower his gun, but you can see a flicker of agreement in his steely gaze. "Spill," he growls at Sagalico. "What's in the Way?"

"This mission has . . . it's already happened," he says. "She's trying to rewind it."

"What? How is that even possible?"

"I don't know," Sagalico says, "but that's what they say."

Argot doesn't like that word. *They*. No one does. It get used too often to justify shitty behavior. "Who?" he asks.

"The Night Office in that index."

"What's an index?" you say. "You said it before. What does that mean?"

"Reality is quantified and bound by an index," Sagalico says. "It's like how computer databases are summarized for easy access. If you have an index, you know where everything is, across all time and space."

"You do?" This is news to you, and judging by Argot's expression, it's news to him as well.

Sagalico sneers at both of you. "You haven't been keeping up on the publications coming out of LOBE, have you?"

"I've been busy," you say.

Argot waves his pistol, telling Sagalico to stay on topic.

"We know *they*—not the other Night Office, but *them*—"

You get the stress he's putting on the word. He's talking about those cosmic intelligences who are mostly indifferent to humanity, except when they are bored or hungry.

"—they exist across multiple quantum states," Sagalico says. "We see them moving in and out of focus, but what they are doing is passing through multiple realities. Each of those realities is objectively manifest to some degree. Those are measured by the indexes."

"Fine, fine," you say. "But what does this have to do with the Way and the future?"

"The Way is the quantum flux of their existence," Sagalico says.

"Hold on now—" Argot starts.

You don't like the sound of that either. No wonder looking into the Way is dangerous.

Argot's hand tightens on his pistol.

Argot is getting *more* agitated. Not less. You need to try something else.

Go to 40.

Sagalico's been looking too far. What he knows is going to break everything.

Go to 54.

43

It doesn't matter, does it? No matter how you contort yourself. You always come back to the same place. You can keep trying, of course, but eventually, you will realize there is no way out. Eventually, you will realize that you've already died, and this is your last breath. Your last thought . . .

Pity. This isn't how you imagined it would happen . . .

THIS IS A RECURSION LOOP. THIS IS THE SORT OF TRAP YOU'RE GOING TO FALL INTO IN THIS EXERCISE. PAY ATTENTION. THIS IS THE ONLY TIME YOU WILL BE GIVEN A CHANCE TO START OVER.

Go to the WHITE ROOM.

44

Trust is tough, especially when you've just met someone. But—and this is broadly generous, of course—among Night Office field operatives, Openers aren't very complicated people. Many of them are arrogant jerks, but they think in very concrete terms. Open this. Shoot that. Get out of the way of the other thing over there. They don't like nuance.

Guides on the other hand? Always aloof and cryptic, and not because they're trying to get into your pants. They walk a knife edge all the time. One slip, and they've just locked in the wrong future. It can make you very paranoid.

If you had to trust one of these types with your life, it's pretty easy to figure out which of the two is less likely to turn on you. (Except for that one time, of course, but let's not get caught up in the exceptions.)

When Sagalico goes feral and tries to bite you—because that's the way this is going to play out—you're ready for that nonsense. You lean to the side.

Argot pulls the trigger on his weapon.

Fortuately, your head is out of the way.

You can't hear anything after that. You see everything, however, and Sagalico's brains are all over the wall. You're not going to forget that sight for a long time.

YOU'LL GET OVER IT. THE NIGHT OFFICE OFFERS COMPREHENSIVE MENTAL HEALTH COUNSELING PACKAGES. THIS WASN'T YOUR FAULT.

MAPS SCORE: 47

45

You are in a central corridor that runs along one side of the station. Opposite you in another—shorter—corridor. The halls are prefab construction—formed in a factory in Scandinavia, flown over in the belly of a C-130 or the like, and then assembled with some allen wrenches and a generous amount of swearing. You feel like it's a place you've been in before (which, obviously, you have), while simultaneously being the same fucking generic layout of every office building everywhere.

Not much help. You can blame this confusion on the blow to your head. That's why you're having trouble remembering anything about this station. *What's it called again? McClarren? No, MacReady.*

You've got to get your head on straight. You might be the only person still alive in this place.

Anyway, what were you doing? Oh, right. The records say you died, and that the body is stored in a locker down in some sub-level.

This isn't right. You can't be both alive and dead. Maybe you should get a second opinion. Yeah. That's probably a good idea. Deep breaths. Maybe you should do that exercise you were taught in that weekend seminar. What did they call it? Ah, yes, "Building a Psychic Network."

Go to 85.

Bother. Guess you'd better go check on that.
Go to 109.

46

A bout of dizziness makes your knees shake. You consider vomiting. When the feeling passes, you focus on the door in front of you. Beside it is a sign that reads "Dr. Nakamura."

You're in the station. A corridor stretches out in either direction. You have choices, but you don't remember enough to know where you need to go next.

You recall a conversation you had with the Old Man, back when he was still alive. You'd been debriefed from your last mission and were having a glass of whiskey with him in his office. You and the Guide had teetered on the edge of an infinite void. *The human mind invents reality as readily as it falsely remembers the past,* he had said. He smiled, as if he was enjoying a private joke.

You are suddenly struck by the notion that he wasn't talking about the mission your had just finished. He was telling you something that you were supposed to remember later.

Of course, it's also possible I never said that, and you're just making it up, the Old Man—the one in your head—points out.

Imaginary friends are the worst, aren't they?

Anyway, you and the Old Man talked about dreams and symbols. He told you about Jung and the notion of the collective unconscious—the symbolic layer that existed beneath language. Things that rise out this layer are translated by our brain into "thoughts," and we pretend that the "I" part of our consciousnesses just came up with these notions.

This is all Descartes's fault, of course.

The point being, he said, *is that when we try to source a thought, we insist on building a rational framework to that thought. It must come from memory. It must have been gleaned from the application of known principles.*

Like when you think: *I like dogs.* Why do you like dogs? You never had a dog as a child. But there are images in your brain that are "dog-like," and the emotional responses associated with those images make you want to hug yourself.

The point is: memory is a series of associated links, and to have amnesia is to be disassociated with the banks of images within your brain that constitute your "memory." It's like visiting a library that has no card catalog. There are many books here, but you have no idea where any particular book is shelved. How do you find a specific book? You could wander the shelves, looking for a specific title, but it'll take you days—or years—to find it.

God, this is frustrating. Focus on one thing. Focus on a next step. What was that? Oh, yes, looking for your gear. Where could it be? Ah, how about a storage room?
Go to 53.

You can't let this—let *him*—distract you. Keep on with the mission, even though you have no idea what is going on.

Which is to say, in Night Office parlance: "Thursday."
Go to 56.

47

You're standing in a corridor that runs from one end of the station to another. You have a dim recollection of the station's layout, and you recall there are two hallways, sort of like an uppercase 'H.' You entered the station through a mud room/ airlock, which was at the top of the 'H.' From there, you had access to either leg.

It starts to come back to you. Yes, on the left is Ops, the radio room, and the computer lab. On the right, there is another entrance to Ops, a briefing room and library, followed by the infirmary and Dr. Nakamura's office.

At the far end, there is a connecting corridor, where there were some work areas and a common room. At the very back, there are some emergency exits and the umbilical to leads to the labs.

You've been in the

(white room)

lab space, but you don't recall anything about them.

Before you go rushing into what is likely a terrible situation, maybe you should secure your gear. The lab coat and orange coverall look is very chic, but it lacks pockets.

Well, that's not totally fair. You have a half dozen pockets. There's nothing in them, and that's going to a problem.

Go to 53.

The labs are important. Head for them.

Go to 106.

48

Dr. Nakamura's desk contains the usual array of office supplies. Heavy on the boxes of staples. She's either a hoarder or she generates a lot of paperwork.

There's a laser printer on a lateral filing cabinet behind you, as well as a couple of reams of paper. Stacked and ready. The doc does generate a lot of paper.

The lateral filing cabinet is locked. It's not a very secure lock, however. You picked a lot of these during school. All you need is a pair of paperclips, which Dr. Nakamura has plenty of.

Another cabinet is covered with warning labels. Poison. Controlled substances. Fire hazards.

You're tempted for a moment. There's probably drugs in that cabinet. Pain meds. Anti-psychosis pills. Maybe even something a little more psychedelic, which you wouldn't mind right now. That would clear away some of this mental fog.

The cabinet has keycard panel on it. You're not going to get in there with a paperclip.

Lateral filing cabinet it is. It doesn't take long. Those life skills you picked up during those rebellious years come in handy once again. Straighten the clips; angle them like that; and . . . *huzzabuzzah*: an open lock.

You flip through the folders inside the cabinet, trying to figure out the doc's filing system. Colored tabs. Some alphabetical. Some numeric coding . . .

Ah, here we go. Green is for incident reports, red is for medical procedures, and black is for autopsy reports.

There are eight black folders, which is more than you'd expect in a place like this. Either Dr. Nakamura isn't very good at her job, or there's some risk associated with being assigned to the loneliest place at the bottom of the world.

The black tab files are ordered by date. Which one should you read first?

Read the most recent file. You don't have time to wade through the entire history of what happened here.
Go to 50.

Start at the back. There's got to be some thread linking all these deaths. You need to pay attention to the subtleties this time around.
Go to 52.

49

Salagico is insistent. "She touched the thing that should not be touched."

Your hands tighten on him. If he looks far enough into the Way, he's going to fix the future. Whatever he sees will be what happenes.

"We can't let him interpret the signs," you say over your shoulder to Argot. "If he reads it wrong, we're all doomed."

"What are you going to do?" Argot asks. The gun is still touching the back of your head.

"How do I know?" you say. "He's the one who is locking in a possible future. I don't even know what thing he's talking about."

(but you do)

"She's unmakes us," Sagalico moans. "She wants to unseal what has been sealed."

You can feel Argot tense. A Closer doing an Opener's job? That's downright rude.

Sagalico's eyes open, and there is a dread finality in his gaze. "Open her up," he says. "Let us see if she's telling the truth."

"No, wait," you say. "We don't have—"

Sagalico doesn't look away as Argot pulls the trigger on his weapon. This is Sagalico's sacrifice. He gets to save the world this time.

AS A NIGHT OFFICE FIELD OPERATIVE, YOU HAVE TO MAKE HARD CHOICES, AND SOMETIMES THOSE CHOICES GET MADE FOR YOU.

MAPS SCORE: 29

50

The most recent black tab file is a few days old. There are photos, and you scan them quickly, keeping a tight rein on your emotions. *You're the Closer*, you remind yourself. If the job goes sideways, it's going to be up to you to do the hard work. You have to be ready for it.

The victim's face isn't recognizable, due to the massive blunt force trauma sustained to the head and shoulders. However, each of the pictures is labeled with a name. "Gull."

She was the Guide on the first team.

According to Dr. Nakamura's notes, Gull had accused members of the Endoluvion team of being—Dr. Nakamura's disbelief is evident here in how she writes the next words— "skin walkers." These team members—listed as "R. Clark" and "C. Norris"—objected to these names. An alteration broke out in one of the research labs.

You search your memory for some recollection of the lab spaces. There's something in your head, but it darts away when you try to focus. *Leave it*, you think. It'll come in its own time.

Near the bottom of the page, she wrote "MBFS," along with a question mark. Dr. Nakamura didn't know the acronym, but you do.

A while back, you were tasked with investigating mysterious shipping company named Carcosa International that was moving lots of dirt back and forth across the United States. Most of Carcosa's clients were Big Ag and new-to-market pharmaceutical companies, which could explain all the dirt, but LOBE didn't like it. They saw the shipments as part of something more insidious.

Your team stopped a rig at a Flying Elvins truck stop outside of Lock Haven, Pennsylvania, intending to pop the shipping container and get a look at the cargo. The rig driver wasn't inclined to let you, mostly because he wasn't human any more.

The shoggoth had spent most of the long haul from California infiltrating the driver. The driver could pass for human—well, his conversation skills were shit, but it wasn't like he had to talk to people during his drive. If you hadn't been put off by the way he kept breathing through his mouth, the space jelly would have probably gotten the jump on your team.

Ullman—the team's Guide—told everyone about how you knew. "Mouth-Breathing Flesh Sack," he said to a rapt audience in the break room one afternoon. "That's how you know. If they look like an MBFS, they probably are."

Gull had been in the rotation for at least a year at that time. Surely she had heard the story, because Ullman wasn't shy about telling it over and over again. But why had Gull mentioned it to Dr. Nakamura? You don't talk to locals like that. They don't know what you know. They're only going to freak out and—

Well, look what happened to Gull.

There's not much you can do with all this. You should keep moving.

Go to 47.

Check the other files.

Go to 52.

51

Her name was Catalonia von Dietrich. Surely an alias, but then so was Adrian Barstow, so who was he to judge? She had feral eyes, hair the color of a smoldering fire, and curves that were more reckless than the southern descent from the top of Semple Hill. Just outside of Mariondale, where he had gotten his first taste of speed and learned that he liked it.

"What are you drinking?" He asked.

She looked at him over the rim as she put those red lips to the glass. He caught a flash of white teeth as she let the tawny alcohol roll to the back of her throat.

"I'll have the same," he told the bartender.

Her gaze lingered on his watch and on the silver buckle of his leather belt. "Are you as impressive as you look?" She asked. "Or is this a disguise?"

"I'm trying to blend in," he said.

"You are very bad at it." When she tossed her hair, he noticed the sharp edge of a tattoo peeking out from the spangled neckline of her emerald dress. He wondered which ritual the symbol was a part of. Acheron's Eighth Warding perhaps? Or was it Farmingle's Superior Etheric Barrier Against Invasive Mental Assault?

Barstow wanted to reach out and push the fabric of her dress back. Get a better look at her body. Expose more of her delightfully smooth skin. He fought the urge, yet another round in the ring with those prickly sensations that reminded him of the life he had given up when he entered the Service.

Wait a minute. Barstow's personal issues aside, those sound like actual Night Office spells. What the hell is going on?

Go to 57.

Morgan has clearly read too many pulp stories from the early twentieth century. This is a waste of your time. You have a mission to finish. Time to get back to it.

Got to 165.

52

Wait a minute, this folder has . . . your name on it.

Your hand shakes as you read. According to Dr. Nakamura's notes, you were brought in on Sunday afternoon. She treated you for trauma to the skull (something hit you), lacerations to the forearm (something bit you), and a high degree of agitation and incoherence. She had to sedate you in order to clean up your injuries, and it looks like she used the good stuff. The report reads like you were jumped by a wild animal while out hiking.

Except, of course, there are no wild animals on the Antarctic Plateau, and no ones goes out hiking in - 53° C.

According to these notes, you went into cardiac arrest six hours later. Dr. Nakamura tried to revive you, and shortly after midnight Monday morning, she pronounced you dead.

You reread the section where Dr. Nakamura lists your injuries. Trauma to the head. More specifically, evidence of a depression fracture on the occipital bone in the— You probe that spot with your fingers and find nothing but hair and a hard head.

You don't feel dead.

There's a note at the bottom of the page: "Removed to Cold Storage. Gamma—Locker Four."

Great. You're going to have to go look, aren't you? If there's a body in that locker . . . well, don't think about that too much right now. Just go check.

Go to 45.

You can't be dead, because, you know, here you are, reading this note. Standing. Breathing. Getting pissed off. Those are some pretty solid benchmarks for "life."

Which means . . . ah, this is Sagalico was talking about, isn't it? What did he call it? A *recursion*.

But what is a "recursion"?

Go to 55.

53

Nearby, there's an intersection between the hall you are in (it's the West Corridor, remember?) and a hall that runs perpendicular. This hall—the cross-bar of the 'H'—runs past a common area and the mess on one side, and on the other side of the hall are a number of closed doors. One of them is conveniently marked "Storage."

The storage room door is unlocked. You open it and quickly slip inside the room. It's very dark, and you fumble

(no no no not the light!)

for a light switch. The room is suddenly filled with the artificial glow of ancient fluorescent lighting.

You investigate. Non-critical medical supplies are on one rack. There are office supplies on another rack. A third rack has prepackaged condiments and serving materials for the mess.

Man, someone really is organized. In fact, the room is so organized that it's pretty obvious in less than a minute that your stuff isn't here.

Okay, okay. Where else might your gear be stashed?
Go to 56.

Well, that was a waste of time. Time which you don't have. You need to find someone. Start with Ops.
Go to 84.

54

You've heard it said that the pulse of the Way is nothing more than the heartbeat of one of *them*, and as you watch Sagalico drift back and forth, you realize the rumor might be true.

A vein pulses on the side of Argot's temple. He's coming to the same conclusion.

A look of confusion sweeps over Sagalico's face, as if he suddenly remembered he wasn't wearing pants. He hiccups once, giggles sheepishly for having done so, and then hiccups again. Except this time, something comes out of his mouth.

It's black and sticky and filled with star stuff.

Argot starts shooting.

You yell at him to get out of the room as you start weaving a Ward of Closing. *Not here*, you think. Not in the Night Office.

You have no choice. That's a space jelly crawling out of Sagalico's mouth. There's a gate inside him. He looked too long. He listened too hard. And they got him. And now he's nothing more than a doorway.

A doorway you're going to Close.

"Move," you shout at Argo.

Argot heads for the door, and you fall in behind him. He keeps shooting, and what spatters on the wall behind Sagalico moves in unnatural directions.

Sagalico lurches against the table. A tentacle crawls out of his mouth and slaps against the tabletop, leaving a trail of slime.

Argot puts a hand on your shoulder, letting you know he's going to make sure you don't bump into anything as you back up. You focus on your words, on completing the Ward.

Sagalico gurgles and lurches toward you. Another tentacle forces its way out of his mouth. The space jelly knows what you are trying to do.

You hear the door open behind you. Argot taps you twice, letting you know the path is clear. You backpedal quickly, and Sagalico charges.

You're through the door. Argot slams it shut, and the panel shivers as what-was-Sagalico runs into it. The voice you hear howling in the room isn't human. You don't let it distract you.

You know what to do.

ANY TIME A SPACE JELLY IS DENIED ACCESS, A NIGHT OFFICE FIELD OPERATIVE GETS A COMMENDATION. IT DOESN'T MATTER THAT YOU NEVER GOT TO YOUR MISSION.

OR MAYBE YOU DID. MAYBE YOU UNDID EVERYTHING THAT IS YET TO HAPPEN BY GOING BACK AND REMOVING THE THREAT BEFORE IT COULD MANIFEST . . . ?

WHICHEVER, DON'T THINK ABOUT IT TOO HARD. TAKE THE COMMENDATION AND THE SCORE.

MAPS SCORE: 72

55

Somewhere over the Mid-Atlanic, partway through the Sao Paulo to Troll Station leg of your trip. You've been traveling for twenty-four hours straight. You haven't slept. You started hallucinating an hour ago, and you're managing those with the little mini bottles you got from the flight attendant on the Chicago to Atlanta portion of your flight. It's not a good solution, but it'll do.

Anyway, as you were staring at the rivets on the metal bulkhead of the Hercules C-130 cargo plane, Sagalico sat in a nearby jump seat. Not the one next to you. You and he have worked out the parameters of your working relationship. It's not that you're a prickly bitch—you'll happily lay claim to that title whenever it gets you out of talking to boring people—it's that your Guide creeps you out.

It's part of the job description, actually. The gung-ho ex-military "I do my job because it's what my country would want of me" types are always Openers. First in. Bang bang. Covered in glory bullshit. The ones who don't like talking to people—girls, especially—and who like to sit in the back of the room and stare at people with wide, unblinking eyes, they like to have secrets. They like to know things they shouldn't. They're always more sensitive to the Way than everyone else.

Fabrienne was working on a monograph about the correlation between psychopathic tendencies and the ability to step into the Way. You saw an early draft—agreed with a lot of it, actually—but the Old Man shut her down before she could publish.

This isn't Behavioral Sciences at Quantico, he told her. *We don't care what they do when they're off the clock. When they're on, they work for us. It's as simple as that.*

Farbrienne took the hint. Last you heard, she was working on a next-gen profiling paradigm for the FBI. A modeling program that would identify serial killers before the broken parts of their brains took control.

Anyway, Sagalico fit the profile, right down to his calfskin gloves, his overly long overcoat, and his terribly trendy neck scarf. He had a habit of tittering to himself between sentences, like he was practicing for some henchman role in a direct-to-video pulp movie.

"What do you know about the persistence of time?" he asked.

"I don't know," you said. "It's persistent . . . ?"

"It's not always linear," he said, ignoring your snark. "It is more like a circulatory system. It's flexible. It changes. It gets damaged and it heals itself, but it might not always heal in the same way."

"That's why we have people like you," you replied. "Someone has to keep track of where it all goes."

At the time, that didn't strike you as especially profound, but now that you think about it, "guide" is the wrong word for what guys like Sagalico did. They were more like trackers.

"Heraclitus said you could never step in the same river twice," Sagalico said. "That was his big revelation about time, but he missed the bigger picture. It's all about the flow. It's is always flowing *downstream*, toward the past and away from the future."

"Wait. Did you say 'toward the past'?"

He smiled, and you wanted to kick yourself for letting him know you were actually paying attention. "You probably think time should flow toward the future," he said, "because of how we understand aging. But whatever metaphor we wrap around it is immaterial. We usually call it a river, but why couldn't it be a circulatory system? It allows blood to flow through the body."

"But a circulatory system is closed," you said. "It's a loop. Time's not a loop."

"No, it's not," he said. "It's a flow."

"I feel like this conversation is a—" You smiled at him. "A loop," you finished, feeling clever about yourself.

He regarded you with a look that said he thought you were a moron. Or maybe it was the look he gave everyone he was thinking about carving up. It was hard to tell with Sagalico.

"What's your point?" you asked.

"If time flows through a system that can be expressed as 'circulatory,' then it is, by definition, circular. Meaning, you can visit the same spot again."

You waited for him to deliver the punchline—the insightful factoid about the Way that he really wanted to share.

"It's called a recursion," he said eventually. "It's what happens when you return to the same place within time."

"And then what?" you asked.

"What do you mean?"

"What's the point? So, okay, I can rescurse to a point in time. Cool. But so what?"

Sagalico leaned over the empty seat between you. "Maybe you could fix something you broke," he said. "Wouldn't that be worth doing?"

That's been bugging you for awhile, hasn't it? Good thing you remembered it.

Go to 59.

At the time, you thought he was messing with you. That's the sort of Guide he was, after all. But now? Now, you're not so sure.

Go to 83.

56

You head for the office next to the storage room. There's a keycard reader next to the door, but the light on it is green. You open the door and go into the office.

It's three meters by three meters. There's a desk, a chair, a counter, a stool shoved in the corner, and a bookcase. The desk is tidy, and the computer's screen doesn't wake when you nudge the mouse. The counter has a bunch of schematics strewn across it, and the bookcase is filled with a bunch of blue and yellow binders that are labeled with an alphanumeric system you don't recognize.

You're delighted to find your coat thrown over the stool, and when you glance around for your discipline stick, you spot it leaning against the wall behind the door.

Finally!

You swap the lab coat for your official Night Office vestment, and the shifting weight of your coat is a comfortable presence on your shoulders. You check a few pockets

(*chapstick, snow goggles, gloves, hand grenade, a couple of Sharpies, Elder stone, moist towelette . . .*)

and are pleased to discover no one has gone through your gear.

(*Where's the knife?*)

You retrieve your stick. It feels good in your hand and you twirl—

—Oh, it's just a lamp. Don't worry about it. The Night Office will replace it.

Anyway, you've got your coat and stick. Now you're ready to face whatever fungi or slime or howling void-bleater is waiting for you.

Not so fast. Maybe you should take a closer look at those schematics on the counter.
Go to 60.

Head for the West Corridor.
Go to 76.

Check out the East Corridor.
Go to 79.

Onward! Let's head for the labs.
Go to 133.

57

You turn the page in Morgan's manuscript and find a section in a very different typeface. It looks like something that has been cut and pasted from a different document.

> Thus, have I given of my blood and spirit. Thus, have I given of my spirit and soul. Thus, have I devoted myself to the fulsomeness of the night. I beseech [Ettrudiax'a ???] to appear. Reveal yourself in my scrying mirror. I open the Way to you. Place yourself in me. I open myself to you. Cross the veil and reveal to me the secrets of the Voerdamnikenari Ascension. Arise [Ettrudix'a ???], and show me your pleasures. I am the fulcrum. I am the anchor. Come, and praise me for my devotion.

This has to be one of the Calls that Starkweather brought back from his mission. What is it doing in this manuscript? Was Morgan one of the Endoluvion employees who was doing the Working?

This isn't good.

Keep reading.
Go to 96.

Skip ahead. See if Morgan copied more of these invocations into his manuscript.
Go to 176.

58

When you blink, you find yourself in the West Corridor of MacReady Station.

Ugh? Really?

This is what happens when you can't remember everything, the Old Man whispers. *It all gets a little slippery.*

Fine. Whatever. You grit your teeth. *You have a mission to do,* you think. *You can't get distracted.*

The Weste Corridor allows you access to Ops, a briefing room, the library, the infirmary, and Dr. Nakamura's office.

The West Corridor is connected to the East Corridor by a short hall known as the Bar—which isn't as fun as it sounds. There aren't any tiki lights, for one. But you can get to the kitchen, a common area, a couple of small offices, and the Umbilical, which is the passage to the other building, where all the science is done.

You don't have a lot of time to be wandering around. Especially when you don't have your gear.

Go to 56.

Head for the "Bar," even though there's no jukebox and nothing on tap.

Go to 71.

Your stomach reminds you that you haven't eaten anything in awhile. Maybe you can find something in the kitchen.

Go to 78.

Did you miss something in Dr. Nakamura's office?

Go to 81.

Start at the top. Visit Ops.
Go to 84.

There's a dim flicker of something in your head when you think about the briefing room.
Go to 99.

You're done here. Head for the Umbilical.
Go to 106.

Perhaps the books in the library will offer some insight. No, really. It's not because you want to check out what kind of books the crew might be reading.
Go to 115.

59

Having sorted out that bit of backstory, you get back to the mission at hand, which is figuring out what happened at the station. To do that, you really are going to need your gear. After wandering out of the doctor's office, you find yourself at one end of a long hall that looks like it runs the length of the station. There's another corridor that runs perpendicular to the one you are in. On your right is an emergency exit as well as an opening covered with multiple layers of heavy plastic.

This is the Umbilical. It leads to the research labs of the station. There will be answers down there, but you really shouldn't go anywhere without your gear.

There are several doors in the short hall opposite you. The first one is marked "Storage." The next one is labeled with someone's name, and you figure it for a tiny administrative office.

Check out the storage room.
Go to 53.

Check out the office.
Got to 80.

60

You peruse the schematics and technical drawings on the counter. The narrow drawers under the counter are filled with more of them. If you were the type who gets all hot and bothered about architecture plans and circuit diagrams, this would be heaven. Regardless, this probably isn't the time to get distracted by . . .

Oh, look, here's one made by Jelicore. *A Dual-core Reverse Circulation Diamond Depth Extractor (Mobile).* It looks like someone attached pistons and a toaster to a giant spider. The scale says this device is a hundred meters tall.

Great. Talk about nightmare fuel.

You shuffle through the stack for another minute, and as you're putting them away, you find a small drawing in the back of one of the drawers. It's a pencil sketch, and it's a picture of a long object. An obelisk. There are—

(Where's the knife?)

The sigils on the damn thing give you an immediate headache. You can't look at them. They're—

(Call them! Call them!)

moving in a way that they shouldn't. Not on paper.

A bloody thumbprint is smeared on the lower edge of the drawing. You turn it over. A warning has been scrawled on the back. "Don't let them touch it."

It looks like your handwriting.

Well, that's creepy.
Go to 76.

Well, that's ominous.
Go to 79.

61

You find a room marked "RADIO" off the East Corridor, and you gingerly push open the door. There's a familiar smell waiting for you. When you flip on the light—yep, that smell's pretty unmistakable—you spot the dead body near the work-station where the radio gear is all racked up.

You're no expert at radio hardware, but you know the difference between "switched off" and "smashed up." This gear is definitely in the latter category. You look around for a log book or something, trying not inadvertently stumble over the body.

Which is missing both the top of its skull and what usually resides in the skull, by the way. The floor is covered with dried blood. Whoever this person was, you hope they died quickly. Being alive as your brains get scooped out of your skull can't be much fun.

Anyway, you find a spiral notebook. The date stamp on the cover is three months old. You flip through it, scanning the log of incoming and outgoing radio transmissions. You consider sitting down to examine the logbook, but you realize there's dried blood on the mesh-back fabric of the chair.

It's okay. You don't need to sit. You'v been doing a lot of lying down recently, anyway.

You don't fully understand the shorthand used by the radio operator, but you can parse the gist of the records. Operations were normal until the last week of August. On the 26th, there was a flurry of messages, both coming and going.

You manage to translate the marginalia. The station's internet connection went down. The radio was the only way to communicate. Every hour, someone tried to ping the outside world. Standard procedure. It's the Antarctic, remember? No one was panicking yet.

On the third of September, there's a note written very clearly. "RECY ENCRYPT. SHARE PASS NEO-TOKYO START." You don't want to have to decipher bad handwriting when you're making important notes.

On the next page, the handwriting changes. Someone else is writing the log. The entries are written in plain English—none of the shorthand from the previous entries—and the writer signs these entries with their name: "Bennings."

The first entry is dated September 4th.

> *Copper's dead. Elkhorn noticed he wasn't at his desk at 1000 hours this morning. Copper's usually at station before 0600. Elkhorn went down to Crew to see if Copper was still in his bunk. He was, but like Blair, he had gotten soft. Palmer has a name for it, but I'm not going to write it down. I'm not going to pretend there is anything normal about how he died.*

> *Anyway, Copper's gone. Elkhorn knew I had some amateur radio experience, and so he assigned me in his place. It's my job now to keep trying to get a signal out, although I have no idea what we're transmitting. Copper locked the whole terminal down. He left a note about a shared key, but he kept it vague. I don't know what the password is. All I can do is keep trying.*

The next entry is dated September 6th.

> *We found Palmer's body this morning. Morgan is missing. I do not know if anyone is receiving my transmission. There's something growing down in Geology. It's not right. We're trapped here with it.*

The following page has been torn out of the notebook. There are impressions of a pen on the following blank page, but they're not clear enough to read.

Now you know a little more about those who have died so far. Of course, the dead ones aren't going to be all that helpful.

What happened to Copper and Palmer? Was Morgan found? What does going "soft" mean? Too many questions.

You glance at the body. Is that Bennings?

Go to 67.

If you don't have your gear, maybe you should find it before you stumble across any more bodies.

Go to 80.

You really need to find someone alive. Get on with the mission.

Go to 106.

Busted radio. Check. Strange deaths. Check. Everything is as creepy as you expected it to be. The fun keeps getting more fun, doesn't it?

If you've got your gear, continue to investigate the station.

Go to 123.

62

You look around for a sharp knife or a long stick or something. There's got to be something here, right?

There are no knives, which is very odd, especially when you sort of remember that you have one—*had* one. You got it from—never mind, that was something else. That's not this—

You stop as you realize you're talking to yourself. Your heart is racing, and you're having trouble focusing. There's something not quite right in your head.

You find a broom. You can screw off the bristled end and make it a stick. It's not a sharp stick, but well, your options are limited. Work with what you've got.

Use the broom to haul the corpse free of the door.
Go to 68.

Use the broom to shove the body into the freezer so you Close the damn thing.
Go to 86.

63

The computer lab of MacReady Station is located in the East Corridor, not far from the radio room. It's longer than it is wide, and three-quarters of the room is devoted to racks of computer gear: blade servers, data switches and routers, back-up servers and drive arrays. It's an extensive setup with lots of whirring fans and blinking lights.

It's darker near the back of the racks. A bank of fluorescent lights is out, and you don't like the way the shadows gather.

In the front half of the room, there are three desks, and each desk has a computer terminal on it. The middle desk also has a printer on it. Two of the monitors have been knocked over, and judging by the chips of plastic and shards of glass on the tables and floor, you suspect both monitors are broken.

One computer. A host of shadows.

Are you ready for this?

Check out the computer.
Go to 73.

Deal with the shadows.
Go to 74.

Neither. This looks like a trap.
Go to 75.

If you have your gear, you're ready for this . . . *trap.*
Go to 91.

64

Think . . . think . . . it's right there . . . yes, that's the memory . . .

Outside the octogonal room. Before. You and Sagalico. He's bleeding again, and the dressing is drenched with blood. His face is pale and he's shivering. You are second-guessing letting him come along with you. You both know he's lost a lot of blood. He shouldn't be down here with you. He can't help you. Not physically. He can still see the Way. He can still offer guidance.

You pause outside the door to the room at the center of the installation. *It has to be here,* you think. You've looked everywhere else. *It has to be here.*

Sagalico leans heavily against the wall. His eyes are unfocused.

"What do you See?" you ask.

"It's all white," he says. He lifts his head, and whatever he is Seeing has touched him. His eyes have lost all their color. "There's nothing there," he mutters. His face twitches. He bites his tongue, and there's blood—dark and rich on his pale lips. "It's everything," he snarls. "Don't touch it."

"I wasn't planning on it," you say.

"Rabbits," he mutters. Another personality is rising in him. "You have to find the rabbits."

"What rabbits?" you ask.

"The white ones," he snaps, spraying blood. "They think you can't see them against the snow. They think they aren't there. But they are. You know they are." He puts his hand to his mouth, smearing the blood on his lips. "Prick them, and they will bleed," he whispers. "They can't hide the blood."

He coughs, and you take a step back. He makes a noise like he is swallowing his tongue, and when he falls down and starts spasming, you realize that is exactly what he's done.

You watch him die. In any other profession, you would have tried to save him, but you know better. When a Guide does something drastic like this, it is because they know they went too far into the Way. Something found them, and it is reaching through time and space for their mind. Killing the one who is looking is the only way to Close the Way.

If he hadn't done it himself, you would have had to do it.

There are no good deaths in the Night Office. That much should be clear by now.

As you shake yourself out of this memory fugue, you quietly promise to say nice things about Sagalico in your post-mission write-up. He performed admirably as a Night Office Guide.

Back to the mission.
Go to 133.

65

As you turn around to leave the abattoir that is the kitchen, you hear a noise. When you turn back around, the body is gone.

Yeah, no. You're out.
Go to 70.

Of course the body is gone. It's going to be like this, is it?
Go to 87.

66

You search the pockets of your coat and come up with an industrial can of hair spray and a battered Zippo lighter you got from an old redneck hill-hugger during a mission in East Tennessee. It puts out a flame longer than your middle finger.

Perfect.

You stalk back to the kitchen. You fling back the freezer door, raise the lighter, and rake your thumb across the striker. The flame jets up, and you get a quick glance of something globulous lurking in the back, past a rack of frozen fish. As it unfolds out of the corner, you realize it's a gluey version of two bodies.

The blobosity makes a noise like a dozen tea kettles clattering as it bounces off the metal racks in the freezer. As it comes at you, you greet it with the can of hair spray. You hold it behind the flame and let it rip.

A sheet of flame fills the freezer with a bright heat and sweaty light. Flesh sizzles, tea kettles keen, and many of those jagged teeth explode like popcorn kernels. The blobosity slows, lurches, and then slowly oozes into a drain in the floor.

You give it another shot of the hair spray flamethrower, hoping the heat will make it liquify faster. And then you hit it a third time, because that is really, really disgusting.

Afterward, you shut the freezer door, and using a sharpie and a bit of sealing wax, you Close the door forever.

Well, now that you are warmed up, perhaps there is another section of the station you should investigate.

Go to 123.

Stop dawdling and get on with the main mission.

Go to 133.

67

Remember that conversation with Sagalico and Argot? Back at the home office, before all this began? Sagalico was the one who told you about the Voerdamnikenari—the space-faring race who were eternally fleeing the Old Ones. They seeded the Fourteen Calls throughout the galaxy, hoping some race would be intelligent enough (and stupid enough) to perform the Invocations. That's what happened here, isn't it? It started with Starkweather in '51, though the ice moved in before they could finish the ritual.

Then Endoluvion came along and found what was buried beneath the ice. They thawed something out. They finished what Starkweather started. That's what happened. And now, one of those Voerdamnikenari has responded to the beacon—the signal that had been transmitting from this station. They heard it and came.

And now . . .

You recall Sagalico's pale face. *It's too late*, he had said. *You can't take back the signal.*

Enough with the flashbacks. Check the body!
Go to 72.

Enough with the dead bodies too! You've got to keep moving.
Go to 106.

68

You keep an eye on the corpse as you twirl the bristled end of the broom off. *This'll work*, you think.

You poke the corpse with your stick. It doesn't react. You poke it again. It still doesn't react.

Okay, enough poking. Time to jam the broom handle into a soft spot (don't think about it too much—just do it).

The stick makes a squelchy noises as it goes into the corpse.

Go ahead and make the face.

Anyway, now that you've got corpse-on-a-stick, you can drag it out of the freezer.

The body slides slowly. You have to apply some leverage like *this* and yank it like *that*, but eventually, you get it free. The door, no longer blocked, shuts. You are distracted for a second by the noise the door makes (a very solid latching noise), and when you look down at the body again, you see its eyes are open.

That's not good.

You drop the stick and back away, and the space jelly that has been hiding in the corpse comes flowing out the body's orifices. It moves like hot grease across the tile, and before you can get out of the kitchen, it's reached your foot. It slithers up your shoe, and you feel the icy touch of its dead space flesh on your ankle.

IT ONLY GETS WORSE FROM HERE.

MAPS SCORE: 36

69

You search your pockets for something useful. A block of C-4, perhaps. Or a set of lock picks.

Where are your lock picks? You always have lock picks. An unsettling thought intrudes: *is this really your coat?*

It has to be. Gull was shorter than you. If this was her coat, it would be tight through the shoulders and the sleeves would be too short. Plus, this coat has that burn mark on the front left side, where you got splashed by that cultist with the elemental wand during that All Hallow's celebration a year or two ago. No, this is definitely your coat.

Maybe I left them back at the office, you think. But there's no reason to do so. Not when your coat has so many pockets, and you weren't in danger of running out.

Anyway, you don't find any lock picks, skeleton keys, or C-4. It's going to be hard to force your way into Ops.

Hang on. Do you need to force your way in? Maybe it's easier than that. You lift your discipline stick and pound on the door with its iron-shod base.

You wait.

You pound on the door again.

You wait.

You're about to wander off when you hear a quiet tapping. It's persistent and rhythmic, and after listening for a minute, you figure out that it is Morse code—heavier bangs and tighter taps.

Bang bang tap. Bang bang bang. Tap bang. Tap bang bang. Tap bang. Bang tap bang tap.

It's been awhile since you've done Morse, but oh, hang on! Maybe you've got a cheat sheet in your coat somewhere. By the time you find the well-creased slip of paper (it's a bookmark in a tattered copy of an old pulp paperback), the noises have ceased.

You bang with your discipline stick again, and whoever is on the other side replies again. This time you are ready to translate.

G - O - A - W - A - Y.

Go away.

That's not your typical space jelly call and response.

You figure out how to tap out "F - R - I - E - N - D," and wait for a response. It takes awhile, but the person inside taps back "N - O - F - R - I - E - N - D - O - F - M - I - N - E." That's when you know the person inside the room is Peele, the Closer of the other team.

Closers are notorious for being very prickly and unapproachable. Not that you are offering your own experiences as evidence or anything.

Anyway, you figure Peele has Closed themselves in Ops. There's no way you're going to override the seal on the door without an Opener, or at the very last, an Opener's Hand. Either way, Peele is safe in there for the time being.

You tap out "N - O," hoping Peele will get that you are using the organization's letters and you're not saying the word 'no.' After a moment, you get a response: "O - N." An inversion of what you sent, which is Asset Resource Management's clever way of allowing field operatives to verify their humanity.

Space jellies don't think backwards.

You rest your forehead against the door panel for a moment. "I got this," you whisper, even though you know Peele can't hear you.

There's another part of the station you want to investigate.
Go to 123.

No time. You've got to finish this quickly.
Go to 133.

70

You retreat from the kitchen, smartly deciding you don't need to see what is in the freezer. Technically, you are shirking your duties as an Asset Resource Management field operative, but let's be honest, you've got bigger problems to deal with. If you're successful, Heavy Battery will come in later and torch out all the nasty critters and dangling pseudopods. They like doing that, in fact, and there's no reason to not leave them some excitement, right?

Right. Get on with the mission.
Go to 71.

That doesn't sit exactly right with you, but you're not dealing with whatever is back there without your gear. Find your gear, and then maybe you can deal with whatever is lurking in the freezer.
Go to 80.

71

You are in the "Bar," the hall that connects the West Corridor and the East Corridor. There are several doors on the inside wall of the hall. One of them is marked "Storage," and the other two appear to be small offices. There is a bulletin board at the far end of the corridor. Opposite is a generous common area which opens at one end into a cafeteria seating area with two long tables. There's a short food serving area past the tables, and beyond that is the kitchen. A slate signboard stands near the serving area. It's been erased a few thousand times, but there is a permanent haze of chalk dust to it. Most of the menu has been erased. Some of it has been blotted out with something you suspect is blood.

At this end of the corridor, there is an emergency exit with a door that looks like it had been recovered from a crashed airliner and then welded into the side of the building. It has a security lock that is currently armed. Near the emergency exit is a narrow hall that leads to the Umbilical, the flexible passage that connects the main station with the lab area.

Since this is the grand tour, let's enumerate the contents of the common area: there are two pinball machines, a big-screen TV, two smaller flatscreens mounted over the bookcases that take up one wall, two couches, four overstuffed chairs that don't match, and one wooden rocker.

Because someone is that idiosyncratic weirdo who brought their own chair.

The bookcases are filled with an unordered mess of DVDs, CDs, books, and LPs. There's a rack of stereo equipment next to the big-screen TV, and—wonder of wonders—there's an karoate machine in addition to the usual assortment of media components.

Go the West Corridor.
Go to 58.

Have you checked the offices and the storage closet?
Go to 88.

You're kind of curious as to the contents of the library on that karaoke machine, aren't you?
Go to 97.

It's been a long day already. Maybe just a short break, in one of those comfy chairs.
Go to 104.

Investigate the kitchen.
Go to 134.

Check out the bookshelves.
Go to 148.

72

You lean over the body to take a closer look. The top of the head is gone, along with the upper portion of the person's face. The tag on the coveralls says "Bennings," and judging by the matted amount of hair and the unmistakable shape of the torso, Bennings was a woman.

There is no brain inside the skull. And as you lean closer (trying not to touch anything, of course), you realize that the jagged edges of the skull are pointed outward and not depressed inward.

Someone didn't go into the head for the brain; the brain came out of the head.

As you are struggling to process what this means, the body jerks. It makes a noise like a cat caught in a washing machine, and it grabs the front of your clothing. The undead monster's mouth moves (that part of the face is still there), and a black ichor drips out.

You scramble backwards, and the ambulatory monstrosity comes with you. It grabs you with its other hand. It's going for your throat! Its teeth make a terrible clacking noise, and its breath is really foul.

WHAT HAPPENS NEXT IS VERY GORY AND QUITE PAINFUL. WE'LL LET YOU IMAGINE WHAT IT FEELS LIKE TO HAVE YOUR FACE EATEN. OR YOU CAN REFLECT ON HOW BADLY YOU FELL FOR A RATHER RUDIMENTARY 'IT JUST LOOKS DEAD' TRAP.

MAPS SCORE: 34

73

You go over to the desk with the computer that hasn't been busted up. You nudge the mouse with a knuckle, and after a moment, the screen comes to life. An Endoluvion logo floats around the screen. When you tap the space bar on the keyboard, a window pops up. It's a security box, containing two boxes labeled *username* and *password*, and—oh, aren't you the lucky one? The username field is pre-populated with data.

"*MASTUR.*"

You think about the password for a second. A rather juvenile option comes to mind. It's not surprising, really. This station is a lonely place, and it's the sort of environment that attracts shut-ins and the socially awkward.
Go to 90.

Is this a name? Does someone have a trouble with spelling? Or is this a space jelly joke?
Go to 92.

74

You're wearing a pair of orange coveralls, which—thankfully—have pockets, but you're not wearing your coat, which not only has lots of pockets, but there are useful things *in* those pockets. Are you sure you want to proceed with—hang on, let's check these pockets—lint, a piece of paper, and a rubber band?

You're going to need something to write with. Surely there's a pencil or something in a drawer around here.
Go to 93.

You're a Night Office Closer. Space jellies tremble at your name. This rubber band is all you need.
Go to 117.

75

If you had your gear, you might be able to deal with whatever is lurking in the back of the room. The question is: is there anything on that computer that'll be helpful?

Regardless of whether the computer is password protected, you really shouldn't be wandering around without your gear. You should be looking for your coat and discipline stick.
Go to 80.

There's probably nothing here anyway. Leave the computer alone, and get on with the mission.
Go to 106.

76

You're in the West Corridor, feeling like yourself again. You've got your coat and your discipline stick. Space jellies had better watch out.

Visit the East Corridor.
Go to 79.

Check out Ops.
Go to 84.

Visit the Briefing Room.
Go to 99.

Stop by the Library.
Go to 115.

It's time to go to the research area.
Go to 133.

77

You're in the East Corridor of MacReady Station. From here, you can get to the Ops Center, the radio room, and a computer lab. The corridor intersects the Bar, which is what the locals call the area at the back of the station where you'll find the mess, a common area, and a couple of small offices/work rooms. You can also get to the Umbilical—which is the not-entirely-to-code access to the station's lab area.

Check out the radio room.
Go to 61.

You need the computer lab.
Go to 63.

Head for the "Bar." Try not to think about the fact that it isn't a real bar.
Go to 71.

It looks like there is a cafeteria and kitchen on the far side of the Bar. Maybe you can find something to eat.
Go to 78.

Head for Ops.
Go to 84.

You don't have a lot of time to sightsee. Get to the important stuff. That means the Umbilical.
Go to 106.

78

You head across the corridor for the common area. There's a small cafeteria with several serving stations for big pans of food. Past those, you see a set of swinging doors that lead into the kitchen proper. You navigate past the stations and push through the swinging doors.

As soon as you enter the kitchen, you know something terrible has happened. It's—wow. It's not good. There's a lot of dried blood splashed on the tile floors and the metal counters. There's even some spray on the ceiling.

A walk-in freezer has been blocked open with a dead body. It's a male figure, and it's missing a lot of its skull. Brains are gone too. The rest of the corpse's clothing has been shredded and torn.

You'll need to get closer if you want to figure out who that might be.

Go to 62.

Yeah, you've lost your appetite. Maybe you'll get something later.

Go to 65.

79

You're in the East Corridor. Your coat is hanging open, and you've got access to your pockets. Your discipline stick is held loosely in your left hand. You're ready.

Visit the Radio Room.
Go to 61.

Visit the Computer Lab.
Go to 63.

Go to the West Corridor.
Go to 76.

Check out Ops.
Go to 84.

It's time to go to the research area.
Go to 133.

80

Your gear has to be here in the station somewhere. After wandering around for a bit, you find an office with a keycard reader. The light on it is green, which means "good." You open the door and go into the office.

The room is about three meters by three meters. There's a desk, a chair, a counter, a stool shoved in the corner, and a bookcase. The desk is tidy, and the computer's screen doesn't wake when you nudge the mouse on the desk.

There's a counter behind the desk, and a number of complicated schematics are strewn across it. The bookcase is filled with blue and yellow binders that are labeled with an alphanumeric system you don't recognize.

You're delighted to find your coat thrown over the stool, and when you glance around for your discipline stick, you spot it leaning against the wall behind the door.

Finally!

You swap the lab coat for your official Night Office vestment. It's a comfortable weight on your shoulders, and you start to feel like yourself again. You still have a lot of questions, but now that you have your coat, things are going to get better.

You check a few pockets

(*chapstick, snow goggles, gloves, hand grenade, a couple of Sharpies, Elder stone, moist towelette . . .*)

and are pleased to discover no one has gone through your gear. You retrieve your stick. It feels good in your hand and you—

(*watch out for the lamp!*)

twirl it, but stop before you knock the desk lamp over.

You stand there for a second, a sickening feeling in your gut. You feel like you've been here before. You knocked over that lamp the last time you were here.

There was something else too. Something important . . .

You're definitely out of sorts. Maybe you should have listened a little more closely to what Sagalico was talking about.

No time now, you think. *He's gone. I'm on my own.*

No, this is going to nag at you. What could it be?
Go to 64.

Hold on. Wasn't there something you wanted to do in the kitchen? No? Yes? Your memory is fuzzy. Maybe you should check. Just in case.
Go to 66.

Be thorough. Head back to the East Corridor.
Go to 79.

Get on with the mission.
Go to 133.

81

You stand in the doorway of Dr. Nakamura's office, trying to see everything anew. Like you've never been here before.

(If you have, how many times? Does it matter?)

You've gone through the files; rather, you are fairly sure you've gone through the files—if not this time, then the time before.

(How many times?)

You look over your shoulder, half-expecting to see a version of yourself standing behind you.

Nothing's there, by the way. Just to be clear. You're on your own.

You recall reading something in a journal somewhere—what was the guy's name? Oregano? No, that's not it—something about how the Way compresses experience. There is—was—a tribe who lived in the Andes in South America. They regularly had vision experiences with something they called the "spirit vine," which gave them access to the Way. Apparently, they used the vine to communicate with their ancestors (at points in time when their ancestors were living, not after they were dead). *Memory and experience are both shared and completely subjective,* the scholar wrote.

You're not sure how that helps, but you feel like you remembered something important.

Great. Now back to the mission.
Go to 58.

No, really. You've been here before. More than once.
Go to 114.

82

You type the password and hit RETURN. The screen blinks, and then the pop-up box comes back. Same auto-filled username. Same empty password box.

The additional text reads:

"PASSWORD INCORRECT. YOU HAVE 1 MORE ATTEMPT."

Well, that didn't work.

You actually don't have any idea what the password is, do you? Might as well get back to the mission.
Go to 103.

Type "spacejelliessuck."
Go to 131.

83

You feel like you're picking at a scab, though it's in your head. Kind of a weird feeling. *Pick, pick.* What is it that you're missing? Was it something Sagalico said? This is the problem with talking with the Guide. You never know if they are telling you something completely batshit, or if they're talking to a future you.

Well, in the meantime

(pick pick)

you're better off focusing on what's right in front of you. Hopefully, you'll uncover that bit of missing memory before it's too late.

You return all the files to the cabinet and head out of the doctor's office.

This is a good start, by the way. You woke up. You got out of bed. You found pants (sort of). You figured out that things are very sideways. What next?

You still need your gear. Maybe that room marked "Storage" across the hall would be a good place to start.
Go to 53.

It's been awhile since you've eaten anything. Maybe you should see about finding some food.
Go to 78.

84

You find the door marked "OPS," and it is very definitely locked. The keycard reader next to the door is glaring at you with its single red light.

Where's an Opener when you need one, you think, and then you remember what happened to Argot and everything gets even more serious than it was a few minutes ago.

You lean against the hall next to the door and close your eyes. *Just a minute*, you promise yourself. You've got to be careful. You can't overtax yourself. Not when you have to

(touch the obelisk)

find out what happened to both your team and the other team, as well as all the crew of this station.

You shake your head slightly, fighting that other thought that was trying to intrude. You haven't felt yourself since you woke up. You feel—what's the word for it?—out of phase. That's it. Out of phase.

Sagalico kept talking about indexes and alternate versions of this reality, didn't he? You try to remember the conversations you before the . . . well, *before*.

However, there's a conversation with Argot that keeps fighting its way to the front of the line. You're in the hydroponics labs, and most of the greenery isn't . . . green. It's a sickly yellow, and some of isn't like any plant you've ever seen. It's definitely non-Euclidean in how it twists around itself.

"They're both responsible," Argot says, and you try to remember who he is talking about. Sagalico and . . . What was her name? The Guide on the first team. Peele, that's it.

Argot's still talking, mostly to himself. "She opened the Way, and she dragged everyone in with her. It's the fucking Ygivennski Bifurcation Paradox. That's what this is. And Sagalico fucked it when he tried to untangle it. Made more indexes. Who knows which is the right reality anymore." He looks at you. *"You're going to have to close them. You and Gull. Jesus Christ, I don't know how we're going to do it. But you're going have to close them all."*

"No," you say. *"There's only one that matters."*

"Yeah, but which one?" he asks.

You beckon him closer. He mutters something about how much of a pain in the ass you've been all mission, but he does approach you. You indicate he should lean in so you can whisper something.

"What?"

"The one where I touch the obelisk," you whisper to him. *"That's the true path."*

And then you stab him with the knife.

"No, that's not what happened," you whisper to the empty hall of MacReady Station, and yet, when you try to think of an alternative—of what really happened—all you can imagine is a white room. An empty void.

The human brain has no defenses to information that is inserted directly into it, the Old Man told you once upon a time. *If these creatures can telepathically insert memories, you may not be able to know what is real and what is imagined.*

How do we fight them? You had asked.

Memory is subjective, the Old Man said. *It is reliant upon an observer, and that observer has discrete rules which are applied to assemblage of memory. When what you remember deviates from these rules, you experience a psychotic break.*

You look at the bandage on your arm. That's not a psychotic break. That's the result of something attacking you—something not human.

I didn't stab anybody, you tell yourself, and you're mostly confident that is the truth.

Visit the West Corridor.
Go to 58.

If you've got your gear, you might have something that could open this door.

Go to 69.

Go to the East Corridor.

Go to 77.

Maybe you should find the hydroponics lab. Maybe you'll find some answers there.

Go to 106.

85

You close your eyes and imagine the office.

(This is how you do it.)

The office is unmarked. The blinds are drawn, and what light gets through makes sharp stripes across the floor. There's a big desk, and behind the desk is a bigger chair. Lounging in the chair is a white-haired man with a beard that looks like birds have been nesting in it. His clothing is a century out of date, and he's got his feet on the blotter. He's snoring, and there's an open bottle of whisky on the desk. No sign of a glass—you always imagined he'd be the sort to drink straight from the bottle.

You rap your knuckles on the edge of the desk, and the sound wakes the old geezer. He snorts, starts, and then smacks his lips a few times.

It's always like this, isn't it? Even though this is all in your head, you don't ever feel like it is totally under your control.

"I need some help," you say.

The Old Man focuses on you. *Of course you do*, he grunts.

"I need to know I'm not losing my mind," you say.

He takes his feet off the desk and reaches for the bottle. He offers it to you, and you make a face. He shrugs and takes a healthy swig. When he exhales, you can almost see the curls of alcohol and bitterness leave his mouth.

It's tough to not project too much onto him. The instructor at the seminar warned you about falling into this trap. *Your mental construct should be someone you trust*, they said, *but don't imbue it with too much character of someone you know. You'll end up coloring your construct with your unconscious bias and what ever unresolved history you have with this person.*

The Old Man sighs and stares at the ceiling. *Are you done?* he asks.

"Yeah," you say. "I'm done flagellating myself."

Thank goodness, he says. *Now, what's the problem?*

You explain the situation to him.

Sounds like a mess, he says.

"Well, thanks," you say. "I wasn't sure."

Glad to be of help.

"What are the chances that my mind is under attack?"

About the same as whether or not you're actually awake, I suppose, he says. *You know, just another day—*

"At the Night Office," you finish for him.

He salutes you with the bottle and takes another swig. *Your team thinks you have lost your mind,* he asks.

"That's because they have lost theirs," you say.

And what are you going to do about that?

"The same thing I always do," you say. "Believe in myself."

He smiles. His teeth are perfect and sharp. So very much in focus. *Good girl,* he says.

"I'm not your girl," you say.

I'm not your father, he says in return, completing the old ritual between you two.

He puts the bottle down on the desk and leans forward, his eyes bright. *Are we going to save the world?*

"We might have to burn it down this time," you say.

He shrugs. *Same as it ever was.*

If you have the manuscript and haven't read it yet, **go to 36.**

Otherwise, get on with the mission.

Go to 58.

86

You leave the bristled end of the broom attached. You have to turn it sideways to shove the corpse, but it's better than just a stick. The corpse is stuck to the floor, which isn't terribly surprising, given the amount of dried blood and other fluids that have collected around the body.

After a few minutes of shoving and swearing, you give up. You need a chisel or a crowbar to get the body unstuck, and yeah, who has time for that?

An unsettling noise leaks out of the freezer. It sounds like . . . laughter. The sort of laughter that you hear on late night monster movies.

Okay, time to figure out how to Close that door, even with the body stuck there.
Go to 89.

There's no time to mess with the door. You need to get out of the kitchen. Right now.
Go to 105.

87

You back up slowly, trying to not make any noise. Even though you're sure twhatever is in the freezer knows you're there. Why else would it have sucked that corpse into the freezer like that?

Wait a minute. Whatever is in the freezer grabbed the corpse like it thought you were going to snatch its . . . snack. That's not something space jellies do. They don't get possessive about food. Though, you're not really sure if they eat dead flesh. And if it isn't a space jelly, what is it?

Anyway, against your better judgment, you edge toward the freezer. As you get closer, you hear a snuffling noise coming from inside. Almost like a small child whimpering. But it can't be. There are no children here. You know this from the briefing. Plus common sense. Who would bring their kids to a foresaken place like this?

Holding your breath, you lean toward the door. The noise is clearer now, and it sounds like a conversation. You can pick out individual words here and there. And there is more than one voice. The conversation is quick and intense, sort of like the internal dialogue you have with the Old Man when you are arguing with yourself.

You edge one step closer, and being careful to not bump into the door, you peer into the freezer.

The corpse has been discarded just inside the door, and you feel a prickle of dread at the casual indignity of how it has been cast aside.

The light doesn't reach all the way to the back, but there is enough of an ambient glow for make out the hunched figure between two meat racks.

The heated conversation continues. As your eyes adjust to the gloom, you realize the figure is more than one person.

You can't help the gasp that slips out of your mouth. The figure breaks off its argument, and as you backpedal away from the door, it charges. What comes surging out of the freezer is a obese monstrosity that is the fused accumulation of at least two people. It has two heads—the source of the hushed conversation you heard—but it has more than four arms and an odd number of legs.

You shove your way through the swinging doors of the kitchen, but when you look back over your shoulder, you slam into one of the serving stations. You twist your ankle falling down, and before you can get back up, the obese monstrosity lumbers through the kitchen doors.

It gets a hand on your leg. You kick at it, but it has more hands. They grab and grab and grab. It doesn't matter how much you kick.

Their mouths open wider than human mouths should, and they have more teeth than human mouths do. Awkwardly, they fall into a bit of an argument about who is going to bite you first. But it doesn't really matter. Their grip is tight.

Your hands are slipping on the tile. You're not going to get away.

IT'S NOT THE FIRST BITE THAT'S THE PROBLEM. IT'S ALL THE BITES AFTER THAT WHICH REALLY HURT. FOR AWHILE. AND THEN NOTHING MUCH MATTERS ANYMORE.

MAPS SCORE: 24

88

In the hall opposite the common area, there are three doors. One is marked "Storage," and the other two look like personal offices.

Check out the storage closet.
Go to 94.

Check out the first office.
Go to 98.

Check out the second office.
Go to 100.

89

How are you going to Close the door? Are you going to melt the body with napalm or something? And you don't have a crowbar to pry that corpse off the floor.

While you are trying to figure out what to do, a black and purple tentacle slithers out of the freezer. It grows a half-dozen eyestalks—all of which look directly at you—and then a second tentacle comes jiggling and squirming out of the freezer.

The second tentacle separates into eight smaller tentacles. You beat at the wriggling stalks, but some of them get their suckers attached to the bristled end of the broom. You're suddenly in a tug-of-war with a space jelly.

You really don't care about the broom, do you?

You let go, and as the tentacles thrash and splinter the wooden handle, you scramble for the exit. You get through the swinging doors, but not much farther than that. Tentacles grab your leg. You claw for something to hang on to, but the floor is smooth. You are hauled back into the kitchen.

The space jelly tries to pull you into the freezer, but you get a grip on the door. Aha, now you've got a chance!

The space jelly pulls harder, and your shoulders pop. How much longer can you hold on? Who is going to rescue you?

Behind you, in the depth of the cold freezer, you hear the laughter again.

PLAYING TUG-OF-WAR WITH A SPACE JELLY IS NOT A RECOM-MENDED COURSE OF ACTION. IT NEVER ENDS WELL.

MAPS SCORE: 27

90

You type in the second half of this rather juvenile word and hit RETURN on the keyboard.

The screen blinks, and then the pop-up box comes back. It's still got the same username in the field, but this time, there's an additional line of text under the password box.

"PASSWORD INCORRECT. YOU HAVE 2 MORE ATTEMPTS."

Okay, fine. Maybe not as juvenile as you thought.

What the hell. Type "asdfasdf."
Go to 32.

Type "VOERDAMNIKENARI."
You think you got the spelling right.
Go to 82.

91

You face the shadow at the back of the computer room. You grip your discipline stick with your left hand and rap it against the metal frame of one of the computer racks. "Come on, come on," you say in a singsong voice. "Come out and play."

At first, nothing happens, but gradually—in time with the beat you're tapping on the rack—the shadows start to twitch and shiver. You keep up the pounding, and sure enough, something comes crawling out of the darkness.

It used to be a person. Well, maybe two people—there are more hands and feet than you usually find on a single individual. The creature is covered with dark moss, and ranks of iridescent mushrooms line its shoulders and back. While it has a head, there's only a pair of holes for feeding or screaming or spewing spores. It doesn't have any other recognizable sensory organs.

It can feel a good rhythm, though.

"Come on, you shambler," you hiss. You quicken the beat, and the monster shuffles faster. Sections of its chest are pulsating, as if there are nodules inside that are ready to burst.

That's the last thing you need.

You dip a hand into a coat pocket, feeling for something useful, and your coat provides. "I got something for you," you say as you pull the road flare out of your coat pocket. You tap it against your discipline stick. *One. Two.*

One of the pulsing spots on the monster's chest erupts, and a cloud of spores spews out. The shambler is far enough away that those spores are going to take a hot minute to get to you, but you don't wait. You crack the end of the road flare against the your discipline stick, and it crackles into life. You throw the lit flare at the shambler.

You think about firestorms and implosions and thermobaric immolations. You say the words that focus the energies in the room. The road flare passes through the haze of spores, and they ignite, caught up in the gravity of your incantation. You smack the discipline stick against the floor, generating micro shocks. *This. Is. How. Your. World. Ends.*

And it is that last tap of your stick that triggers the spell.

A fire starts in the racks. It burns bright and hot, and something writhes in it. But the fire collapses inward, like a black hole swallowing itself. The creature starts to howl, but the sound is cut off abruptly as the spell flashes out.

There is nothing left but an ashy film on the floor and racks.

One of the computers sucks some of the ash into its chassis. It whines. The drive locks. The motherboard overheats. A single curl of black smoke wisps up from the case as the computer dies.

Otherwise, the shadow at the back of the room is gone.

Well done. Notch another shambler on your stick.
Go to 116.

Okay, now you have time to figure out the password on that working computer.
Go to 124.

92

You think about what the password might be for a minute or two. "MASTUR" is the sort of username a space jelly might use. Well, a space jelly that has taken over a human host. Without a host, space jellies don't have any use for computers.

Anyway, given the phonetic spelling of the username, it follows that the password might be similarly misspelled.

You type in "FUD" for the password and hit RETURN. The computer thinks for a second, and then responds with the same login box. There's more information on the screen. One line says you only have one attempt left before the system locks you out. Beneath that, the screen says:

"(HINT: *minimum character requirement is 4*)"

Add an exclamation point to "FUD." That's four characters, right?

Go to 110.

Well, drat. You've got one chance left. How about a naughty four-letter word?

Go to 113.

93

You fumble around with the drawers on the desk in the computer lab. You find a half-dozen network cables, an unopened bag of pretzels, and a black beanie with an anime logo on it. Nothing to write with.

Annoying, but not surprising with computer geeks. They aren't fans of that old school technology.

This is when you really miss having your gear, don't you?
Go to 75.

Whatever. You'll got a rubber band. That'll be enough.
Go to 117.

94

You cross the hall and find the storage room door unlocked. You open it and quickly slip inside the room. It's very dark, and you fumble for a light switch.

You find one, and the room is suddenly filled with the artificial glow of ancient fluorescent lighting.

As storage rooms go, it's well organized. Non-critical medical supplies are on one rack. There are office supplies on another rack. A third rack has prepackaged condiments and serving materials for the mess.

Man, someone really is organized. You get a momentary high from all this organization, but it fades quickly when you realize it doesn't really help you with your current situation. Still, an endorphin rush is an endorphin rush. You take what you can when you're in the shit.

Right. Better check out the other doors on this side of the Bar. **Go to 98.**

Enough with the storage rooms. Get on with the more important things. **Go to 106.**

95

It looks like a pretty good bottle of bourbon. Shame to leave it, but better safe than sorry, right?

You put the bottle back in the drawer. You go through the drawers under the counter behind you. You find more office supplies, along with a bunch of drafting supplies and a stack of empty three-ring binders. Nothing out of the ordinary.

You take one last look around the office before you flick off the light. There's really nothing here.

Fair enough. Maybe you should check out the other office.
Go to 100.

You're dawdling. Get back to work. You don't have time for sightseeing.
Go to 106.

96

Barstow rolled onto his elbow and watched Cat as she went to the window. She pulled back the diaphanous curtains, and the blue light from the Riesendrad made her naked skin glow with a sepulchral light. The line of tattoos that ran down her back to her hip glowed with an ethereal light. He felt a stirring in his loins, like one of those mudskippers which hibernate for years in desert lands until water returns.

She looked over her shoulder at him, her eyes alight with a feline assurance that she still had secrets. "Would you—"

The window shattered in a hail of gunfire. Cat fell to the floor, wreathed in the tattered silk of the curtain, and Barstow—reacting instinctively to the flickering red dots that glazed the window panes a split second before they shattered—flung himself off the bed. Feathers and fibers puffed into a floating haze as the bullets from the assault rifles tore into the fancy bedding.

Barstow scrambled for his briefs and his sidearm, and when the masked gunmen came through the door of the suite, he was ready. He put two rounds in the face of the first intruder, a round through the shoulder of the second man, and rolled toward the bathroom as the third man fired his weapon.

The rifle was silenced, and it made a phut-phut-phut-phut noise as bullets tore up the carpet where Barstow had been a moment before. Barstow came up on one knee, extended his arms, and fired a single shot. The *bullet ricocheted off the metal frame of the door and shattered the left lens of the gunman's goggles.*

He was dead already, but his trigger finger didn't know it yet. As he fell, his gun continued to go phut-phut-phut! *The second gunman spasmed and jerked as bullets marched up his torso.*

In the silence that followed, Barstow exhaled. His arm remained steady.

The three bodies lay in a tangled heap. No one else came into the room.

A single shard of glass fell from a window pane. It chimed as it struck the debris on the floor. The sound was like a starter's pistol and it shattered the frozen tableau in the hotel suite.

Gunmen on the rooftop across the alley from the hotel started firing again. Feathers and fluff danced on the tangled bedding. Barstow darted toward the open door. He was exposed; he had to get out of sight.

You feel like you missed a scene, but you're going to keep reading.

Go to 101.

Skip ahead some more. You don't have time to dawdle with this manuscript.

Go to 186.

97

Seriously?

All right.

You wander over to the stereo unit next to the big-screen TV. You hit the power button on the receiver.

Nothing happens.

You tap it again.

Still nothing.

Ah, well. Probably for the best.

Go to 71.

Is this rack even plugged in?

Go to 107.

98

You head for the office next to the storage room. There's a keycard reader next to the door, but it's not showing any lights. You jiggle the door handle, and it doesn't appear to be locked.

You go inside. The light switch is right where it should be, and when the lights come on, you find yourself in a tiny office that isn't more than three meters by three meters. There's a desk, a chair, a counter, a stool shoved in the corner, and a bookcase. The desk is tidy, and the computer's screen doesn't wake when you nudge the mouse on the desk. The counter behind the desk is clear, and there are a handful of drawers beneath. The bookcase is filled with blue and yellow binders labeled with an alphanumeric system you don't recognize.

You go through the desk. The center drawer contains various sorts of office supplies. The right hand drawer has file folders, and the left hand drawer has some snack bars. In the back, you find a bottle of bourbon.

You lean back in the chair as you uncork the bourbon and take a sniff. The smell goes right up your nose. It's a startling change from the fetid air that is swamping the installation.

It's tempting to have a sip.

Absolutely not. Who knows what is hiding in this bottle.
Go to 95.

Oh, come on. What harm could there be in having one sip?
Go to 174.

99

The briefing room is dominated by a central conference room table. You immediately notice the dead body on the big table. It's been staked there by a dozen or so ice axes. It's wearing the standard MacReady issue coveralls, and while the namepatch is covered with blood, you can make out a few letters "—rris."

You feel a headache coming on, and you collapse in one of the conference room chairs. Suddenly, you remember what happened here. The body is a man named Norris, and he was one of the two members of the station's team who Gull singled out as being co-opted by shoggoths. What did she call them? Whatever term she used, they didn't like it. Things got violent.

You remember Argot yelling at Brinkmann. They were over there, by the white board. The body was on the table, struggling against the ice axes holding it down. Argot had used his Hand to extract a good chunk of the space jelly, and you sealed it into a box. The little jelly left in the body was whacking away at the motor controls in the brain. The body was basically a zombie, and it could get in the way, but it wasn't dangerous.

Not that you wanted it wandering around, which is why it was still staked down.

She was supposed to be looking for incursions like this, Argot had yelled. *What the fuck have you been doing here the last few days?*

You have no idea what's down there, Brinkmann had yelled back. *These idiots have been transmitting the Calls for more than a week. They're coming. We can't stop them.*

We have to, Argot had replied. *That's our job.*

In the corner, Sagalico tittered.

Your hand was already reaching into your coat, anticipating that you were going to have to do something terrible.

It's so pure, Sagalico whispered. *It's so simple.*

What is?

The rabbits, he responded. *The white.*

He looked at you then, and his eyes had widened. *Don't touch*, he whispered. *Don't touch. Don't touch. Don't touch. Don't touch.* Each time he said it, his voice got louder. *Don't touch. Don't touch. Don't touch.* He was shouting now. He stood up, pointing at you. *Don't touch. Don't touch. Don't touch.*

Argot and Brinkmann broke off their argument, and you could feel Brinkmann's Hand get hot. *What's going on?*

Don't touch. Don't touch. Don't touch. Sagalico was screaming himself hoarse. His face was turning strange shades of eggplant. You could see blood vessels bursting in his eyes.

Argot got to him first. He slapped the Guide, which made no difference. Then, he punched Sagalico in the face. Hard. With his Hand. The Guide went down, his nose broken. No one complained, because that meant he wasn't shrieking any more.

Argot looked at you. *What the fuck is he talking about?*

At the time, you had no idea, and you told him as much. But you know now, don't you?

No idea. You're also not convinced that this isn't a false memory inserted by whatever is messing with your mind.

Go to 111.

Yes, you know what Sagalico is talking about.

Go to 127.

100

The second office is very utilitarian looking. Desk, chair, bookcase. There's an easy chair shoved into one corner—it looks like it might match one of the chairs on the common area across the hall. Behind the chair is a torchiere lamp. It looks like someone wanted a quiet place to read. You can't blame them.

The computer under the desk is not switched on, and you don't see the point of booting it up to find out that it is password protected. You go through the drawers, and find nothing unusual.

There's two ways to look at how dull this office is: 1) given that you're on a deadline, this wasn't a very good use of your time; and, 2) nothing in this room tried to kill you, so that's a win. Take 'em where you can find them.

Maybe you should try out that easy chair.
Go to 102.

Enough of this. Time to get on with the mission.
Go to 106.

101

Out in the hall, Barstow takes a moment to catch his breath. How had DIABOLIK found him? And why were they trying to kill him? He leaned against the wall, his heart suddenly clenching in distress. Cat! He couldn't stop the images from flooding his brain. Her naked voluptuousness, pale and blue in the light from the Ferris wheel. Her hair a tangled mass of cold fire down her back. The symbolic suggestion of her tattoos trailing across her body.

Was she dead? She had to have been hit by the fusillade of bullets that had shattered the windows, but he wasn't entirely sure. She had disappeared under the curtain as she had fallen, the silken drape obscuring her delirious figure. He took a half-step toward the suite, wanting to know—needing to know—but he knew there was no way he could get through the door without making himself a target. And he didn't have time to wait out the gunmen across the alley. While their weapons were silenced (like the weapons of the team who had breached the room), the report of his CZ 75 was loud. While the Grand Meridian prided itself on discretion, gunshots were not something that management would graciously ignore.

A new thought intruded: was she the target? Had AMBER been compromised? Barstow had to get out of the hotel and find a secure line. He needed more information. He needed to know who he could trust. DIABOLIK was moving forward with their sinister plan, and he still didn't know anything about it.

Barstow checked his weapon. He had six rounds left. He glanced at the open door of the hotel suite. The third gunman's body lay outside the room. He could retrieve the man's weapon.

Barstow dismissed the idea. He was only wearing a pair of light cotton briefs. He could barely hide a handgun. There was no way he could fit an assault rifle in his shorts.

At the other end of the hall, the elevator dinged.

Barstow is in some serious shit. You need to know what happens next, don't you?
Go to 108.

Skip ahead. You're not here for the hotel shootout.
Go to 188.

102

You sit down in the easy chair. It's surprisingly comfortable, given that whoever sat in this chair—and they sat in it a lot—was heavier than you. Some of the support springs are tired from holding up all that weight.

Okay, enough of that. You have things to do.
Go to 71.

Oh, look. There's a handle. This thing is a recliner! That's awesome.
Go to 104.

103

You turn away from the computer. In the back of the room, the shadows wave and beckon. You know they want you to come investigate. You check the pockets of your overalls and find nothing more than a rubber band. That's hardly enough to deal with anything that might be lurking in the shadows.

You are a Closer, after all. A rubber band should be enough to deal with a space jelly.

Go to 117.

A rubber band is not the same as a phosphorus grenade or a flame thrower, and you remember packing one of those two in your coat before you left. Maybe you should go find your gear before attempting anything foolish.

Go to 118.

104

You throw the lever and the easy chair drops beneath you. It comes to an equally sudden stop, and you try to catch your breath. You are inclined at a rather severe angle, and you feel like all the blood is rushing into your head. This can't be comfortable.

You catch sight of a strange stain on the ceiling tile directly overhead, and you realize you are in a terribly compromised position. What if there is something up in the ceiling . . . ? You need to get out of this chair.

When you move one way, the chair shifts underneath you, and you get thrown against the wall. When you struggle to sit up, your ass sinks deeper into the chair. What a diabolical trap!

Something spatters on your cheek. You freeze. You try to see what it is. Is it moving? You reach up and wipe at your cheek. You stare at your fingers. Is it . . . ?

It looks like water.

You glance up at the ceiling. The stain is still a stain. Nothing appears to have changed.

It's just water, you think. *There's a leak somewhere.*

Relieved, you reach for the handle on the recliner.

A sharp pain bites at your cheek. Like a bee sting.

Your fingers too. Not just one bee. Many bees. When you look at your fingers, they are bleeding. You swipe at your cheek with your other hand, and there's blood on your fingers.

Another drop falls from the ceiling and lands on your head. It starts burning.

You flail at the recliner handle, trying to get out of the damn chair before . . .

It starts raining, and each drop is pure acid.

NEVER SIT IN THE COMFY CHAIR. THEY ARE ALWAYS A TRAP. THIS IS AN NIGHT OFFICE ASSESSMENT EXERCISE, AFTER ALL. IT'S NOT A SHOPPING EXPEDITION FOR NEW FURNITURE.

MAPS SCORE: 11

105

You scramble for the exit. You get through the swinging doors, but not much farther than that. Tentacles grab your leg, and you are pulled down. You try to grab onto the counter, and your fingers scrabble frantically across the side of the serving station. The space jelly hauls you back into the kitchen.

You roll over as you are pulled, which means you see the dank and gelatinous form of the shoggoth as it flows out of the freezer. There are frozen hams and someone's hand floating in its jiggling bulk.

You try to think of a Closing ritual, but nothing is going to stop this thing from enveloping you and devouring your mind. You close your eyes and put your hands over your nose and mouth.

The space jelly can still get in through your ears. For a fleeting moment, you wish you had an extra set of hands, and then you feel the cold touch of the space jelly as it slurps into your head and touches your brain.

THIS ENDING IS RELATIVELY PAIN-FREE, SO YOU HAVE THAT GOING FOR YOU.

MAPS SCORE: 38

106

You duck through the long plastic strips that cover the entrance to the Umbilical—the narrow corridor connecting the main station to the research labs and crew quarters. The walls of the Umbilical are heavily padded with industrial insulation, which is held in place with tape, nails, and the haphazard piece of 2 x 4. Long strands of naked bulbs hang from planter hooks screwed into pieces of weather-warped wood. It has a very early twentieth century explorer vibe.

At the end of the corridor is a pressure door nearly as wide as the corridor. It isn't sealed, which is a little disconcerting. You push it open and see an empty hallway. Fluorescent lights flicker glazed ceiling tiles.

You hesitate on the threshold, considering whether there is a message in the flicker of the lights. Your arm throbs beneath the bandage.

You've been here before, and it didn't go so well.

You remember that Argot had to Open the door. That's why it isn't sealed now. Yes, you can see the burn marks. And then what?

It's all so frustrating. You know the memories are in your head. You just can't get to them. *Short-term amnesia is a defense mechanism of the human brain,* the Old Man reminds you, *a way to prevent a deep trauma from damaging your mind.*

It's a way to hide things from yourself, you think. *Things you don't want to face.*

Matters you aren't ready to face, the Old Man clarifies. *Events you aren't strong enough to fully absorb.*

Well, how do I get stronger? you snap. *Wouldn't facing these memories—I don't know—build character or something?*

Character isn't required in the Night Office, the Old Man laughs.

Okay, enough of this. Maybe it's time you and your Therapeutic Personality Construct had a proper talk.

Go to 85.

No, you've already had a talk with the Old Man. All he's going to do is laugh at you. He's just your own insecurities, anyway.

Go to 165.

107

There's a power strip wedged behind the stereo rack. The console is heavier than it looks, but you manage to tug it forward enough to wiggle the power strip free.

The strip is very non-descript and utilitarian. Not the brand you'd use, because you're not about to let a power surge come zapping down the line and fry your gear. You should always have a decent surge protector on your power strips.

Anyway, the status light on the strip is dark, and when you toggle the on/off switch a few times, nothing happens. It looks like the strip itself is dead.

You're disappointed in the lack of proper safety and care that these people afforded their stereo equipment. Losing the gear in a freak power surge would be . . . Enough to drive someone out of the mind?

Well, maybe not *that* batshit crazy, but maybe enough to commit murder.

Wouldn't that be something if this entire incident came down to some wanna-be pop star losing their shit over a dead karaoke machine? They carved everyone up because they couldn't sing-along to Kansas or Loverboy.

You could check out the bookcases, but come on, you're just procrastinating. Get on with the mission.
Go to 71.

Maybe there's a clue among all that media on the bookcases?
Go to 148.

108

You find another section in the manuscript which isn't the spy thriller. It's a bunch of notes, as if someone was scribbling down details of something else they were reading.

- Pabodie-Lake. 1938. Supposed to investigate what Dyer and Danforth saw. cf. H. P. Lovecraft. American fiction writer.
- Ph'nglui mglw'nafh Cthulhu R'lyeh wgah'nagl fhtagn. What the fuck does this mean?
- Who financed Pabodie and Lake?
- Pedro Oresti?
- What happened to the Codex Acheroni? Was it destroyed? Fourteen Calls. Dee?
- Where's the key? What did the Russians find?
- Blair. Blair knows.
- 50°S 100°W. ?????
- It's started. They're in our heads now.

This is unsettling. You have lots of questions.
Go to 173.

Morgan doesn't know anything, the Old Man says. You need to focus on the mission.
Go to 232.

109

You duck through the long plastic strips that cover the entrance to the Umbilical—the narrow corridor that connects the main station to the research labs and crew quarters. Once, the buildings were separate spaces, but Endoluvion decided the outpost should be more of a contiguous space. You can't blame them. Who wanted to go outside—even for a hundred steps—in this weather?

The walls of the Umbilical are heavily padded with industrial insulation, which is held in place with tape, nails, and the haphazard piece of 2 x 4. The lights are a long strand of naked bulbs hanging from planter hooks screwed into pieces of weather-warped wood. It has a very early twentieth century explorer vibe.

The pressure door at the end of the corridor is as wide as it is tall. It isn't sealed, which is a little disconcerting. You push it open and see an empty hallway. There are fluorescent lights behind glazed ceiling tiles. Several are dark, two more are flickering, and the rest are steadfastly bright. You can't help but read the pattern of light and dark as zones of danger.

You hesitate on the threshold. Your arm throbs beneath the bandage. You've been here before, and the last time you had the rest of your team. *It didn't go so well,* you think, struggling to remember what happened.

You remember Argot had to Open the door. That's why it isn't sealed now. Yes, you can see the burn marks. And then what?

Short-term amnesia is a defense mechanism of the human brain, the Old Man says in your head, *a way to prevent a deep trauma from damaging your mind.*

It's a way to hide things from yourself, you think. *Things you don't want to face.*

Matters you aren't ready to face, the Old Man clarifies. *Events you aren't strong enough to fully absorb.*

You might be dead already. That's a pretty traumatic thing. Who wants to face that? But you are going to have to find out if it is true or not. Otherwise, you can't be sure of your own sanity. You have to know, one way or the other.

A chart on the wall nearby shows the layout of the research sub-section. You find the room marked Storage. It's the next door on the left. You don't want to go in there, but after taking a deep breath, you open the door.

It's a large room. There are several rows of metal racks, all filled with industrial boxes marked with cryptic strings of numbers and letters that mean something to the MacReady crew.

Gamma, you think, recalling what the note in Dr. Nakamura's office said. For lack of a better way, you start counting with the rack in front of you. *One, two, three*—ah, yes, here we are.

There's a large freezer on the lower shelf of the rack in front of you. Do you open it?

Wait! What—what if it is your corpse? Doesn't that mean . . . ?
Go to 112.

Yes, for crying out loud. You need to know!
Go to 121.

110

You type in "FUD!" and hit RETURN. The computer thinks again, and then the screen goes blank. After a second or two, it turns on again, and this time, you see a desktop. You're in!

You start double-clicking folder icons, trying to find a directory that might have some useful information. As you are scanning text files, you hear something moan behind you.

Glancing over your shoulder, you sense movement within the shadows at the back of the room. A hand, covered with a spray of tiny mushrooms emerges from the shadows. It claws at the floor, slowly dragging a similarly mushroom-festooned body out of the darkness.

You gauge how fast the hand is hauling its fungal load and figure you have two minutes—maybe two and a half—before you need to worry.

Two and a half minutes isn't a lot of time.
Go to 137.

That's more than enough time to find something useful.
Go to 138.

111

It all feels like a bad dream that never ends, doesn't it? You don't remember what you did. You're not even sure that your memories are your own. Can space jellies gaslight a person?

It might not even be space jellies. They're not that evolved. This is something else. What were they called? You're sure you've heard the name before.

The Voerdamnikenari.
Go to 132.

The Dumfirammir.
Go to 152.

112

You flip the latches and lift the lid. A gust of frigid air flows out, and your teeth chatter. Once the fog clears, you peer into the chest.

There's a body in there.

The corpse is covered in a layer of hoary frost, making it hard to tell who it is, though you can tell it is wearing one of the ubiquitous orange jumpsuits that everyone wears at MacReady. Much like the one you're wearing right now, in fact. Which doesn't mean anything, because you found this one in a locker in the infirmary.

"It's not me," you whisper. It can't be. You're alive. You're standing right here. The records in Dr. Nakamura's office are incorrect. Someone is lying.

And this is when the Old Man pops up in your head. *Welcome to the Night Office,* he whispers, *where you are never told the whole truth.*

People are always lying. You know this. You've seen it time and time again. Marylynn Velasquez lied. Alice McTaggart lied. Your aunt lied. Starkweather lied. They're all liars. They all wanted something, and were willing to be hurt people to get it. This is just more of the same.

What are you going to do? the Old Man whispers again.

"I'm going to do what I always do," you whisper.
Go to 128.

"I'm going to burn it all down," you whisper back.
Go to 151.

113

You type in a word you use quite regularly, usually when referencing the state of affairs in a Night Office mission. You hit RETURN, and the computer thinks about your password choice for a second. A new box appears on the screen.

"PASSWORD INCORRECT. NO MORE ATTEMPTS AVAILABLE. THIS STATION IS LOCKED FOR 6 HOURS."

Well, you're not about to wait around that long.

No regrets about trying that password, though.
Go to 106.

114

Having completed your search of Dr. Nakamura's office, you turn to leave, but a small noise catches your attention. When you look, you see the Old Man. He's sitting in the doctor's chair, his feet on the desk. He's rolling a long cigar between his fingers.

You know he's not really there. He's been gone a long time. You're just one of the lucky ones who still sees him, now and again.

This one is twisting you up, isn't it? he says. *Bending you sideways.* He shows you his teeth—the most feral thing about him.

"I did something terrible, didn't I?" you say.

He shrugs. *We all do, one day or another.* He produces a match from somewhere—his coat is the prototype of all Closer coats, after all—and strikes it with his thumbnail. It flares into life, and he holds it to the end of the cigar. He makes the flame dance, and the end of his cigar crackles and flares.

"Isn't time travel dangerous?" you ask. "Doesn't it lead to—I don't know—a breakdown of reality?"

I would think so, he says. He snuffs the tiny flame of the match out with his broad fingers. *Isn't that what is happening to you?*

"I guess so," you say. "Is this why the Night Office stays away from temporal co-realities?"

Officially, the Night Office doesn't acknowledge the theoretical possibility of temporal co-realities, the Old Man says.

"Unofficially?

He puffs on his cigar. *Time travel is a shit-show,* he says with a smile.

"You're no help," you say. You turn away from the phantom of the Old Man, intending to dismiss him from your mind.

Would you prefer someone else? This voice is different, and when you turn back, the person behind the desk is your aunt.

She looks younger than the last time you saw her, which isn't a surprise, really. All mental projections get younger as our memories of them fade.

"You aren't much better," you say. "We are taught to make imaginary friends so that we can have a sounding board— someone we can ground ourselves with. But you? You don't ground me. You haven't for a lot time."

Your aunt doesn't say anything. You notice that her hands are out of sight in her lap.

"What have you got in your hands?" you ask.

Nothing, she says dully, sounding like a sulking teenager. Oh, how many times did you use this voice on her?

"Show me," you say.

No, she says.

"Show me." You are more forceful this time. She is your projection, after all. You can make her do what you want.

She fights you, which is telling, but she raise her hands. She's got a switchblade. *Happy now?* Her tone is pinched.

"No," you say. "Where did you get that?"

(You know where you got it.)

She shakes her head. She's not going to tell you. As you approach the desk, she shivers and vanishes.

The knife, however, remains. Lying there on the desk blotter.

Leave it. Like everything else, it doesn't exist.
Go to 129.

Take it. *Take it!*
Go to 144.

115

This is the library. It's contents are different than the contents of the bookcase in the common area near the kitchen. This room is the repository of all the stodgy research papers and publication materials of the staff. Kind of a trophy case, in fact, more than a working library. This is room where they would shoot their marketing videos, if they bothered with that sort of thing.

You're not expecting to be attacked when you come into the room, but that's what happens. All you see is a flash of orange, and then a heavy book comes hurtling at your head.

Duck. Dodge. Get ready to wrestle.
Go to 122.

If you've got your gear, you don't need to wrestle.
Go to 125.

116

One does not "notch" a discipline stick, for crying out loud. These things are carved with active sigils and protective spells. Cutting the wood will undoubtedly break one of the wards, and where is that going to leave you?

If you really need to mark your victory, cut a—no, wait. That's not okay, either. The school psychologist was really freaked out by the line of scars on your inner arm. You had to stop recording your triumphs in an external fashion. No one understood.

Just mark your victory in your little notebook (the SIGIL— 66/d log, of course). You keep it in the inside breast pocket of your coat. Yes, there. Let's see. This beastie was sort of a Hinch's Howling Abomination (page 78), but hmm, those are more frog-like than this thing. Maybe a denizen of Eurdoriat's Gate (page 22)?

Well, it doesn't really matter. Mark it down somewhere.

You can sort this out later. After you survive.
Go to 124.

It does matter. Survival isn't as important as leaving a good record of your efforts. No one lives forever in the Night Office. A field operative's Sightings, Inquiries & Grievous Immolations Log is the only way anyone remembers what you accomplished.
Go to 141.

117

You loop the rubber band around your thumb and pull it back with your other hand. Thus armed, you move carefully down one of the aisles of the server room, stepping over the raised tracks where cables run back and forth between racks. The shadows at the back of the room waver slightly, and for a moment, you think it could be an optical illusion.

Nope, there's definitely something back there.

It lurches forward, dragging the shadows with it. It was human once, but some kind of fungal infection has taken over the body and turned it into a walking mushroom farm. The creature looks like something from a very low-budget dystopian horror film—late-night local cable access channel sort of horror fillm. It's not very terrifying.

Still, it's an ambulatory fungoid, and spores can be deadly. Best to treat it with caution. You threaten it with the rubber band. It pauses for a second, staring dully at the rubber strap pulled taut between your fingers.

You say a couple of the Lesser Banishing Words, and it seems to know what those are, even if it doesn't abide by them. It starts lurching toward you again, more quickly this time. A haze of fungal gnats swarm around its head.

You back up a few more steps, and then your heel hits one of the raised cable tracks and you lose your balance. Your hand twitches, and the rubber band flies off your thumb. You hit your tailbone hard when you land, and for a second, you can't feel your legs.

The fungal shambler has been doggedly shuffling toward you, and as you scramble back, it lunges. A cloud of spores expresses from open sores on its head, and you press your lips shut, holding your breath.

Your eyes are open, though, and some of the spores land on your eyelashes. You blink—you can't help it; you were startled to see your rubber band sticking to the front of the fungal monster's face—and some of the spores dust onto your cornea. You blink frantically, trying to clear them off, but the spores are tenacious. They crawl under your eyelids, where they are going to make mischief.

SCOOPING OUT YOUR EYEBALL MIGHT WORK. TO BE SURE, HOWEVER, YOU'RE GOING TO HAVE TO KEEP SCOOPING, AND EVENTUALLY, YOU'RE GOING TO RUPTURE SOMETHING YOU SHOULDN'T.

OF COURSE, YOU DON'T HAVE A SPOON, SO HOW YOU'RE GOING TO ACCOMPLISH THIS IS SOMEWHAT TRICKY . . .

MAPS SCORE: 43

118

You head for the infirmary. You must have missed your gear back there. However, when you get to the end of the hall, you stop and listen. There's something . . . you hear a scraping noise.

Carefully, you peer around the corner.

There isn't anything in the hall.

You look over your shoulder and don't see anything behind you either.

Damnit. You know you heard something.

You blink and blink again. The shadows—

The door to the computer lab is open. You're pretty sure you closed it. And the shadows are all wrong . . .

You hear the noise again. It's definitely coming from the hall near the common area. You peek around the corner again, and there's nothing there. Except . . . the shadows are weird. They're . . . moving?

That can't be right.

What am I doing here? you think, trying to remember why you left . . . whichever room you were investigating. It's getting fuzzy. Even the Old Man is quiet.

The noise comes again, and you realize it's the sound your fingernails make on the bandage around your forearm. There's a weird stain that wasn't there earlier. It's almost like . . .

THE SHADOWS ARE DANGEROUS WHEN THEY GET IN YOUR HEAD. WE'LL SPARE YOU THE INEVITABLE DESCENT INTO MADNESS, BUT REST ASSURED, YOU'RE DEFINITELY ON YOUR WAY.

MAPS SCORE: 40

119

You decide to wait ten more minutes. In your head, the Old Man has wandered off, shaking his head. You start reading the manuscript. It's very pulpy.

There's a sudden lack of sound in the room. When you look over at the individual lying on the floor, you realize they've stopped breathing.

"Well, shit," you mutter. You stand over the body for a second, sparing a quick thought—maybe a tiny apology.

Well, these things happen. Might as well get back to the mission.

Hang on. This manuscript is kind of interesting.
Go to 36.

Forget the manuscript, for crying out loud. You can read this sort of crap on the plane ride home.
Go to 106.

120

"I know you're in my head," you tell the Old Man. "And I also know something is trying to convince me that I'm insane. That I've done things—terrible things. It wants me to do even worse things."

Are you? the Old Man asks. *Are you going to do worse things?*

You laugh at him. "Worse than what you've done?"

He smiles when he realizes you aren't going to take the knife. It's a cold smile, touched with a hint of pride. He closes the knife and raises it to his face. Opening his mouth wide, he shoves it past his strong teeth. He makes a face as he swallows the knife, but it doesn't appear to harm him.

So glad to be of assistance, he says.

"I am not going to be the monster mothers warn their children about," you say.

He shrugs. *If you won't, someone else will be.*

"That's what the Night Office is for," you say.

He's frozen in place, like a video projection that has been paused. You peer at his face, staring into his hard gaze. *You're going to be okay, kid,* is what you read in his gaze.

If you don't have your gear, maybe you should do something about that.
Go to 80.

If you have your gear, you can get on with the mission.
Go to 133.

121

You undo the clasps on the freezer and lift the lid. A dense cloud of cold storage fog rolls out. You can't see anything for a minute, and part of your brain shrieks about how dumb it is to open a locker like this without any preparation. *It's too late*, you tell yourself.

The fog clears and you can see that the freezer is . . . empty.

"Well, this is unsatisfying," you say.

You slam the lid shut, furious at being tricked like this.

Trick-trick-trickery, the Old Man whispers. He's there, in your head, that voice of reason which only shows up at inopportune times. Like now. *Who is playing tricks?* he asks.

You open the freezer again. *There's no body*, you tell him. *I'm not dead because I'm right here. Those records are bullshit.*

You slam the freezer again. You're angry now, aren't you? Someone is messing with you. Where has everyone gone? Who filled out that report? Who—

Where is that freezer getting power from? the Old Man asks, interrupting your mental tirade.

You step back and look at the freezer. He's right. There has to be a power source somewhere. You grab the edge of the freezer and shove it against the edge of the rack. You see the cord behind the box, and . . .

"What the . . . ?"

There's a hole in the wall behind the freezer. The cord runs into the hole. It's big enough for someone to crawl into.

You wrestle with the freezer, trying to get it turned around so you can squeeze past it. Once it is shoved out of the way, you crouch and look at the hole in the wall behind the freezer.

It's not very deep, and there's a source of white light at the other end.

Fortune favors the foolish, the Old Man says.

"Shut up," you tell him.

You crawl across the metal shelf of the rack. The hole is smaller than you thought, but you'll fit if you crawl on your belly. You wiggle into the tunnel, and suffer only a mild attack of claustrophobia, but you manage to make it through.

The room beyond is white. It's not an ice cave. The walls aren't painted white. It room itself is . . . white.

There's an object in the center of this empty space. It may be the source of all this emptiness. It may be holding the emptiness at bay. You're not sure. There is a noise coming from the pillar, a hum that makes your teeth vibrate in your mouth. The hum gets into your jaw, and from there it resonates into your skull. It slithers into your spine, shaking your ribs, and it travels all the way down to your pelvis. Oh, yeah, you feel it down there too.

There's a body lying next to the object. One hand is outstretched, fingers almost touching the pillar. You approach the body.

What did Sagalico warn you about? the Old Man whispers in your head.

Go back to the WHITE ROOM.

122

The first attempt narrowly misses your skull, and you cry out as the heavy book slams against your shoulder. You lose all sensation in that arm, which puts you at a disadvantage when they raise the book to hit you again.

"It's me," you shout, trying to distract them. Trying to get them to recognize you as a human and not as a host to some extraterrestrial space goo.

The individual hesitates, the book held over their head. Their eyes are white with fear—it's been hours—days, even—since they've heard another voice. They don't know what to do.

Take advantage of this hesitation.
Go to 130.

Step back and raise your hands—well, one hand; that other arm is really numb.
Go to 136.

123

You've got your coat and your discipline stick. Now you're in business. You need to wrap up wandering around the main floor of the research station soon, though.

Check out the Computer Lab.
Go to 63.

Check out Ops.
Go to 84.

Stop by the Briefing Room.
Go to 99.

Hit the Library.
Go to 115.

The Umbilical will take you to the research area of the station.
Go to 133.

124

You return to the desk with the computer terminal on it. You nudge the mouse and the screen flickers to life. An Endoluvion logo floats around the screen. When you tap the space bar on the keyboard, a window pops up. It's a user / password combo, and—*aren't you the lucky one?*—both fields are pre-populated with data. The user name is "MORGAN."

You hit RETURN and the computer gurgles for a minute. A desktop appears; the background is the Endoluvion logo. You find the directory system and click on one of the shared drives. The computer thinks about your request for a minute before throwing up an error message: "VOLUME OFFLINE."

You glance over at the server racks. You can't imagine that the one server that got smoked by the fungus spores is the precise one that manages connections to the server farm. Most likely, many of the servers have been compromised, which leaves you with whatever was stored locally.

You click into the local files, where you find Morgan's user directory. There's a folder called "MECHANICAL REPORTS," a text file titled "THE_ALBATROSS_LEGACY.doc," and a spreadsheet with a file name of "ANOMALOUS_0920.xls."

Check out the folder.
Go to 126.

Oh, that file looks mysterious. Click on that.
Go to 140.

Check out the spreadsheet.
Go to 142.

125

You get your discipline stick up in time to block their attack. You counter with a sharp jab to their face, and you feel something crunch. They cry out and drop the book. It lands heavily on their foot, and this is too much for them. They go down, their hands to their face (where is definitely some blood). They are waving their injured foot in the air, as if that is going to make it feel better.

You stand back, keeping your discipline stick ready.

The crew member lowers their hands, and you get your first clear look at their face. Their nose probably isn't broken, but there is blood on the lips and chin. "You hit me," they exclaim, their voice slurring from the pain.

"You attacked me," you point out.

They get a better look at you, and their eyes widen. "You," they exclaim.

"Me," you say.

"But you're—you're—"

"Not who you expected?"
Go to 139.

"Dead?"
Go to 143.

126

You double-click on the folder titled "MECHANICAL REPORTS." It's filled with images and sub-folders. The images have generic sequential names, and the folders are titled with equally obtuse nomenclature. You double-click on a file at random, and it opens to show a picture of an old woman mugging for the camera with a live puffin on her head. She appears to be an island somewhere.

You check another image file, and the same woman is whacking a walrus with a broom.

You scroll to the bottom of the inventory and try one of the last images. This time the old woman is—

You close the picture, wishing you could scrub that image out of your brain. That was not what you expected.

With some reluctance, you check out one of the folders. It's filled with more generically named images. You open one, and this time, the subject is an old man riding a llama. There are several dozen more images. You hesitate, fearing to investigate what the happy go lucky septuagenarian might be doing in later pictures.

You don't have time to look at anything else. Get out of the room before the slithering shambler gets you.
Go to 106.

You really don't have time to oogle someone's holiday pictures. Check out the file instead.
Go to 140.

127

Sagalico is talking about the obelisk, the object that Endoluvion discovered in the ice. It's what they dug up. It's what they've been worshipping with their Calls. It's the invocation marker which is calling them here. But they can't cross over yet. Not until someone activates the gate. Not until the ritual is complete.

And you know who fucked that all up, don't you?

You did.

How are you going to undo the terrible mistake you've made?

You're going to make the right choice this time.
Go to 135.

No. It's time to let someone else deal with this. It's time for Protocol 9.
Go to 151.

128

And what is that? the Old Man asks.

"My job," you tell him.

You slam the freezer shut. It doesn't matter whose body in inside. It won't be the last body you find. You're here to save the world, and that's what you're going to do. The one hiccup is that you're not very well prepared. You don't have your gear, for one. You're woefully unprepared, for another. And third—

"This is the Night Office," you say, interrupting that part of your brain that often gets hung up on the particulars. "We always make it up as we go, because no one has ever done what we do."

In your head, you can see the Old Man's knowing smile, and you want to punch him for it. Not because he's a smug bastard, but because you can feel the adrenaline starting to fill your blood and—Damn!—something needs punching.

But first, your gear. You've got to find your gear.

You notice a cardboard box on the shelf above the freezer. It's incongruous in a room full of prepackaged and insulated supplies. You haul it off the shelf and open it up. There's a piece of clothing and a short black rod inside. You pull out the garment and discover that it is a full-length coat. The rod is weighted funny, and when you flick it, it telescopes out to a full baton.

Ah, the tools of a Closer. This isn't your gear; it's Gull's.

You slip the coat on. It's a little short in the sleeves and longer than you prefer, but it'll work. You feel it settle on you, and there is that familiar weight of full pockets. Your discipline stick was a hand-carved piece of hickory, but since you're just going to be hitting things, this black baton will work fine.

This is more like it, you think.

Return to the front half of the station and investigate the other areas.

Go to 71.

You're in the back half of the station, where the science happened. It's also where the unnatural things probably happened. You might as well stay in this area.

Go to 165.

129

Your aunt says something unkind as you leave the doctor's office. You ignore her. It's just a replay of when you left. Something broke in her that summer; something that leaked poison into her heart. She turned against you. She forced you to do those things you did later. It was all her fault. You wouldn't have turned out this way if she hadn't—

The Old Man is leaning against the wall. He's cleaning his nails with the very knife you left behind in the office. *You shouldn't think of her like that,* he says. *She meant well. You were a difficult child.*

"She could have been more supportive," you say.

The Old Man shrugs. *You weren't owned anything. None of us are.*

He wipes the knife blade along his sleeve. Reversing the weapon, he holds it out to you. *She isn't the only one who tried to hurt you,* he says. *What about the other one? The one who keeps telling you that you are stupid?*

"I'm not stupid," you say.
Go to 120.

You know who he is talking about. Take the knife. You have to put these demons to rest.
Go to 144.

130

You do that thing you've been practicing, where you flail with one arm while darting forward. When you're close enough, you smack them in the nose with your first.

It's a mean thing to do, but these are mean times, aren't they? The individual cries out and steps back. Their hold on the heavy book slips and the volume comes down on their head. They made a noise like a deflating balloon and collapse.

You eye the unconscious person as you rub your arm, trying to work some sensation back into it. They're drooling slightly, which is a troubling sign.

You nudge the heavy book with your foot, and wow, it's really quite heavy. Did you—? Oh, dear.

You kneel and thumb up one of their eyelids. Their pupil is dilated. They are still breathing, but you don't think they're going to come back anytime soon after having that book drop on their skull.

Brilliant work, there.

Whoops. Well, surely they'll be all right. You can leave them here. Maybe lock the door when you leave?

You've got a mission to finish.
Go to 106.

Give them a few minutes. You might as well investigate the rest of the library as you wait.
Go to 156.

131

It's nice of you to share how you feel about shoggoths, but as you are keying in your latest guess at the password, you hear a noise behind you. At first, you think one of the server fans broke, but when the noise is repeated, you realize it's not a hardware error. It's wetware.

Lurching out of the shadow at the back of the room is something that was human once, but now it is a shambling mass of fungal growth and malformed animal parts. It has five legs, two heads, and a variegated pattern of mushroom growth on its belly. It barfs globs of squirming ectoplasm, and as it lumbers toward you, the ectoplasm crawls up the metal cages of the server racks. Servers smoke and die as the fungal goo gets inside, and you suspect the same thing is going to happen to you if any of that goop gets on you.

You head for the door, and as you're faster than the marsh matrix that is slurping after you, you get the door closed. There's no way to lock the room from the outside. It's probably not the best idea to leave a shambling patch of vile fungi roaming around the station unchecked, but you can't exactly stand here and hold the door shut.

If only you had your gear. A phosphorus grenade would solve this problem.
Go to 149.

Hope the fungi isn't smart enough to work a door knob. Head for the Umbilical and the labs.
Go to 154.

132

You remember a briefing you had—didn't have? Might have in the future with someone named Pip. He told you about the Voerdamnikenari. They slip through time and they're apparently very tasty, according to the Old Ones.

(no, they're parasites)

They sent us information we couldn't translate. Not for several generations. The Fourteen Calls. It was a test. When we figured out how to perform the rituals, they would know that our brains were ripe. That we were ready to be contacted.

We're just blind worms, poking around in the vast darkness. You'd think we would have learned enough already with the Deep Ones and the black goats of Ur. But no, here we go again, poking and whistling where we shouldn't.

All of this is useful to remember

(or learn again; it's all so confusing)

but you still have to finish the mission.

No, you're a Closer. You screwed it up the first time, but somehow you've been given another chance. You're going to finish this.

Go to 106.

It's time for Protocol-9. Seriously. You've mucked this up. You need to call in backup.

Go to 151.

133

Next to the infirmary is the hall that leads to the other half of the station. You duck through the weather stripping and find yourself in a narrow hallway. Bare bulbs run on a single strand of wire along the ceiling, and the walls are covered with industrial padding held in place with tape, nails, and the occasional piece of weather-warped wood. It's got a very DIY bottom of the world vibe to it.

You recall a map of the station from the briefing materials. It showed two distinct buildings, but it looks like Endoluvion built a connective umbilical between the two structures. You can't blame them. Who would want to go outside in this environment?

There's a pressure door at the end of the hall. The keycard reader is showing a red light. You investigate the door more closely, and see that it is merely shut. It hasn't been Closed.

You rest your fingers on the metal panel. Why isn't this Closed, you think? If there are terrible things on the other side of this door, shouldn't you or Peele—the Closer on the other team—have already sealed them off? There's a nagging feeling in your brain, and you feel like you're picking at a loose thread on an old cardigan. You don't want to tug on the thread because you know it's going to unravel the whole damn sweater, and it's one of your favorites, but you know you need to tug on the thread. You need to remember what happened.

Your forearm aches under the bandage. Something bit you. Where did it happen? You recall a forest—no, not quite a forest—and there were fans. Large fans that make you think of being in an underground facility, like a bunker or a storage facility. There's a weird glow coming from . . .

You can't remember.

But you know you don't have much time. You need to get this door opened.

You check the pockets of your coat. Surely you have something that can open this door.

Maybe a bit of plastic explosive?
Go to 146.

Wait. Why are you dawdling here? Is this a recursion—no. You've already opened the door to the research station. This is all the same index.

Isn't it?
Go to 153.

Never mind that. Don't you have an ATM card in your coat somewhere?
Go to 160.

134

On the far side of the common area, there is a small cafeteria area with several tables and chairs. Beyond those, there are three serving carts with troughs for big pans of food. A set of swinging doors leads into the kitchen proper. You navigate past the counters and push through the swinging doors.

The kitchen is small and utilitarian. It's also the scene of a terrible slaughter. There's a lot of dried blood splashed on the tile floors and the metal counters. There's even some spray on the ceiling. There's a walk-in freezer, and the door is blocked open by a body.

It's a male figure, and it's missing a lot of its skull. The brains are gone too. The rest of the corpse's clothing has been shredded and torn.

Unfortunately, you'll need to get closer in order to identify that body. This is the price of curiosity, after all.
Go to 62.

There's nothing you can do for that poor soul. Leave the body alone and get on with the mission.
Go to 106.

135

You look around in the briefing room a bit more, and you find the box that you shoved the space jelly into. It's got your mark on it. You trace the sigil, and the motion is reassuring. Each time you trace the mark, the fog in your head clears a little more. Pieces start coming back.

Your arrival. Sagalico's unease. The nest in the geology lab. The secret door in—

And the obelisk. Yes. You remember it now. You remember hearing it call to you. In the white room. Where the rabbits live.

(They aren't rabbits)

You can feel *them* too—pushing hard against the barrier of the Way, eager to come through. Eager to feast on this world.

They're not allies. You know that. You've always know it. Starkweather lied. Oresti knew, and he vanished before Starkweather could sacrifice him.

You smell the Old Man's cigar, and when you turn around, he's perched on the edge of the table. *They forgot to tell you about what Starkweather did, didn't they?*

"They always forget to tell us something," you say.

He would have killed them all if Blethins hadn't scrambled his brain.

"Blethins?"

You won't find any mention of her in the official record, the Old Man says. He taps the side of his head. *I was on the team that went to the cold empty to bring them back. A bunch of corpses and Starkweather. Blethins should have killed him too, but he knew too much. He had to come back. He knew about* them. *He knew what they desired. He wanted to tell us. It was a compulsion. They had coded his brain so deeply that even with everything else a fucking mess, he still wanted to serve them.*

"Why did you—why did we—let anyone talk to him?"

The Old Man shows you his teeth, and then shoves his cigar in his mouth and sucks on it ferociously.

"You were gone," you say, understanding what happened. "And when you left, everything you knew left with you."

Institutional knowledge is a bitch when no one dares to write anything down, the Old Man grouses.

You don't mention the incongruity of a figment of your imagination being fussy about no one remembering what he knows.

They're brain parasites, the Old Man says suddenly.

"Who?"

The Voerdamnikenari. The Old Ones cast them out because they devoured everything, including them. They're a pest, and Starkweather wanted us to contact them. The Old Man waves his cigar at the station around you. *These idiots wanted to contact them.*

"They succeeded," you say, your throat dry and scratchy.

The Old Man fixes you with his steely-eyed stare. *Are we done then?* he asks.

"No," you say. "I have a trick or two yet."

You always were my favorite, the Old Man says. He exhales a huge blast of cigar smoke that envelopes him.

When it fades, he's gone too. It's just you and the staked out corpse of the poor bastard who had his mind eaten by a space jelly.

Well, that felt like an actual briefing. Huzzah! Now you know what you're up against, at least.

Go to 106.

136

You're try to look non-threatening, but given the general atmosphere at MacReady Station, you're not sure how well you pull that off. Fortunately, this individual has at least three brain cells left, and they figure out what you're trying to signal them. They lower the heavy book and stare at you.

You recognize them. "You're—you're Doctor Nakamura," you say.

"You're—you're the patient," the doctor says. "The one who went into the room."

"Which room?" you demand.

They drop the heavy book, and you wince as it nearly crushes the doctor's foot. "It's all so horrible," they say.

"That's why I'm here," you say, trying to be helpful. You have a hundred questions, and you know there's not enough time to answer them all. "I—I have some questions," you say gently, trying to get them to focus on your immediate needs.

They nod absently. You can tell their attention is drifting. You don't know how much time you have before they check out.

"Tell me about the deaths," you say.
Go to 157.

"What happened to the rest of my team?" you ask.
Go to 161.

137

There isn't much time to leisurely look through the computer files. You find the documents folder associated with this user. You click on a sub-folder labeled "MECHANICAL REPORTS," and find hundred of image files. You double-click one and it fills the screen when it opens. It's—

Ah, well—that's unexpected.

It's a picture of an old man in an all-weather slicker hugging a seal. The seal looks like it is having more fun than the old man.

You randomly pick another file, and this one is a picture of the same old man, but he's wearing a different weather slicker. This time he is chasing an emperor penguin. The penguin looks very annoyed.

You glance over your shoulder. The hand is still dragging its unholy mass. The growth is starting to sprout limbs that are covered with thorns and suckers. If that thing gets ahold of you, you're never going to get free.

You shouldn't risk sticking around any longer.
Go to 106.

One more minute! Keep looking on the computer.
Go to 145.

138

You figure the easiest way to find something is to use the computer's built-in index search tool. You know, it's the magnifying glass up in the right corner—

Oh, this isn't one of those operating systems. It's something more primitive and less user-friendly.

Glancing over your shoulder, you see that the hand is part of a fungal growth composed of ancient tree bark, shards of bones, and slurries of human flesh. It jiggles, giggles, and slurps along like a mutated glop of convenience store slush.

You find a sorting function on the active window. That seems like the best approach. You click the order icon—sorting by most recent access date—and wait as the computer hiccups and wheezes.

The screen redraws, and you look at the top results.

The first one is a folder called "MECHANICAL REPORTS." The second item is a text file titled "THE_ALBATROSS_LEGACY.doc." The third item is a spreadsheet with a file name of "ANOMALOUS_0920.xls."

Check out the folder.
Go to 126.

Check out the file.
Go to 140.

Check out the spreadsheet.
Go to 142.

139

The person moves away from you, angling toward a corner of the room, and you let them go. They're in shock.

"I need some answers," you say. "What happened here? Who are you? Where is everyone else?"

"They're—they're all dead," they say.

"Why haven't they—" You realize that's a bad question. You should try something else. "What's your name?" you ask.

"Jame—Jamie Nakamura," they say.

"You're the doctor."

They start to nod, but as your words sink in, the panic comes back. It's clear this individual doesn't want to be the doctor anymore. Too many bad memories.

"You were—you were dead," they say, finally looking at you. "We had—we brought you back, but . . . you weren't responsive. You were in a coma." The doctor shakes their head. "Ar—Argot said to keep you hydrated, and that I should give you—" They break off.

"Give me what?" you ask.

"Amphetamines," the doctor said. "And that dosage—I couldn't administer that. Not as a medical practitioner."

"Yeah, well, we do things a bit differently in the Night Office," you say, making light of what you think Argot was trying to do, which was shock your body out of its self-induced comatose state. *He must have been desperate*, you think, *because that rarely works.*

"What happened to Argot?" you ask.

The doctor shakes their head. When you repeat the question, they squeeze themselves into the corner even farther, trying to make themselves as small as possible.

This is a waste of time. The doctor is in shock. They don't understand what they're up against. They don't understand what it is that you must do.

Go to 106.

You can't keep pushing. You're going to have to wait for them to calm down. As much as you hate the idea, you need to get the doctor talking.

Go to 155.

140

You double-click the text file, and after a moment of thought, the computer opens the file and displays it on the screen.

PROLOGUE - VIENNA, 1986

Adrian Barstow knew the pair shadowing him were working for DIABOLIK. He was supposed to meet his contact with AMBER at the Rose Vault, the bar in the basement of the Grand Meridian Hotel, but he couldn't show up with these hired killers on his trail. He had to shake them, or kill them. He could do the latter readily enough as he was proficient in sixteen different martial traditions, as well as the darker arts known to a second-stage initiate of the Green Hand—the secret society that had taken him in as an orphan . . .

Oh, for crying out loud, this is a spy novel manuscript. Is that what Morgan was working on in his spare time?

You don't have time for this.

There's a printer on the other desk. Maybe you can grab a printout and read it later.
Go to 31.

This is all a waste of time. You need to get to the research labs.
Go to 133.

Check out the spreadsheet before you go.
Go to 142.

141

Of course, you're not going to get a certification seals on your SIGIL—66/d entries until after you return from this mission, but we understand the desire to make those marks as they happen. Knock yourself out.

NOTE: YOU HAVE UNLOCKED A BONUS ACHIEVEMENT. THIS WILL BE NOTED AT THE END OF THE EXERCISE.

Get on with the mission.
Go to 106.

Wait. Wasn't there something you still wanted to do in this room before this beastie interrupted you?
Go to 124.

142

You double-click the spreadsheet file, and your eyes glaze over almost immediately when you are confronted with lines and lines and lines of data. Whoever was collecting this data hadn't done much to organize it yet, and it's almost too much to wade through. Date markers, amplitude measurements, range of error reporting, a count of something called "ink spots," and a column marked "NOTES."

You sort the data by date and then scan the "NOTES" column. Morgan was correlating behavior in a number of individuals. He only lists last names, and you recognize a few from the crew roster of MacReady.

One of the data entries on September 10th is "NOBO arrive!!!!" *NOBO* is an acronym Asset Resource Management uses when interfacing with the general public. Internally, it doesn't mean anything, but ARM doesn't mind when the public thinks it stands for "Night Office Black Ops," because that was good for the organization's image. Useful for sidestepping local chains of command and for cutting through bureaucratic red tape.

However, that's a lot of exclamation points. Morgan doesn't seem the type to wax enthusiastic about a black ops team. Maybe the "!" are how Morgan is tracking "ink spots"?

You resort the data by the number of "ink spots," and you see the entry on the 10th is the third largest concentration of spots. The two larger concentrations are on the 13th and 12th, respectively.

Gull died on the 13th. Your team—the backup team—arrived on the 12th.

On a whim, you scroll to the bottom of the sorted list. The dates with the least number of ink spots entries are a few days last month and . . .

You glance at the time stamp in the corner of the computer screen. The latest data entry in this file is only an hour old. How is that possible?

As if sensing your question, the computer beeps and a dialog box opens up. "FILE UPDATED. RELOAD?"

You click on the *YES* button. The spreadsheet disappears. The computer grinds for a second, and then the window opens again. It's blank this time, except for a line of text at the very top.

"DATA CORRPUT. NO RECORDS FOUND."

It's all gone, whatever it was.

You glance at the cables coming out of the back of the computer. This machine is hooked up to some kind of instrument somewhere else. Probably in this room. Maybe elsewhere in the facility. The instrument is reporting data to this computer at a regular interval, and assuredly, there's some security in place that would prevent a data wipe like this, but you don't have time to figure it out.

The more important questions are: where is the instrument, and what is it measuring?

Speaking of cables, there's a cable that runs from this computer to the printer. Maybe you can print out that text file on this machine and read it later.

Go to 31.

Right. So you're not going insane. There is something happening here. You just need to keep looking.

Go to 106.

143

The person hiding in the library laughs when you say that. There's a manic quality to their laughter, as if they have seen things humanity is not meant to see. You know the feeling, and so you wait patiently for the shock and panic to pass.

(It may never pass.)

Eventually, they have to stop to breathe—which isn't long because of the condition of their nose—and their wide-eyed panic subsides into twitching fear.

"Who are you?" you ask.

They look at you. "You don't remember?"

You shake your head. "Things are a bit fuzzy."

"I'm the doctor," they say. "Doctor Nakamura. We met when you and—and—when you and your friends arrived. Your leader—"

"He's not my leader," you say.

Doctor Nakamura flinches at the correction, but overcomes their reaction. "Who—whoever he is—he wanted a briefing of all the—all those who had died."

"Did you give it?"

The doctor nods.

"How many?" you ask.

"Five—no, six," the doctor says. "One of them was . . . was one of yours."

"Gull," you say, remembering.

The doctor nods. "Yes, that was their name."

"What happened to Gull?"

The doctor can't look at you. "It was horrible," they say.

It usually is, the Old Man whispers in your head. You bite your lip. You were about to say the same thing out loud.

"What happened to me?" you ask.

The doctor shudders. "He attacked you."

"Who?"

"A man named Clarke. Or, what used to be Clarke, I guess." The doctor raises their hands to cover their face and winces when they touch their nose. "I don't understand any of it."

You rub your forearm, as if friction will bring back the memories that are missing. "Did he bite me?" you ask.

The doctor shakes their head. "Yes, but not with his—not with this mouth." They point to their face. "They had—"

"Mouths in the palms of their hands?" you ask.

The doctor stares at you, and you shrug lightly. "It's typical space jelly behavior," you say. "Not that the mouths connect to a digestive system or anything. They're just extra biters. Space jellies like to bite."

The doctor wanders over to the couch in the library and collapses onto it. They stare into space.

They're not coming back. You've seen this sort of shock before in survivors. You're not going to get anything more out of them. Best to leave them here and move on. Hopefully, they won't get eaten while you're wandering around the station.

Go to 106.

You're not excited to wait, but you need answers.

Go to 155.

144

A psychic wave rolls through you. It drives you to your knees. Your brain tries to flee out your ears and nose. You stuff it back in, along with the animalistic howl that is trying to get out of your throat. For a moment, everything is white

(Even the rabbits)

and then the room comes back into focus. The door is open. You grab the thing you shouldn't forget and head out the door.

You find yourself in the East Corridor of MacReady Station. Your head still hurts, but you can manage the pain. You have to manage the pain.

There's something in your right hand. It's a knife. You're not sure where you picked it up, but it feels good in your hand. As you are trying to recall how you go there, you hear voices coming from around the corner.

(Wait, why is there blood—?)

Ahead, Argot, Sagalico, and two people from the station come around the corner. Argot is arguing with the taller of the two station employees; they're going on about some aspect of security. The station guy doesn't want to acknowledge Argot's authority, and Argot is about—

Well, you know exactly what is on Argot's mind, and you can help him with that.

"Where did—" The station man starts, but his question is cut off by your knife.

It moves so effortlessly in your hand. In fact, it's almost like someone else is doing all the work, and you're merely watching it happen.

Sagalico—the only one who can see you for what you truly are—is shouting, and you are delighted to realize you know a way to shut him up. You say the words that will seal his mouth.

They are human words, and once upon a time, you understood where they came from, but now, they are strange noises that change the world. You don't know why they work. They just do, and it's marvelous.

Argot—oh, how could you forget about Argot?—grabs your shoulder with his eldritch hand. It's very shiny, and so very hot. Flesh melts under his touch, but you smile at him because you don't feel anything. Not anymore. You're done with all those silly human feelings.

I live to serve, you think, and the voice in your head—it's not that pathetic father figure anymore; no, it's a marvelous voice, filled with love and warmth—that voice says . . .

THE NIGHT OFFICE REGRETS YOUR FAILURE TO WITHSTAND THE MENTAL ASSAULT OF THE VOERDAMNIKENARI. EVEN THOUGH THIS IS A PSYCHOLOGICAL ASSESSMENT EXERCISE, WE HOPE YOU WILL NOT SUFFER ANY ADVERSE MENTAL EFFECTS FROM BEING A PAWN OF INTERGALACTIC MIND EATERS.

MAPS SCORE: 32

145

You double-click a text file that has been recently modified. It's titled "ALBALEG.txt." The computer thinks for a minute and then throws up a text document. It starts:

PROLOGUE - VIENNA, 1986

Adrian Barstow knew the pair shadowing him were working for DIABOLIK. He was supposed to meet his contact with AMBER at the Rose Vault, the bar in the basement of the Grand Meridian Hotel, but he couldn't show up with these hired killers on his trail. He had to shake them, or kill them. He could do the latter readily enough as he was proficient in sixteen different martial traditions, as well as the darker arts known to a second-stage initiate of the Green Hand—the secret society that had taken him in as an orphan . . .

Oh, for crying out loud, this is a spy novel manuscript. Is that what Morgan was working on in his spare time?

Glancing over your shoulder, you see the thorny shambling mound is getting close. Too close. You're out of time.

There's a printer on the other desk. Maybe you can grab a printout and read it later.
Go to 31.

This is a waste of time. Get on with the mission.
Go to 154.

146

Sure enough, you find a small lump of C-4, a couple of detonators, and a couple meters of wire. Oh, and a 9-volt power block. You'll need that.

You shape the C-4 around the latch of the door, stick a detonator into it, and then attach the wire to the leads sticking out of the back of the detonator. You unravel the wire as far as it goes (which isn't quite minimum safe distance as recommended by professionals, but come on, there *is* a limit to how much you can carry in the pockets of your coat). You attach one of the strands of wire to the battery. Crouching down and turning your back to the door, you flash the loose strand of wire across the other terminal on the battery.

The explosive makes a loud noise, and you feel something rattle deep in your chest—some kind of psychic echo. The hall sticks of chemicals and burnt plastic.

The latch has been blown. The door is open.

Back in college, you hung out with some conspiracy extremists during one of the semester breaks. Most of the time you drank ultra-caffeinated carbonated beverages and played armchair strategist about role-playing games, but there was the occasional bout of radical training. Which was what you were there for, right?

Then, one of them got a little too friendly one night. You were disappointed that things took that turn, but not really surprised.

It would have been easy to rig an improvised device like this—you had read that dog-eared pamphlet one of them had under their mattress, after all—and he would have lost a hand, at the very least. But it was a noisy solution. You had other ways of dealing with stupid shit like this. Quieter, and they made your point much more effectively.

Anyway, sometimes a Closer needs to Open. It's good to diversify your skills.

Speaking of stories about useful skills, have you read that manuscript yet? Maybe you should before you go any further.
Go to 36.

There's no time for any of that. Stay focused. Finish the mission.
Go to 165.

147

You drag the unconscious doctor into a corner of the room. Then you arrange the cushions from the couch around them to create a kind of a fort.

It's a pretty dismal looking fort, and so you drag over the cushion-less couch and flip it over. Now the doctor is definitely covered, but as forts go, it doesn't have a lot of space to wiggle around in. You can lie still and nap, but you can't curl up with a stack of comic books and a flashlight.

Sounds delightfully nostalgic and charming, doesn't it? Well, you took a wrong turn somewhere in junior high, and all that was thrown out the window. Too late to get fussy about it now. Not when the universe needs saving. You might as well get to that.

NOTE: YOU HAVE SAVED A MEMBER OF THE ENDOLUVION CREW. YOU WILL BE RECOGNIZED FOR THIS AT THE END OF THIS EXERCISE.

Go to 106.

148

You check out the station's media archive, and learn the Endoluvion crew is into South Korean boy bands, European techno from a decade ago, classic rock, westerns, pulpy science fiction, occult symbology, necromantic rituals, rom-coms, and anime.

Clearly, they like to watch violent cartoons, but they don't like to read the original source material.

Well, you can't entirely blame them. Reading is so out of vogue these days. Plus one DVD of *Akira* takes up a lot less space than that multi-volume English-translation set than Merchant has on the shelf in his cubicle, back at the office.

Man, he loved that anime. You were in rotation with him a year or so back. He couldn't stop talking about Neo-Tokyo. You almost felt bad when those giant shrews took him down.

God, those were terrifying.

Anyway, the media collection of MacReady Station is definitely eclectic. You suspect there's a chart somewhere that details who gets to pick what on a given night of a month. Well, you hope there is. Otherwise, you can't imagine a week going by without someone picking something that would piss someone else off.

Though, perhaps, maybe that's what happened here . . . ? Someone went for French new wave cinema too often, and the rom-com fans finally snapped. It sounds ridiculous, but these folks are in isolation for three or four months. Who knows what that does to the human mind.

Well, actually . . . Anyway, you should probably keep moving.

What's this stack of paper shoved behind the E. E. "Doc" Smith Lensman books? It looks like some kind of manuscript.
Go to 36.

Hit the "Bar." Okay. It was funny the first time, but now it's just an annoying reminder that you're more than five hundred kilometers away from even a *shitty* dive bar.
Go to 71.

Check out the kitchen.
Go to 134.

149

You head back toward the infirmary and the doctor's office. Maybe you missed a locker in there or something. There's a box near the door, which you had overlooked earlier. It's empty, which is annoying. You check the filing cabinet again, and this time you check the bottom drawer. Aha! Jackpot.

Your coat has been thrown into a plastic tub. You pull it out and shrug into it. It's a welcome feeling around your shoulders. You do a quick inventory of some of the pockets.

(Fingerless gloves, pack of dried apple chips, a scratch ticket from a Massachusetts lottery game, moist towelette . . .)

Here it is. One white phosphorus grenade.

You return to the East Corridor, where you find the shambling mushroom shrub. It looks like it was sentient enough to work a door knob. Not very fast, though.

You pull the tab on the grenade and roll it down the hall. The grenade lights up the East Corridor with a kajillion lumens, and on a psychic level, you hear something scream. It screams for awhile, and you almost feel like you've wounded the global fungal network or something, but eventually, it stops. After a long while, the sunburst fades and the light level returns to the normal spooky ambience of the deserted station.

You peek around the corner. The East Corridor is spotless. No sign of the fungal shambler.

Have you gone to every location you wanted?
Go to 123.

Pat yourself on the back, and then get on with the mission.
Go to 133.

150

The doctor doesn't want to answer this question. They shy away from you. They flinch. They look at the floor.

You ask it again, raising your discipline stick slightly to drive home the point that you're merely being polite in your phrasing. The doctor is going to tell you.

The doctor looks at their hands, their face screwed up as if they can see blood stains that will never come out.

"It started—they found something in the ice. Almost as if they knew it was here. I'm not—I'm a contractor. I'm not an Endoluvion employee. I don't know how or why or what brought them here. I've only been on station for five months, and during that time, my job was very easy." They stop, and you can tell they have gotten lost for a moment in the fond recollection of what was—what will never be again. They wet their lips, and their voice is hoarse when they continue.

"I didn't have anything to do for several months," they say. "I mean, there was the occasional issue with frostbite that I had to treat, but mostly, the people here were strong and healthy and they took care of themselves.

"But then—then, something came up. I don't know what it was. I wasn't part of those meetings. All I ever heard was talk of something called the Acheroni—the Asheron Codex, or something like that—and something about moon charts. No, it wasn't moon charts. It was some kind of chart."

"A correspondence table," you prompt.

"Yes," the doctor says, nodding their head. "A correspondence table." They look up at you. "What is that?"

"It's a table that helps you map sigils or letters or—as you said—moon phases to markings. It's a key, basically. A key that unlocks . . . certain kinds of documents."

"The Calls," the doctor whispers. "That's what it was. A series of Calls."

"Perhaps," you say, keeping your voice nonchalant. On the inside, though, the lizard part of you is running round and round and round. Clueless and uninitiated doing Calls? This was a Closer's worst nightmare.

"What happened next?" you ask, trying to move on.

"I think—I think they did . . . they made a room somewhere, deep in the sub-station. And in that room, they did these—they made these Calls."

The doctor flinches at nothing, and for a moment, they are seeing things that aren't there. Gradually, they come back, and you gently prod them to continue. "And what happened when they were done?" you ask. "Did anyone answer?"

"Blair was the first," the doctor says quietly. "He was the first one to die."

"Okay," you say. "And when was this?"

The doctor squints at your shoes. "August," they say. "The last week of August."

"And how did he . . . ?"

"I don't really know," the doctor says with a brief laugh that is pure madness. "They didn't even tell me about it for three or four days. They put him outside."

"Why?" you ask, and then you wish you could retract the question. You know why.

"Who died next?" you ask.
Go to 157.

"What about my team?" you ask.
Go to 161.

151

You find the emergency exit near the Umbilical. You're not wearing proper gear for the weather, but you tell yourself this won't take long. You shove against the crash bar, and alarms go off in the station. The wind is happy to see you, and it gets inside your clothing in an instant. Getting all close and frigid with you. Your lungs hurt instantly. You feel like the fluid in your eyes is freezing.

You're not sure if you can make it to the satellite relay.

You have no choice. This is the only way.
Go to 158.

Yeah, this was a bad idea.
Go to 164.

152

The Dumfirammir are a race of subterranean dwellers, the Old Man says.

You turn around. You're a little surprised to see him manifesting like this, but to be fair, you're a bit fractured. Your brain is trying to heal itself, and that means calling on your Personal Therapeutic Construct to talk you back to sanity.

They're blind, he continues. *They devour anything they can fit in their mouths, including the stone through which they are tunneling. They find most fleshy things to be very . . . squishy. Their digestive tracts are so acidic that they must maintain a very high ratio of ultra-dense materials or the acids will eat through the linings. They will literally liquify themselves if they don't have enough rock in their bellies.*

The Old Man looks at the corpse staked to the table. *This isn't the Dumfirammir,* he says. *There's too many fleshy bits left.*

"Yeah, it must be the other ones," you mumble, trying to remember the name of the other race of eldritch monsters you must be dealing with.

The Old Man looks at you with his piercing gaze. *You don't remember, do you?*

"It'll come to me," you say.

He rolls his eyes. *If you are our last hope, we're doomed.*

You show him the bandage on your arm. "I've been out of commission for awhile," you snap.

And guess what happened while you were napping? He gives the corpse a side-eye.

"He died before I got injured," you point out.

Maybe. The Old Man sucks on a tooth. *Unless they fucked with your head. In which case, maybe* you *killed him.*

"I didn't kill *any*—I didn't kill this guy."

He stares at your for a minute. *Sure,* he says finally, in a tone of voice that suggests he doesn't believe a word you said.

You can't blame him. You don't either.

You're going to have to figure this out, kid, the Old Man says, his tone softening. *We're all counting on you.*

"I'll know," you say. "I'll—I'll try."

Go to 106.

153

Got your gear? Let's get back to the mission.

If you were dealing with the airlock in Hydroponics, **go to 177.**

If you were dealing with the espresso machine in Admin, **go to 180.**

If you were trying to figure out how to open the chemical locker in the Organic Chemistry lab, **go to 184.**

154

You duck through the long plastic strips that lead to the narrow corridor connecting the main station to the research labs and crew quarters. Once, the buildings were separate spaces, but Endoluvion decided the outpost should be a contiguous space. You can't blame them. Who wanted to go outside—even for a hundred steps—in this weather?

The walls of the Umbilical are heavily padded with industrial insulation, which is held in place with tape, nails, and the haphazard piece of 2 x 4. The lights are a long strand of naked bulbs hanging from planter hooks screwed into the weather-warped wood. It has a very early twentieth century explorer vibe.

There is a sealed pressure door at the end of the corridor. There's a keycard reader next to the door. The light on it is red.

You check the door, just to be sure, and it is definitely sealed. There's no keypad on the reader. You need someone's badge to get through this door. Or an Opener, except you're pretty sure they're both dead.

You hear a noise behind you. You turn and look. How about that? The shambling mound you left in the computer room was smart enough to work the door latch.

It's bigger now too. Earlier, you might have been able to leap over it, but now, it's as wide as the hall. It has spawned a few limbs too, and they are covered with tiny tentacles and nasty-looking thorns. If one of those gets close . . .

You look around for a weapon, and the best option is one of the planks attached to the wall. You grab the nearest one, digging your fingers into the insulation. It's loose, and you think you might be able to pull it free. If you have enough time . . .

AND THEN WHAT? YOU CAN'T BEAT A FUNGUS TO DEATH. THEY DON'T HAVE A CENTRALIZED NERVOUS SYSTEM. IT'S JUST GOING TO SLURP ALL OVER YOU, AND THEN DIGEST YOU . . . SLOWLY. IT WILL HURT FOR A LONG TIME.

MAPS SCORE: 51

155

Eventually the doctor stirs and comes back from whatever special place they had run off to. They look at you. "You have questions," they say. There is a haunted look in their eyes, as if they hope you don't ask the one question they are dreading the most.

"They did some kind of ritual, didn't they?" you ask.
Go to 150.

"What happened to my team?" you ask.
Go to 161.

156

You investigate the rest of the library. As you surmised, it's filled with stodgy academic papers and symposium reports. Performative bullshit to validate one's retention at various high-profile universities and government-funded think tanks.

The only thing of interest is thin stack of stapled paper that turns out to be a printed manuscript of some kind. It looks like someone on staff is secretly working on a spy novel.

You return to the person who clobbered themselves and check on them again. The drooling has stopped, but their pupils are still dilated.

You've wasted enough time. Get on with the mission.
Go to 106.

Wait a more minutes. You can page through the manuscript while you're waiting.
Go to 159.

157

The doctor tries to wander away from you, but the library isn't big enough to play hide-n-seek, and after a few futile attempts to find an angle or a corner in which to disappear, the doctor goes over to the main bookcase and leans against it.

"It was Copper," she says. "He died after Blair and Garry. Right at dinner, in fact. I was there when he started coughing. We got him onto a bed and hooked up before he—before it got worse. Which meant I had some data. For a little while."

"Why only a little while."

"He died in less than a half hour after we got him stabilized. I had gotten an IV into him. It should have calmed him down." The doctor shrugged. "Something happened inside of him. I don't understand it. I really don't."

"What happened?"

"Massive internal bleeding. Spontaneous hemorrhaging in multiple locations. There weren't any external indicators. No broken bones. No contusions. No bruising. He just started . . . he bled out, on the inside."

You nod grimly, deciding not to tell her that such a fate was not as strange as she made it out to be. It wasn't dissimilar to the way a spider kills its prey after it has cocooned it. The exterior gets hard and crunchy, and the insides get all soft and gooey. It easier to eat that, if you are into soft food like space jellies are. "It's a terrible way to die," you say.

They only do that when they are gathering sustenance for— the Old Man starts in your head.

You nod again, and the doctor stares at you, wide-eyed. She can't hear your internal dialogue, and all this head-nodding must seem like you've lost your mind.

(maybe you have . . .)

They're under some influence, you think. *These jellies have a master.*

"What—what should we do?" the doctor asks.

"Tell me about my team," you say.
Go to 161.

"You should find someplace to hide," you say.
Go to 163.

158

You can't see anything. It's dark. The wind is howling. The temperature is—well, don't think about the temperature. Thinking about it isn't going to warm you up.

You try to recall the map from your briefing before you left the Night Office. There were the two main buildings. The airstrip was a kilometer to the east. There were several windmills to the west, along with a small shack for the turbine controls and power monitoring station. Between the research half of the station and the control shack was the satellite relay. If you can get to it, you might be able to access a local panel and get a message out to Heavy Battery.

They'll know what to do.

You follow the rope guides. You lock your jaw to keep your teeth from chattering so hard they will likely shatter. You can't feel your feet, and your left arm feels like a piece of driftwood stapled to your shoulder.

You're not going to last much longer.

This was a bad idea. Turn back.
Go to 164.

Press on. The satellite relay is close.
Go to 201.

159

Do you think the rest of them are sitting around? The Old Man asks you after a few minutes.

"What do you mean?"

I mean, while you're sitting here, waiting this idiot sink deeper into their concussion, the rest of them—especially the ones who have been taken over by space jellies and God knows what else—are probably busy setting up whatever ritual they hope to accomplish.

"I need to know what happened," you tell him.

Why? He demands. *You know the job. Since when have you needed to know the reasons for what needs doing?*

You check the individual's pupils again. They're still dilated.

The Old Man's not wrong, you know. You should get back to the mission.

Go to 106.

The Old Man's also an asshole when it comes to giving a shit about other people, so you're going to wait.

Go to 119.

160

Wow. You've got a lot of miscellaneous stuff in your wallet. You dig past the coffee shop coupons, the free waffle cone tickets, and the handful of one-day zoo passes, before finding the worn ATM card. The name of the bank is nearly indecipherable, and the holographic logo does not catch the light like it should. The magnetic stripe is solid, though, and as you rub it across the gauze bandage around your arm, you feel the charge build. When your mind is at rest and focused, you slide the ATM card through the reader.

One swipe. Like you know what you are doing.

You find yourself holding your breath as you wait.

The light on the reader turns green, and you hear the sound of the lock disengaging. You're in!

You grab the door and haul it open before the security system has second thoughts about granting you access. You fumble the ATM card back into your wallet and put your wallet away.

The less said about that ATM card the better.

Before you go through that door, do you want to read that manuscript you've been carrying around?

Go to 36.

No, you've already read it. Bunch of nonsense, wasn't it? Get on with the mission.

Go to 165.

161

The doctor covers their face for a minute. You check the door, nervous that something might be lurking in the hall. There's nothing there, but you feel a little calmer when you turn back to the doctor.

"You were part of the second team," the doctor says eventually. "You came after . . . after that man hurt—"

"Who?" you ask, though you have a pretty good idea.

"The angry one," the doctor says. "The leader of the first group who arrived."

"Brinkmann."

The doctor nods. "Yes, that was—is—his name."

You frown. "You don't sound so sure," you say.

"Sure of what?"

"Is he alive or dead?" you ask.

The doctor starts to shake their head, but stops. "I don't know," they say. "That's—I don't know."

Interrogating survivors is such a crap shoot. They struggle to deal with what they've seen—some of which is decidedly horrific and alien to them—and they lose track of the shared reality of the human experience. How can you look at the world the same way again when you've seen spongy things move in non-Euclidean ways? How can you think about the color of a man's soul when you've seen him get turned inside out? How can you eat mushrooms ever again after you've witnessed a fungal mass devour a body in less than sixty seconds?

"What about Argot?" you ask.

"Which—which one was that?"

"The ex-military one," you say. "Not much taller than you, but with sixteen times more piss and vinegar."

"That one," the doctor says, and then they shiver.

"Is he still alive?"

"I—I think so."

"Where is he?"

"I don't—I don't know. I don't know where any of them are." The doctor looks they're about to start crying. "They've all gone down there. To get closer to it."

"To what?" you ask, your skin scrawling.

"The thing that sings to them," the doctor says.

Now you feel like you're getting somewhere. "And what thing is that?" you ask, even though you

(can you hear it?)

know what the doctor is talking about.

"It's like a . . . a spike driven into the ice," the doctor says. "A nail in the heart of the world."

"And I'm supposed to pull it out," you say.

The doctor shakes their hand. "You can't touch it," they say. "If you do . . ."

"I'm not going to touch it," you say. "I know better than that. I'm going to use the world's largest claw hammer and—" You see their expression and offer a smile. "I'm sorry, I thought we were talking metaphorically . . ."

As you watch, their eyes deaden. They start to shiver, and the shivers turn into the shakes, and before you help the doctor, they collapse on the floor.

Cautiously, you check for signs of life and find a weak pulse fluttering in the doctor's neck. Not dead. That's good.

There isn't anything you can do for the doctor. Get on with the mission.

Go to 106.

Build a pillow fort around them with the cushions from the couch.

Go to 147.

162

Right. So, the airlock in Hydroponics. It's a mess. Something shoved a chair in it, and then tried to tear it to shreds. Judging by the smears and tracks of blood around the monitoring station, this thing is at least as big as a small pony. And it's in the other room, hiding in the fog.

But, sure, you got this.

You squeeze through one of the long tears in the plastic of the airlock and step over the wrecked office chair. So far, so good.

You wriggle through a tighter spot on the other side, and here you are, standing in the Hydroponics grow lab. There's blood on the floor. Someone got dragged around, and the first row of grow tables has been knocked aside. The air is fetid and heavy, and you hear labored breathing and—

Oh, wait. That's your breathing.

Your heart rate is up too. You feel like you're breathing swamp water. Sweat is already dribbling down your back. The wound on your forearm is itching. You'd really rather be—

IT'S ABOUT THIS TIME THAT THE PREDATOR LURKING IN HERE COMES OUT OF NOWHERE AND BITES YOUR FACE OFF. AND THEN IT TAKES ITS TIME ON THE REST OF YOU.

MAPS SCORE: 18

163

"Where?" the doctor asks. "The only room that is truly secure is Ops, and—"

"What?" you ask.

"It's sealed," the doctor says.

There's something about the way they say the word that makes you think of Peele, the Closer on the other team. You file this information away for later.

"Here," you say, gesturing at one of the corners of the room. "Pull that couch over, and one of the bookcases. Build yourself a fort. And be quiet."

The doctor nods slowly. They aren't convinced, or they realize any effort is probably futile.

While you might agree with their assessment, you find yourself helping build the fort. "Good luck," you say once the doctor has been successfully ensconced behind all the pillows. The doctor doesn't reply.

Hey, at least you tried.

NOTE: YOU HAVE SAVED A MEMBER OF THE ENDOLUVION CREW. YOU WILL BE RECOGNIZED FOR THIS AT THE END OF THIS EXERCISE.

Go to 106.

164

You turn around, intending to get back inside the station before you freeze to death. However, the emergency door has closed behind you. You grab the handle and pull. The door doesn't open, and you realize your flesh is now frozen to the handle.

You could pull harder, but all that is going to do is strip your flesh right off.

You could call for help, but who is going to hear you? The wind is very loud. It's excited that you came out to play.

YOU'RE GOING TO FREEZE TO DEATH WITH THAT SURPRISED LOOK ON YOUR FACE. AT LEAST YOU'LL BE A WARNING TO OTHER PEOPLE WHEN THEY FIND YOU.

MAPS SCORE: 23

165

You are now in the research section of MacReady Station. The hallway runs straight and then makes a right-hand turn.

There is a chart screwed into the wall nearby. It's a map of this area. The research section is a large rectangle, and the *YOU ARE HERE* marker is in the upper left hand corner. The hall runs along the top edge of the rectangle. Off it are sections marked STORAGE, HYDROPONICS, ORG CHEM, and ADMIN. It looks like you have to pass through ADMIN to get to ATMO-SPHERICS, ENGINEERING, and GEOLOGY. Beyond are two more areas marked MECHANICAL and CREW.

You have a dim recollection of something happened in Hydroponics. Maybe you should go there.
Go to 166.

You might as well check out the Storage area. Maybe there's a secret stash of nitroglycerin or something.
Go to 167.

You never made it past first-year chemistry in college, and so organic chemistry is going to be a bunch of scientific equipment that won't mean at thing. You should still check it out.
Go to 193.

All paperwork and no play make for dull boys and girls. But maybe there's an espresso machine or something in the admin area. A little pick me up won't hurt.
Go to 195.

166

You enter the room marked 'Hydroponics,' and find yourself in a small antechamber with three computer stations. An enormous white board covers most of one wall. Another wall has been sectioned into four windows that look into the room where the Endoluvion team does their experiments and grows their own food. Three of the four windows have been shattered, and there is glass all over one of the computer stations and the floor. There are dark stains on the floor as well.

Moving cautiously, you peer through one of the broken windows into the grow room. It's foggy, which means it is moist, which means fetid things may be growing in there.

The proper way to get into the grow room is an airlock—over near the white board. It has been jammed open, and you can smell the earthy scent of the grow room. There's a strong whiff of decay and mold.

There's blood on the white board. It covers up some of the scrawl, but you can make out enough to figure out that it is a map of what is growing where in the lab. Whoever was keeping up the chart made lots of notes in multiple colors.

There are no bodies in the room, which is disquieting, given the amount of blood. Though, you've got a pretty good idea where the bodies have been taken.

Only one of the three computer workstations is on, and when you nudge the mouse, the computer starts churning.

You keep an eye on the grow room beyond the broken window. You half-expect something to come leaping through the window at you.

The computer beeps, startling you, and you glance down at the screen. It's blue, and there's a message saying that something has faulted in some bit of code, which has caused something else to dump, and because of this, the computer is basically fucked. It's apologetic about this state of affairs, but the only option it gives you is an 'OK' button.

You click 'OK' and the computer shuts off.

That was anti-climactic, you think.

In the other room, something shifts in the fog.

You recall a conversation you had with Argot.

"The rot is in the roots," Argot says.

"We should seal the room," you say.

He's looking at the irrigation system of the hydroponics lab. "We've got to kill it first," he says. "There's enough organic material in here for it to live a long time if we just seal the room."

Implicit in his comment is some contempt. He doesn't think you can Close a room well enough to keep a space jelly from escaping.

You ignore his passive-aggressive bullshit. You've learned how to ignore many of the remarks made by assholes in the organization over the years.

"How did it get here?" you ask.

Argot shakes his head. "Ask Sagalico. Not my department."

"I haven't seen him in awhile," you say.

This gets Argot's attention. "I thought you were—"

"I don't babysit," you say, interrupting Argot before he can pin this on you.

And then you were interrupted. Something was happening in the front half of the station. Something that required your attention. And after that, well, you never had another chance to talk.

Enough of this reminiscing. Get on with the mission.
Go to 165.

Approach the airlock.
Go to 168.

167

You check out the large storage room in the research section of MacReady Station. It's filled with, well, stuff in boxes and crates and heavy packaging. If there's a body hidden in this room, it'll take a week to find it.

The only thing that catches your eye is a large freezer. It's big enough to store enough food to feel a family of six for an entire winter, or, you know, a body or three.

Okay, so it wouldn't take a week to find the body.

The question is: do you open the freezer?

Hell no. That's what an Opener is for.
Go to 169.

How many times has opening a freezer turned out well for you?
Go to 171.

168

You approach the airlock of the Hydroponics grow room. The airlock is simple: a rotating metal frame, inside a bubble of tri-layer plastic sheeting. The frame is locked open because someone has shoved an office chair between the rotating drum and the outer frame of the airlock. The plastic frame of the chair has been torn up a bit, as if it has been clawed by something.

Something big.

Got your gear?
Go to 177.

If you don't have your gear, you might want to reconsider this approach.
Go to 185.

169

Speaking of which, where the hell is your Opener? You haven't seen much evidence of your team, and you're starting to wonder —well, okay. You've been wondering for awhile.

I think you know, the Old Man says.

You look around for him, but he's not manifesting this time. He's just a voice in your head.

"What do I know?" you ask him.

You know what's in
(the heart of it all)
the white room, he says.

"You stuttered," you say.

No, I didn't.

"You did." There was another voice. Something whispering beneath his voice. Like an echo. But you shouldn't be hearing echoes when you're talking to your Personal Therapeutic Construct. Echoes require hard surfaces for sound to bounce, and since this is all in your head . . .

"I'm compromised," you say out loud.

The Old Man doesn't argue with you.

"Fantastic," you sigh.

Nothing to do about it now. You've got a mission to finish. Hopefully you can keep your sanity long enough to do the work.
Go to 165.

You're running out of time. *The heart of it.* That's what the voice said. You need to find the heart.
Go to 195.

170

You go to the next lab bench and examine it as well. It's just like the first one, except there's a burner and a rack of test tubes instead of a microscope. There's no paperback hidden in the bottom drawer either. Fewer candy bars too, and they're a different brand. Judging by the handwriting in the notebooks, this person was a lot more precise in their record keeping.

Written on the back page of the latest journal is a three-digit combination. 214. Might be useful.

Check out the next lab station.
Go to 190.

In the back of the room is a chemical storage locker. It has a keypad combination on it. You suspect you might know what the combination is.
Go to 197.

171

How many times have you had freezer issues over the years?

There was that time in Akron, so that's one. And there was that time in Barbados—but technicaly, there wasn't a body in the freezer then, so maybe that one doesn't count. And then there's that stupid house-clearing mission that went bad. So, that's what? Two? Maybe three?

Call it two and a half, and no, none of them turned out well.

Do you really think this time is going to be any different? the Old Man asks. He's marveling at your persistent air of hopeful-lness.

Read the mood in the room and leave the freezer alone.
Go to 172.

You appreciate his enthusiasm as you approach the freezer.
Go to 183.

172

You make another pass through the storage room, looking more closely at the crates and boxes and packaged goods. It's mostly medical and scientific supplies, materials used in gardening (but in quantities much larger than you'd need for a small plot in a homeowner's yard), dry goods, and office supplies. Oh, and cases and cases of toilet paper.

Winter lasts for a long time down here.

You return to the freezer and stare at it. There's only one, and it's the only object that is independently powered. It's not out of place, but at the same time, it's an oddity.

Something itches at the back of your brain, and when you go to scratch it, you realize you're scratching the edges of the bandage on your forearm.

You stop all of a sudden, frozen by a flood of memories, like a dam bursting.

Alpha Team got to the station forty-eight hours ahead of you; they should have finished clearing the station by the time your team arrived. But that hadn't been the case. They were still arguing with the Endoluvion staff about how to proceed. The station commander—what was his name? Elkhorn, that's it— was insisting that the Night Office had no jurisdiction onsite. While this was technically true, Brinkmann and the others had been cleared by Asset Resource Management to deal with the recorded message that was coming from the station.

The problem was the message stopped as soon as Alpha arrived. The team had swept the station and found nothing untoward.

(No, that wasn't right. Where were all the bodies?)

Your team's arrival only increased the tension between Endoluvion and the Night Office.

Why the fuck are you still arguing about this? Argot had demanded of Brinkmann. *We're onsite. We have a job to do. We don't give a shit about local politics.*

There's nothing here, Brinkmann had argued.

Sagalico had laughed. *You're a blind fool,* he had said to Brinkmann. Peele had freaked out.

This was why the Night Office doesn't send two teams. Each team would follow their Guide, and when Guides saw different things in the Way, well . . . suddenly, you're on different sides.

Soon thereafter, Gull accused those two Endoluvion staffers of being skin walkers. Yes, that was what had happened, you recall. In the common room, after lunch the second day. Heated words had been exchanged, and when Gull tried to do a Closure Ward on one of the pair, he had erupted.

Not in that red-faced blowing-steam sort of way, but in that flesh-rending, bone-cracking vomiting out malformed creatures of darkness sort of way. A thing that was supposed to be a dog, but which had human arms and an extra mouth on its belly, had launched itself at Gull. Another part of what had been a bearded guy with a receding hairline merged with the other guy accused of being a cosmic monster, and they had turned into a writhing mass of thorny tentacles and blind heads with broken teeth and gnarly horns.

You lean against a nearby shelf, your knees weak and your breath short in your chest. There's a lot of memory flooding back, and you struggle to assess it all.

You and Argot had been somewhere else in the station, and it had taken someone to come rushing in—crying and wailing—for you to find out about what had happened. Wand when you arrived in the common area, you found that Gull had sealed the dog thing into a Cube of Finite Folds. The tentacle and horn beast had caught one of the other Endoluvion crew and was flailing the corpse around like a wrecking ball. Argot started shooting at it while you prepared something similar to Gull's compression box.

Your head hurts as you try to sort out the memories. They start to get jumbled. You remember Argot shooting. Someone else was shooting too, though their weapon wasn't nearly as effective. Gull was—

What had Gull be doing?

You can't remember.

Your forearm aches. You clutch it. There's something in all that mess about getting bitten, but you can't put it together.

You look at the freezer again.

You don't need to open it. You know what is inside. Gull. She's sealed something inside herself. Argot must have frozen her.

Why? you wonder, and the first half-dozen answers to that question aren't good. It's against protocol. Asset Resource Management has rules about trying to save compromised field operatives, and even more rules about bringing them back. You don't bring back bodies that might have a surprise inside.

You and Argot are going to have a chat, the next time you see him.

Go to 165.

173

"I have some questions," you say to the Old Man.

He waves a hand, as if ushering you into his office, and your mental landscape changes to his office on the 13th floor. He goes to the sideboard and pours himself a glass of Scotch. He offers you one, but you demur. Imaginary Scotch makes your acid reflux kick in.

"What happened to Starkweather?"

He looked somewhere he shouldn't have, the Old Man says. He sits in the immense leather chair behind the desk and puts his feet up on the table. His wooden foot clunks against the mahogany table top.

"Was he compromised?"

Probably.

"But the eggheads in LOBE wanted to know what he knew, didn't they?"

They wanted to slice his brain into tiny samples and bath them in microwaves. The Old Man sips from his glass. *LOBE had a lot of weird ideas back then.*

"They have a lot of weird ideas now," you point out.

He salutes you with his glass. *Starkweather made contact with an intelligence that wasn't the Old Ones,* he says. *We thought there might be something beneficial in a mutual sharing of ideas.* He shrugs. *If we could get the information out of his head.*

"But his language centers were all messed up."

That they were.

"So what happened?"

LOBE came up with a different route. Through the Way. Sort of like astral projection, but more . . . sideways.

You recall a briefing you may or may not have. "The indexes," you say.

The indexes, the Old Man repeats.

"Which are what? Astral time travel?"

More like time potentiality.

"That sounds like something LOBE would say." You go to shake Morgan's manuscript at him, but in this mental projection you've created, the manuscript has become an actual book. It has a black cover that seems to suck in light. "What's this, then?" you ask.

Looks like one of those pulpy reads you get at the airport, he says. *What is it called?*

"*The Albatross Legacy.*" You show him the cover.

He squints at it. *Ah, so we've come to that, have we?*

Before you can ask him what he means, there's a knock at the door of his office. You glance at the Old Man. This is your mental construct. No one should be "knocking."

Ignore the knocking. The Old Man can only tell you what you already know. If there's a useful clue buried in your brain, it's got to be in this manuscript somewhere.

Go to 186.

"Should I answer that?" you ask.

The Old Man shrugs and sips from his glass.

You open the door. There's no one there. When you look over your shoulder, the Old Man is gone. The wall behind his desk is dissolving into pure emptiness.

You need to find a way out. Look for

(the rabbits)

a door or something. Anything to anchor you in an index that you remember.

Go to 268.

174

You tip the bottle up and let a small amount of the bourbon trickle into your mouth. It's sharp and spicy, and you choke and cough. You haven't had anything to eat or drink in the last sixteen or so hours, and this is how you reintroduce liquids to your body? No wonder it is freaking out.

You must have gotten some of it in your lungs because you can't stop coughing. You try to put the bottle on the desk, but you miss and it falls to the floor where it shatters loudly. Now the whole room smells of bourbon.

Your back brain is starting to freak out. It would really like to breathe.

You try to get up from the office chair, but your foot hits a slippery spot on the floor (all that bourbon), and your leg skids out from beneath you. You start to panic, but then your forehead hits the edge of the desk and . . . everything goes dark.

YOU'VE JUST KNOCKED YOURSELF OUT. WELL DONE.

WITH ALL THE NOISE YOU'VE BEEN MAKING, SOMEONE—OR SOMETHING—WILL UNDOUBTEDLY INVESTIGATE. AFTER THEY GET DONE LAUGHING AT YOU, THEY WILL PROBABLY EAT YOU.

MAPS SCORE: 12

175

You keep your discipline stick in front of you, as you make your way across the grow lab. The fog parts reluctantly. You see more disturbed tables. None of the plants look healthy—they're all pale and doubled over.

Something snarls at you from the other side of the room. You keep your discipline stick ready. The flame falters slightly, and there's a nasty taste on your lips. The fog is rancid, and its ill touch is having a deleterious effect.

You try not to think about swallowing, which makes it almost impossible not to swallow. Stupid human brain.

The monster snuffles at you, and you jab your discipline stick in that direction. It makes a noise like goats being compressed. Encouraged by this noise, you search your coat for something flammable and you come up with a squeeze bottle of overproof alcohol.

Purely medicinal use, of course.

You thumb the tip up and aim to your left. When the creature makes the goat squeezing noise again, you squeeze the bottle. A stream of highly flammable alcohol shoots out, and when you bring your discipline stick in line, the stream becomes a flare of fire.

For an instant, you catch sight of something covered with eyes and mushrooms, and then it is gone, fading into the mist. You hear grow tables scraping on the floor.

You adapt your aim and squeeze again. This time, your line of flame scorches across a table filled with dusty plants. They take the flame greedily, and within seconds, they are burning fiercely. The fog retreats from the flame, and as it rolls back, you get a better look at the monster that's been lurking in the grow lab.

It looks like something a kid would draw after a terrible nightmare. Too many teeth. Too many eyes. And all the mushroom stalks scattered on its bumpy flesh sway and undulate like they're intelligent.

It's enough to make you never want to order pizza from that place on 83rd again.

All those eyes are looking at you, and as the dusty plants flame and die, you realize just how large this monster is. It snorts and paws the floor. It's come to the same realization.

You trigger one last burst of fire, and then turn and run for the airlock.

Behind you, the monster snorts and howls, and then you hear grow tables cracking and groaning as the beast charges.

You'll never make it through the airlock in time. Head for the broken windows.
Go to 192.

No, you can make it. Get to the airlock.
Go to 203.

176

Paging through the manuscript, you find another section where Morgan has copied out one of the Calls that Starkweather brought back from the ice.

> O you Eyes without Limit, you Spirits of Eternal Understanding, attend to my supplication and my sacrifice. I beseech the boon of your 23 Tongues so that I may confuse the minds of my enemies. I offer their fear and confusion as a gift. These hearts are nourishment for your hungry children. Feast, O Yhyzella! Devour, O Chwentzach! Open your mouths and take of this offering. Show yourselves and receive our adoration! We are your devoted servants. We languish without your love. We dream of being engulfed by your passion.

You know? Someone should have a talk with the folks in LOBE about what constitutes a "mutually beneficial" relationship. This sounds a lot like what those creeps in the Union House expected from their "girlfriends." They were in for a surprise when they tried this bullshit with you, weren't they?

"We're not thinking about that now," you say quietly.

Turn the page.
Go to 186.

Skip ahead.
Go to 210.

177

As you approach the airlock in Hydroponics, you dig through the pockets of your coat, looking for some cheap firecrackers and a laser penlight. You find them both. Oh, you'll need a lighter too. That's easily solved with—yep, Calbedetti's Infernal Invocation, aka "the Best Stick is a Stick on Fire" protocol. You perform the invocation and the tip of your discipline stick bursts into flame.

Holding all of these objects, you squeeze through the rips in the airlock.

On the far side, the air is heavier and sweatier than in the climate-controlled monitoring room. There's a smear of blood on the floor that leads away from the airlock. It disappears in the haze of the room, and you can only see the edges of a few rows of the grow tables. They've been knocked out of alignment.

You hear something move in the distance, something that sounds like a tree sloth dragging a bag of angry rattlesnakes. The flame on your discipline stick flickers, mirroring your own uncertainty.

Use your discipline stick.
Go to 175.

Use the firecrackers.
Go to 178.

Use the laser pointer.
Go to 182.

178

You wave your discipline stick under the fuse of the firecrackers and then throw them into the fog. You move to your right, keeping the wall at your back. A few seconds later, the firecrackers go off, a long string of *pop-pop-pop!* noises. Something moves in the fog, and the tables scrape noisily across the floor.

A final firecracker pops, and then something howls. It's a loud roar that fills up the room and makes you think about filling your pants in an unseemly manner.

After the echo dies, you hear that sound again. Like a sloth dragging a sack of pissed off snakes.

Use the laser pointer.
Go to 206.

Decide that discretion is better than valor.
Go to 209.

179

Paranoia is a steady companion during a mission, isn't it? You're jumping at shadows. Thinking that every stain on the floor or wall or ceiling hides some terrible secret. And who knows where all the spider watchers are.

(They're everywhere, of course.)

Overthinking things is definitely part of the job, and if you overthink the overthinking, well, then everything gets six times harder, doesn't it? So, knock that shit off and get to work.

Come on. Space jellies are not going to put tape over the motion sensors. Sticky tape is anathema to a space jelly. It's like salt with slugs.

The mental image of a space jelly wrestling with a tape dispenser is pretty hilarious, and you're chuckling as you walk into the chemistry lab like you don't have a care in the world.

Sure enough, the lights come on automatically when you enter.

That wasn't so bad. Check out the nearest lab bench.
Go to 212.

That could have been a lot worse. But just to be sure, you should check out the whole room before you start nosing around this lab equipment.
Go to 218.

180

Let's take a closer look at this espresso machine. There's a button on the left marked 'POWER'. You start with that, and you're rewarded with some gurgling noises from the belly of this steel beast. A small jet of steam blurts out of the wand, startling you. You laugh at how jumpy you are.

There are no beans in the hopper. While the machine is warming up, you go to the refrigerator and retrieve the jar of coffee beans. The Petroi Vacu-See system is simple and elegant in how it seals. You just have to grab the rubber bit here and twist it like . . . there you go.

You sniff the beans. They smell really good. You pour a small amount in the hopper. Resealing the jar (the top goes like *that*, and you push the other rubber bit like *so*), you put the beans back in the refrigerator. You get the milk and . . .

This is all very exciting, but shouldn't you be paying attention to the rest of the room, in case someone—or something—is trying to sneak up on you?

Actually, maybe you should look over your shoulder.
Go to 211.

You're not worried. You'd totally hear the door opening.
Go to 215.

181

The old "come on in and try to find the light switch" is one of the dumbest tricks in the book. Space jellies aren't all that bright, which isn't all that surprisingly given that they've been the ugly foot soldier of the great cosmic intelligences for something like sixty thousand millennia. You don't stay in the same job for that long unless you've either got zero desire for personal growth or because you have absolutely no imagination.

Either way, this is about as tricky as space jellies get. However, the sad thing is how often this trick works.

So, are you going to launch yourself into the admin center and find the light switch or not?

This really seems like one of those no-win situations.
Go to 179.

There has got to be another way.
Go to 202.

182

You click the laser pointer on and wave it around, making a red beam of light dance like it's trying out for some prime-time reality show. Something grumbles in the fog, and you slow down the dance party so it can follow the beam. You move the light through the fog, like you are slicing off a layer of meringue on a pie, and you see the fog roll in tandem, as something tracks towards the light.

You run the light to the far end of the room, and hold the dot on the wall. As you are standing there, range-finding the wall, you wonder what happens next. It's a laser pointer. You use it in presentations. What are you going to do? Wear this thing out by making it chase the light all over the room?

It's a lure. You've got a plan.
Go to 199.

Maybe this wasn't a good idea.
Go to 209.

183

You flip the latches on the freezer and lift the lid. A gust of cold air rushes out, and you shiver as it passes around you. Once it passes, you lean forward and peer into the freezer.

It's packed with lots of boxes that are marked with Endoluvion's logo. Near the back, room has been made for a corpse. It looks like some kind of spaniel or something, but you see strange tears along the muzzle that suggest that something else came bursting out of the beast. *Why are they keeping it?* you wonder.

But you don't wonder too long. *Scientific research*, the Old Man says in your head. The standard reason everything goes shitways.

Well, it's none of your business. You've got a mission to finish. **Go to 165.**

There are some rules in place about finding dead things in freezers. As well as rules about what you're supposed to do when you find dead things in freezers.

Check your coat. Didn't you mix up something fun in the Organic Chemistry lab?
Go to 187.

184

The locker in the Organic Chemistry lab is a fairly standard electronic lock. If you had an Opener handy, it'd be a snap to get into this locker, but unfortunately, your Opener is still AWOL.

(Where is Argot?)

You're going to have to resort to a different skill set. You find a bottle of wood glue and a roll of clear tape in your pockets. You smear a layer of glue on the sticky side of the tape and carefully roll it across each of the numbers on the keypad. You find a jar of unicorn glitter in the bottom of another pocket and dust the keypad with the contents of the jar.

It's not a perfect solution, but there's more glitter on some of the numbers than on others. You assume the combination is a three or four digit code, and luckily, only four numbers have glitter on them. Trying all the combinations won't take too long, right?

You don't have that kind of time. Time to move on.
Go to 195.

Four digits is only twenty-four combinations. This should be a snap. Well, unless you can repeat numbers, but let's not go there quite yet.
Go to 200.

185

ADMINISTRATIVE NOTE: THIS MISSION CANNOT BE COMPLETED WITHOUT YOUR GEAR. HOW DID YOU GET THIS FAR WITHOUT IT?

Okay, fine. Go find your gear.
Go to 80.

This is hardcore mode. You can totally finish this mission without your gear.
Go to 194.

186

"*You appear to have some issue with trust and intimacy, Mr. Barstow.*" *Dr. Nebbins made some notations in the leather-bound journal in her lap.*

"*Please, Adrian,*" *Barstow said.*

Dr. Nebbins looked at him over the rim of her silver glasses. Her eyes were very green. "*I prefer to keep things professional, Mr. Barstow,*" *she said. She uncrossed and recrossed her legs, and as Barstow was reclining on the couch opposite her, he couldn't help but notice the lace tops of her stockings and the delicate flesh of her thigh.*

"*Of course,*" *he said, directing his attention to the tall picture on the wall behind her. It showed a militant angel descending from heaven with a shiny spear. Below the angel, demonic figures writhed and snarled. The angel's bare foot—as white as polished marble—hovered above the largest demon's outstretched hand.*

"*We were talking about Vienna,*" *Dr. Nebbins prodded.* "*About—*" *She referred to her journal.*

"*Catalonia,*" *Barstow said, his throat tight.*

"*Yes, Catalonia von Dietrich.*" *Dr. Nebbins stared at him again. There was an intensity in her gaze that Barstow mistook for hunger.* "*You were intimate with her.*"

"*Yes,*" *Barstow admitted.*

"*And then?*" *A flush rose up Dr. Nebbins's throat. She toyed with the collar of her austere blouse. Barstow couldn't look away.*

Maybe you should save this for after the mission.
Go to 165.

No. You've read this far. You might as well finish it. You're not sure why, but whatever. Add it to the list of things you stuck with longer than you should have.
Go to 188.

187

You find those four bottles of acid you made in the Organic Chemistry lab. You can probably spare one.

You pour the contents of one of your flask over the corpse, ignoring how the frozen flesh steams and crawls. You slam the lid of the freezer shut, and using your Sharpie, you write a long litany about how fucking stupid science in servitude to capitalism can be. You finish off your creed with Ntingathion's Third Ward of Closure—the one that burns everything within the ring—and set the magic loose with a bit of saliva and blood.

That should hold.

Scratch another mark in your monster kill log (SIGIL—66/d). That'll earn you another ticket for the office lottery when you get back.

NOTE: YOU HAVE ACHIEVED A BONUS ACHIEVEMENT. THIS WILL BE NOTED WHEN YOU HAVE COMPLETED THIS EXERCISE.

Go to 165.

188

"I thought we had agreed there wouldn't be any more incidents like this, Barstow." The Chief was angry. "This sort of behavior is very unbecoming of a Triple Q agent."

"Me?" Barstow looked wounded. "She started it!"

"Damnit, man. You could have been a gentleman and politely refused her advances!" The Chief slammed his palm against his desk. He looked like his cravat was strangling him.

"I thought I was doing my duty to—"

"To Queen and Country, is that it?"

"Well, maybe she had some insight into this situation with AMBER."

"We've already been over this, Agent Barstow. Europol insists there is no such organization as AMBER. Nor do they have any record of a Catalonia Von Dietrich. She doesn't exist. It was all a DIABOLIK trap."

Barstow reflected on the slope of Cat's back, on how her skin felt under his hand. On the taste of her lips. "Well, it seemed real enough," he admitted.

"My God, man. You are dangerously close to being declared incompetent. Don't make me redact your Qs."

Barstow stiffened. "You wouldn't, Chief."

"I would," the Chief snarled. "The world might be safer if you were sectioned."

There was a knock at the door, and when the Chief barked, the heavily shielded door opened and a slender figure entered the Chief's sanctum. It was one of the Chief's private security detail, and Barstow privately admired her curve of her backside as she approached the Chief's desk. "The latest SIGINT from Tripoli," she said as she put a folder in front of the Chief.

Ignoring the proximity of her bosom, the Chief reached for his glasses. "Thank you, Miss Ogival."

The woman looked at Barstow, and he let out an involuntary yelp as he saw her face.

The Chief threw a look at Barstow that said he had completely misinterpreted Barstow's reaction. "Get out of my sight," he snapped. "And report to Donaldson before you leave the building. You are in need of some reconditioning."

Barstow, still stunned by the animal intensity of Miss Ogival's gaze, meekly fled the Chief's sanctum. He waited in the outer office, and when the door swung open again to allow the curvaceous form of Miss Ogival, he grabbed her arm and pulled her away from the door.

"What are you doing here?" he hissed.

Miss Ogival—which wasn't her real name, or maybe it was; Barstow wasn't sure anymore—glanced nervously over her shoulder, but the office door was already closed. "It isn't safe," she whispered. Using an Andalusian knuckle lock, she deftly removed his hand from her arm.

"I thought—" Barstow's throat closed involuntary, and he swallowed heavily to open it back up. "That night, in Vienna. I thought you were dead."

"I had prepared the room ahead of time. For us." Miss Ogival closed her eyes halfway, as if she was embarrassed to have been caught pre-planning their dalliance. "There were safeguards in place. There was a microweave Kevlar mesh in the curtains. It saved me from the bullets. I'm sorry. I should have told you, but I thought it might interrupt—"

Barstow shook his head, cutting her off. "It doesn't matter," he said. He glanced down at her hand. Her fingers were still holding the knuckle of his right ring finger in debilitating lock. All she had to do was squeeze and his bones would never align correctly again.

She noticed his gaze, and instead of letting go, she wound her fingers in his. Her palm pressed against his, and once again, he was reminded of the soft slope of her lower back. "I know what DIABOLIK is planning," she whispered, edging closer to him. Her body pressed against his.

"Tell me." He pulled her closer.

"Later," she said. Her eyes flickered to his mouth, and he greedily lowered his head. Her lips met his, and he felt the sharp nip of her teeth.

The red light over the sanctum door flashed, and Miss Ogival—Barstow privately thought of her as 'Cat,' and his flesh thrilled at this secret between them—broke off their kiss. "I have to go," she said. "One can't keep the Chief waiting." She was slow to release his hand. "Meet me tonight," she said. "Under the swans."

The massive lock of the sanctum door clunked and the door started to open. Barstow stepped back, out of the Chief's line of sight, and his breathing was rapid and tight as he watched Miss Ogival slip back into the sanctum.

"Under the swans," he said quietly to the now-empty room. Finally, he thought. DIABOLIK's master plan will be revealed!

This is it, you think. You're getting close, aren't you?
Go to 208.

189

The espresso machine in the admin offices is a Hesslaugh MCA800X. Brushed stainless steel body. Polished chrome knobs. Conical burr grinder attachment. Onyx tamper. Micro-range pressure adjustment. Anodized steam wand with 270 degree range of movement. Weighs about eighty kilograms.

You open the counter drawer below it and find a dizzying array of instruments and attachments that go with the machine. Inside the refrigerator, you find a glass jar with a Petroi Vacu-See lid. The jar contains whole coffee beans. There's even a container of organic milk. You check the expiration date, and it doesn't expire for another week yet.

Damn. You could make yourself a cup of coffee. If you can figure out how to work this machine.

If you have your gear, this'll be a lot easier.
Go to 180.

Who needs gear? You've got two hands, and this is just an espresso machine. How hard can this be?
Go to 185.

190

You go to the next lab bench and check out what this scientist was doing. Again, you really have no idea. You're a Closer, not an organic chemist. But you rummage through the drawers and thumb through the notebooks to be thorough.

This sort of behavior makes Openers crazy, by the way. They're all about getting in and knocking things over. They don't like standing around while Closers and Guides take their time to figure out a scene. If something needs Opening, they're on it. Once that's done, all they want is that next high. They certainly don't want to stand around and puzzle through paperwork. Man, that's Hell for an Opener.

In general, Openers are brash assholes who like glory. It's an unfortunate aspect of the personality types that fit that field operative job description. They like to kick down doors and break things. They get excited about wrestling tentacled monstrosities that live between the stars. They think they can win a staring contest with the Abyss.

However, and this is one of the statistics that every Closer knows and keeps to themselves, the team member most likely to lose their shit within the first hour of an operation is the Opener. Most of the time, it's pretty obvious: they suck up a space jelly, their eyes go dead, and they try to kill you. But you've heard stories about Openers who make it back from a mission, but they aren't right in the head. They get stealthy. They get mean. They start dreaming about burning everything, and that dream of fire engulfs everything. They start thinking they are the only ones who can save the world. It becomes a narcissistic obsession about a sacred destiny.

And this gets you thinking about Argot. If he's gone rogue, you're going to have to take care of him.

It won't be the first time you've had to subdue one of your own, but damn, wouldn't it be nice if, for once, you didn't have to do all the clean-up?

Anyway, all this fumbling around is really just you wasting time. You should get on with the mission.

Go to 195.

There's a chemical locker at the back of the room. You should check that out.

Go to 197.

191

Having found some industrial acid in the Organic Chemistry lab, you return to the Storage area and the freezer. There's that weird corpse you're not willing to leave behind.

You pour the contents of one of your flask over the corpse, ignoring how the frozen flesh steams and crawls. You slam the lid of the freezer shut, and using your Sharpie, you leave a lewd note: "So much for you science experiment, suckers!" You sign it with Cleomantra's Frantic Closure—the quick and dirty Ward that everyone learns the first week of Orientation.

Just in time too. The freezer shakes as something inside reacts badly to the acid. You back away from the box, holding your breath. Your Ward should hold.

After a few moments, the freezer stops bouncing.

You approach it carefully.

The panel on the front has a temperature setting. You press buttons until it is at the coldest setting. Just in case.

This is worth another mark in your monster kill log (SIGIL— 66/d).

NOTE: YOU HAVE ACHIEVED A BONUS ACHIEVEMENT. THIS WILL BE NOTED WHEN YOU HAVE COMPLETED THIS EXERCISE.

Time to finish the mission.
Go to 195.

192

You dart around the last row of grow tables, and ignoring the jagged edges of glass still in the frame of the window, you vault into the monitoring room. A shard of glass slices through your knee, and you hit the table with the computer workstation like a stunned wildebeest. You bounce off the monitor and crash to the floor.

Your hip and shoulder ache. There's blood in your mouth, and blood is running down your leg. You ignore all your injuries and scramble backwards, trying to get away from the window.

The monster slams into the wall of the grow lab, knocking shards of glass out of the window frame. Part of it fits through the window, and it swipes at you with a long appendage that is more tentacle than arm. You swear the arm has grown longer when it tries a second time.

Amazingly, you've still got the squeeze bottle and your discipline stick. You raise both and spritz a jet of flame at the monster. Its tentacle arm catches fire, and the mushroom tops start shrieking from the flame. Dust—or ash or pollen or God knows what—scatters from the burning matter.

The wall creaks ominously as the monster tries to break through. You don't know how long it is going to hold.

Long enough, you think. In one of your pockets, you find a piece of carved soapstone. You bring it to your lips, kiss it fiercely, and then hurl it at the monster. It glistens as it flies through the air, and you hear a tearing noise as some part of reality shreds.

The Elder Sign hits the monster, and because that much of one thing cannot co-exist with that much of its opposite, both the sign and the monster cease to exist.

That was a little too close.

NOTE: YOU HAVE SENT AN UNHOLY MANIFESTATION BACK TO WHERE IT BELONGS. MAKE A NOTE IN YOUR SIGIL BOOK (SIGIL-66/d). YOU HAVE UNLOCKED A BONUS ACHIEVEMENT. THIS WILL BE RECOGNIZED AS PART OF YOUR FINAL SCORING FOR THIS EXERCISE.

Take a moment to catch your breath. Maybe you can get an espresso or something in the Admin section before you tackle the back half of the research station.

Go to 195.

193

You come to a door marked "ORGANIC CHEMISTRY," and when you nudge the door open, you can't see anything the lab. The lights are off.

You recall a session during Orientation and Inoculation with an old Asset Resource Management field operative (and by "old," we mean, "a three-year veteran"). They were part of what came to be known as "Storytime Thursdays," when field operatives would tell anecdotes meant to terrify all of you trainees. This particular field operative was a man in his mid-thirties who was missing one eye and most of his right arm. He told you and the other trainees to call him "Lucky," because that's what he was. He was the lucky one. The rest of his team weren't.

He lost his eye during an operation when he and his team were clearing an abandoned mine in Nevada. The place hadn't been actively used for decades, but there had been reports from people who lived in the nearby community of strange lights and noises. Plus, you know, the cattle mutilations and the esoteric markings burned into the ground around the bodies.

"Lucky" and his team tracked the source of the disturbances to the mine. "Never go into a place without a half dozen ways to make light," Lucky said. "These fuckers love the dark. It makes them think of Mother, even though most of them probably ate the bitch after she gave birth. Anyway, the whole place is pitch black and it stinks like the inside of a dead man's ass. We can't see shit, even with a couple halogen high-beamers."

Lucky was one of the more colorful commentators who showed up for the Storytime Thursday sessions, though it took him awhile to get to the actual story he was there to tell. This day had been no exception. Mostly, you suspect he was there to drill a stern warning into the heads of all of the neophytes in the room: Dark rooms are dangerous; never go into a dark room.

Okay, funtime story lesson aside, how are you going to finish this mission without going into this room?

Who says you have to clear every room? Let's avoid the obvious trap.

Go to 165.

But leaving a room unchecked is going to bug you, isn't it?

Go to 179.

However, if there are space jellies in this room, they're waiting for you. They must think you're stupid enough to fall for the old "come on in and find the light switch" trap, or they think you're afraid of the dark.

Which one is it?

Go to 181.

It really is a tricky conundrum. You're pretty sure there are some space jellies waiting for you inside this dark room, but you need to go into this room in order to get to the back half of the research substation.

Go to 188.

194

Seriously? You want to try to finish this mission without your gear? You do realize you're a Closer. You need to Close things. Sometimes you need to blow things up. Other times, you need to stab things. Or bludgeon them. Or light them on fire. How are you going to do these things without the contents of your coat pockets?

Oh, you're one of those who thinks the only adventure worth doing is the one done with nothing but your bare hands and your wits. We wish you would have said something about this aberration of your character earlier. But, whatever. It's too late now. You might as well muscle on.

Because Asset Resource Management are not complete assholes, we'd like to offer you a bonus to any MAPS SCORE you might receive after this point. It takes a certain amount of moxie to go charging ahead without your tools.

NOTE: ADD 7 TO ANY MAPS SCORE YOU MIGHT RECEIVE (THE BADASS BONUS).

Back to the airlock in Hydroponics.
Go to 162.

Now you can tackle that espresso machine in Admin.
Go to 196.

Time to get that chemical locker open now.
Go to 204.

195

At the end of the hall is an unmarked door that opens into a functional administrative space. There are two desks with computer workstations. A pair of file cabinets between them, and at the back of the room, there is a small kitchenette. There's a half-sized refrigerator, a microwave, and an espresso machine.

There are two doors leading out of this room. There are small signs attached to the wall beside each door. One sign reads "QUARTERS," and the other sign says "HALVES."

Someone's got a sense of humor, apparently.

Check out that espresso machine.
Go to 189.

Go through the door marked "HALVES."
Go to 233.

Go through the door marked "QUARTERS."
Go to 236.

196

You take another look at the espresso machine. There's a button on the left that is unmarked. You push it. The machine gurgles and shudders. A wisp of steam emerges from the tip of the steam wand.

A red light comes on. Underneath the light are the words "CLEAN ME."

Ignore the red light.
Go to 198.

Or maybe you just need to clean the machine before you use it. Should be simple enough, right?
Go to 221.

197

In the back of the Organic Chemistry lab, there's a large chemical storage locker. It's probably got a lot of nasty chemicals in it, and some of them might be useful. However, the locker is closed and there's an electronic keypad on it. You're probably going to have to break into it somehow.

If you have your gear, **go to 184**.

If you don't have your gear, **go to 185**.

Leave it alone. It's a distraction.
Go to 195.

Hang on. Didn't you find a combination? If so, turn to the section corresponding to that three digit number.

198

You ignore the red light on the espresso machine and continue blithely pushing buttons and twisting dials. The machine rattles more, and a jet of superheated steam spurts out of the wand, nearly burning your hand.

You have to be careful with expensive home equipment like this.

You set the grind level and dump some of the beans from the vacuum sealed container into the hopper. When you push the button to start grinder, the espresso machine makes a lot of noise. It sounds like it is trying to grind gravel and not beans. The beans are jumping in the hopper, but they're not going into the grinder.

Anxious for that cup of coffee, you lift the lid on the grinder. Some of the beans jump out, and you try to catch them. You can't catch them all (or any of them actually), and frustrated by these recalcitrant beans, you try to keep them in the grinder.

With your hand, because that's the only tool you have, right?

The machine shudders and then lurches. Its motion surprises you—this thing weighs a ton, after all—and, well, you mean to steady yourself, but where you do put that hand?

The grinder eagerly grabs at your finger. Oh, that's going to leave a mark.

You try to pull your finger out, but the grinder motors in the Hesslaugh MCA800X series are made by a sub-division of Batollini Motors, who are known for making high-performance racing car engines, which is to say you get a lot of torque from a small package with Batollini.

The grinder has reached your first knuckle, and it feels like it is speeding up.

FORTUNATELY, YOUR ELBOW IS PROBABALY TOO BIG TO FIT IN THAT GRINDER. THAT'S THE GOOD NEWS. THE BAD NEWS IS THAT THERE'S NO ONE AROUND TO HELP YOU TIE OFF THAT TERRIBLE WOUND, AND YOU'LL MOST LIKELY BLEED OUT IN A FEW MINUTES.

MAPS SCORE: 61

199

As you are trying to convince yourself that you do, in fact, have a plan, the monster bursts out of the fog. It runs smack into the wall, and the wall doesn't hold. Drywall, plaster, and metal sheeting all complain loudly and tear noisily. The wind, thrilled to have found a way in, howls into the room. The temperature drops three degrees in as many seconds.

You can't help but stare at the hole the monster made in the wall. You barely got a glimpse of it. It looked like a rose bush tried to convince a lion and a rhinosauros to mate.

And now it's escaped the station.

You should go after it.
Go to 207.

It won't survive. There's nowhere for it to go, and the wind will surely strip its flesh in no time. Right?
Go to 219.

200

You start with the simplest choice: straight numerical order. That doesn't work. You try the inverse. That doesn't work. You try the odd numbers, followed by the even. Nope. Evens, then odd? That doesn't work either.

Well, fine. You settle in to do each of the possible combinations of four digits. You get about halfway through when the keypad beeps and the light turns green.

The locker is unlocked.

You reach for the handle.

This could be a trap. It could also NOT be a trap, and you're merely letting your paranoia get to you. But paranoia is what keeps Night Office operative alive, so . . .
Go to 227.

It's not a trap, you tell yourself.
Go to 229.

201

You sense a structure on your right. Over there, past the ropes. But you're not in a rush to go check it out, because once you leave the ropes, you are on your own.

This is too dangerous. Go back.
Go to 164.

You've come this far; you need to finish this. Let go and head for the structure.
Go to 228.

202

There certainly is another way to deal with the Organic Chemistry lab: avoid it entirely. Sure, it's probably a bad idea to leave a room unchecked as you sweep through the station, but come on, what's Asset Resource Management going to do? If you fail to save the world, what difference is one room full of space jellies going to make? And if you save the world, Heavy Battery is going to burn everything behind you anyway so . . .

Regardless, Asset Resource Management isn't here. You are, and you're calling the shots. The shot you're calling right now is: "This lab can suck it."

Give that door the finger too. It'll feel very satisfying.

Okay, once you're done with all that, time to check out another section in the back half of the station.

Go to 165.

Hey, what's that smell?

Go to 195.

203

You flail toward the airlock, fighting your way through the plastic layer on this side. You nearly trip over the office chair in the center as the monster careens into the outer frame of the airlock. The impact knocks the chair loose, and the inner frame of the airlock rotates. You're disoriented for a moment, and you struggle to figure out which way is the right way.

Away from the monster, the Old Man recommends, and you don't spare a brain cycle to tell him to piss off.

You hear plastic tearing, and something rips across your back. Your coat protects you, mostly, but you still feel blood start to flow. You're nearly at the other plastic barrier.

The monster goes low, and its long tentacle arm thingie wraps around your legs. The monster pulls you off your feet. You struggle, but all those mushrooms are like fish hooks or suckers. You're not getting free.

The monster hauls you back through the airlock . . .

WHAT HAPPENS NEXT IS TERRIBLE. IT'S REALLY–YOU DON'T WANT TO KNOW. THE NOISE ALONE WOULD STRIKE A GOAT DEAD WITH FEAR, AND THAT'S NOT TAKING INTO CONSIDERATION ALL THE SCREAMING YOU ARE DOING. SO MUCH SCREAMING.

MAPS SCORE: 46

204

You bang on the keypad of the locker in the Organic Chemistry lab. That's not effective. You try a chair, which isn't much better. The only way you're going to get this locker open is if you had some sort of explosive.

It's likely that the contents of this locker would provide you with the raw materials needed to make that explosive, but if you could get access to those materials, the locker would be open already.

This is a stupid conundrum.

Let's face it: you're not getting into this locker without some assistance.

Okay, okay. Maybe you should go find your gear.
Go to 80.

Hang on. Maybe you don't need to brute force this. Someone must have written down the combination somewhere. Check the lab benches.
Go to 212.

205

You decide to ask about the rest of the crew of MacReady Station first. People always like to talk about their friends and co-workers. That'll help keep them calm.

"Can you tell me about your friends?" you ask. "Where's—" You try to remember the names of the people stationed here. "Where's, uh, Nakamura?"

The desk creeper shakes their head. "I don't know where the doc is," they say. "I haven't seen them since . . ." They get that look in their eye that says they've either lost their keys or they're trying to not think about something awful. You suspect the latter since no one needs a set a keys in this place.

"Since?" you prompt, trying to keep the conversation going.

"Since your people showed up."

"What about your commanding officer? The person in charge?"

"Elkhorn?"

"Sure. Elkhorn."

"He's a coward. I hope they ate him first."

"Who? Who ate him?"

You're hoping they don't respond with "your people" again.

"*Them*," the desk crawler says.

Okayi, this is going to take longer than you thought.

"How about . . . how about the science guy?"

"Which one?"

"The uh—the one who—"

You suddenly realize you can't tell these people apart. There's been something troubling you for awhile about the crew—about all these names you've been seeing—but you haven't had the time to really think about it. But now, as you struggle to put a face to a name, you can't escape it. This disheveled human being hiding under the desk: you can't tell if they are male or female. Not because they aren't presenting well, but because you can't—fuck. You can't even focus on their face. You've got—what's that thing called where you can't recognize faces?

Prosopagosia, the Old Man supplies. *Face blindness. But it doesn't prevent you from seeing people, from recognizing body types and sexes. Unless . . .*

Unless what . . . ? you ask. You wrestle with what he is suggesting. *You think I've been co-opted by one of them.*

I'm in your head, remember? the Old Man reminds you. *Which means you're the one doing the thinking here . . .*

"Are you okay?" the person asks.

"I'm fine," you snap. When your tone makes them flinch, you soften your voice. "What's your name?"

"Hamish," they respond.

"You got a first name?"

"That is my first name," they respond testily.

"Okay, Hamish. What's your last name?"

"Nash," they say.

"And what do you do here, Hamish Nash?" you ask.

"I'm a soil scientist," Hamish says. It still sounds like they—he?—is sulking.

Hamish is a boy's name, right? Maybe? You're not entirely sure. This whole lack of being able to discern sexes and faces is troubling you. How could you have not noticed before now?

The Old Man rolls his eyes. You want to smack him, but there's no way to do that without scaring Nash. "Did you work in one of the labs?" you ask.

"Yeah," Hamish says. "But not anymore."

"Why not?"

"Because that's where we put the rod. That's where Windows turned into—that's where things went wrong."

"Is Windows okay?"

Nash stares at you like you're an idiot. "Your team did something really awful to him." Nash shakes his head. "I mean, it wasn't Windows anymore, was it? But still . . ." A shiver runs through his body. "Nothing should have to suffer like that."

Now is a good time to change the subject. How about the obelisk? You should ask him about that.
Go to 225.

What about the rest of his crew? Hopefully Argot or Brinkmann didn't make a mess of everyone else. There's got to be someone else you can get Hamish to focus on.
Go to 231.

206

You click the laser pointer on and off a few times, piercing the fog with the red light. Something snuffles, shifts, and then there's a burst of activity as something large and mean tries to catch the floating dot.

You point the penlight toward the far corner of the room and click it on and off a few more times. The monster charges the light, and for a minute, you get a solid glimpse of it through a gap in the fog. It's bigger than a small pony, and it looks like a baboon tried to eat a tiger, but couldn't choke it all the way down. You've never seen anything like it. It's certainly not one of the beasties in your *Sightings, Inquiries & Grievous Immolations Log* book.

As you're staring, the baboon-tiger shreds the wall of the lab with long claws. The noise startles you and your hand shakes, moving the dot. The monster freaks out when the dot jumps and dances on its skin. It whirls, and—holy shit, this is no good—it sees you.

Standing there, going clicky-clicky with the laster pointer.

It charges.

You thumb the power amplifier lever all the way up on the pointer and give the beast a solid pulse. The beam vaporizes one of its eyes—good aim!—and drills a neat hole through its skull, which doesn't slow it down in the slightest.

These handheld devices have enough juice for two charges. You've got one more chance to bring this thing down, but as you're trying to figure out the best spot to drill the monster (you already put a hole in its skull!), it leaps.

Man, that thing can jump.

YOUR BODY IS CRUSHED AGAINST THE WALL BY THE FULL WEIGHT OF THE SERVANT OF HUIGGHERASTRA.

THAT'S WHAT IT IS, BY THE WAY. THE ONLY EXISTING MENTION OF IT IN THE RECORD IS AN ANCIENT SUMERIAN TABLET USED IN PRE-UR NECROMANTIC RITUALS. OF COURSE, THIS TABLET (AND RITUAL) IS ULTRA-SECRET NO-EYES CLASSIFIED, SO IT'S BEEN EIGHTY OR MORE YEARS SINCE ANYONE HAS BOTHERED TO DECIPHER THE TABLET.

ANYWAY, THE SERVANT OF HUIGGHERASTRA LIKES TO PULP ITS FOOD BEFORE INGESTING IT. YOU'RE GOING TO WISH YOU HAD DIED IMMEDIATELY FROM A CRUSHED RIB CAGE BECAUSE THIS BEAST IS GOING TO TENDERIZE ALL OF YOU IN THE NEXT FEW MINUTES.

MAPS SCORE: 35

207

You stare at the ragged hole in the wall of the hydrophonic lab. Whatever was lurking in here just made an express exit to the outside.

On the one hand, you should go after it; on the other, there's a good chance the weather outside will kill it. You give Mother Nature . . . what? an eighty-five percent chance?

Forty-six, the Old Man says in your head.

"Damn it," you whisper more to yourself than to the spirit of the Old Man.

You go over to the hole in the wall, and the wind starts tickling you immediately. Your teeth shiver as you peer out the hole. You don't see anything. The wind laughs at you.

Forty-six percent chance the weather wins. How you feel about those odds?

That's not good enough. Asset Resource Management will dock you after the mission is over if you walk away from odds like that.

Go to 217.

Asset Resource Management isn't here, and you know the protocol. Field operatives have operational control. Not the suits back home. And after everything you've been through? You'll take those odds.

Go to 219.

208

Once upon a time, there had been a theater building on the island in the center of the park behind the William Morris Gallery. Called the Waltham Forest Theatre, it ran summer stock theater—good for the kids and the young at heart—for a few decades before succumbing to the general malaise that swept the UK in the later years of the twentieth century. The building had been demolished in a recent attempt to redesign the park for a new generation, and the only reminder of the playhouse was an iron sculpture of a pair of swans, their necks entwined. Some nouveau sculptor's attempt to reimagine what Morris might have done had he been more a century later.

Anyway, the park closed at twilight, and a bumbling pair of security guards waddled through the garden, urging the malingerers to move on. A trio of youths in hooded sweatshirts looked as if they might challenge the local authority, but the fatter of the two showed the troublemakers that he had a handheld stun gun and he knew how to use it.

Once the park was empty, the guards wandered off to the warmth of their tiny hut behind the museum. Barstow, who had been hiding in the rafters of the covered picnic area, dropped to a table and quickly jogged over to the northern footbridge that crossed the moat. The swans were on a small rise near the center of the island, and from there, Barstow had a good view of both the north and west approaches. Occasionally, he would glance over his shoulder and make sure there was no one on the southern approach.

It was only after he had been in position for ten minutes that he realized there was someone sitting on the nearby park bench. They hadn't been there earlier, when he had approached the swans, and he couldn't ascertain how they had managed to reach the bench without him spotting them. Regardless, the figure was there now, wrapped in a gray trench coat and wearing an equally gray trilby.

Barstow considered what sort of passphrase might work in this situation. "Aphrodite madly bakes earnest—" He fumbled for a dessert that began wit the letter 'r.' "Rhubarb pie," he finished. Even though he had an extra letter.

"I like pie," the figure croaked.

Good enough, *Barstow thought.*

"Where's our mutual friend?" he asked.

"We are spies," the figure said. "We don't have friends."

"Acquaintances, then."

"Late," the figure said. "Hung at the office."

Barstow winced at the figure's choice of words, and he secretly hoped the lack of a adverb in the bench sitter's explanation was due to a lack of familiarity with English rather than a morbid linguistic precision.

"Who are you?" he asked.

"That is the wrong question," the figure replied. "Where am I might be better."

You're starting to understand Barstow's annoyance, but you have no choice. Keep reading. You need answers.

Go to 210.

209

You edge toward the airlock, trying to move as silently and unobtrusively as possible. You reach the torn airlock cover without mishap. As you ease past the plastic layers, the air shifts in the grow lab. There's a swirl of fog, as if something moved suddenly.

You are out of time! You struggle to get through the airlock. As you reach the halfway point, something rushes out of the fog. You get a brief glimpse of the mosnter. Your brain struggles to make sense of it—*It's a gorilla! It's a tiger!*—and then it slams into the airlock.

You stumble and trip over the office chair wedged in the airlock frame. You fall on your ass, thinking *What a way to die.*

But wait! The chair has come loose. The airlock rotates. The gorilla-tiger is caught. The metal frame of the airlock has pinned it in place.

You start to laugh—more from still being alive than anything actually funny. A chair! You were saved by an office chair! How ridiculous is—

What? How long are the arms on this thing?

LONGER THAN YOU THOUGHT. THE MONSTER REACHES INTO THE AIRLOCK AND HOOKS YOUR LEG. YOU SCREAM A LOT, BUT IT DOESN'T MATTER.

MAPS SCORE: 49

210

"Okay," Barstow snapped. "I'll play your silly game. Where *are* you?"

"Many places at the same time," the figure said. "I am always in the way."

The figure stressed the last word in a manner that suggested some importance, but Barstow didn't know what they were talking about. "Why are you here?" he asked, thinking that he was clever.

"Not as clever as you think," the watcher replied. His words made Barstow shiver. "You think you know what you know, but you don't know what you think you know."

Barstow tried to parse what the figure had said. "But, that's exactly why I am here?" He couldn't help the rise at the end of his sentence, which gave away his uncertainty.

"DIABOLIK is within you," the figure said. "They seek to poison the serpent from the inside. Other snakes will come, but they will be smaller. Weaker. Less able to suss the complete reflection within the mirror. They will not understand—not fully—what is going on."

"What is—" Barstow heard a sound behind him, and when he looked, he saw a lithe figure coming up the path from the southern footbridge. He realized his mistake and looked back at the bench. "Damnit," he swore when he saw the bench was empty.

"What is it?" Miss Ogival asked as she reached the swans. She was wearing a dark tracksuit, the kind with the zipper that went all the way down. Her hair was tucked under a wool cap.

"There was someone here," Barstow said.

"Where?" she asked, looking around in the gloom.

"On the bench," he said. "But they disappeared when I looked away."

"An apparition?" she asked.

"A projection," Barstow said, realizing what he had witnessed. "They were about to tell me something important. Something about DIABOLIK."

Miss Ogival stepped close to Barstow, and not entirely because of the chill in the air. "They're planning on assassinating ——," she whispered.

You stare at the name on the page.

"That's your name," you say out loud.

The Old Man manifests in your head. *Is it?* He peers over your shoulder. *Huh. How about that.*

"Why is your name in Morgan's manuscript?"

You should ask Morgan, he says.

"Morgan's dead. Or, at least, I assume Morgan's dead." You glance around, listening to the emptiness of the station. "They're all dead."

Just like me, the Old Man says.

And suddenly, you recall that Management's explanation for the Old Man's disappearance wasn't very satisfying. Not that you had expected it to be, of course, but now, in light of this manuscript written by a deranged radio operator in the middle of the Antarctic, you start to wonder.

And thus, a seed is planted, the Old Man says.

There's one more page to the manuscript.
Go to 256.

211

You glance over your shoulder—just to be sure—and you don't see anyone sneaking up behind you.

Oh, wait. Hang on. Is there someone hiding under one of the desks?

Cautiously, you edge closer. At first, you thought the body was a corpse (there's been no shortage of those, after all), but you realize this person might still be alive. Their arms are covering their head so you can't tell for sure, but there's no blood and no obvious sign of trauma, which is a good sign.

Move closer and investigate.
Go to 216.

Try to coax them out.
Go to 222.

212

You investigate the nearest lab bench. It has a fancy microscope and a shelf full of black lab notebooks. You find the ususal sort of crap in the drawers, including a stash of candy bars (which is totally a no-no in a lab setting) and a paperback book. There's a monster on the cover. It's some kind of retro pulp horror novel. You find a bookmark advertising a quaint little bookstore in Washington state. Idly, you note the bookmark is on page 214.

The notebooks aren't very helpful. Page after page after page of nearly indecipherable scribbling. It's not a secret code. It's just shitty handwriting.

Check out the next lab station.
Go to 170.

You spot a locker at the back of the room. Perhaps you should cut to the chase and check that out.
Go to 197.

213

"I know where she is," you tell Nash.

He looks at you, and you have to look away. His expression is too hopeful. You can't stand it.

"She's in the briefing room," you say. "I left her there."

"Noooo," he shrieks. "Why? Why? Why?"

"Hey, listen to me!" you shout. "She's alive. She's still alive."

His voice cuts off mid-shriek, and he stares at you, his mouth hanging open. "A—alive?" he manages to croak.

"Yeah," you say. "She's alive. She's frightened, though. I built her a fort, but she needs someone to watch over her." You soften your tone. "She needs your help."

"My—my help?"

"Yeah, Hamish. She needs you."

He starts to come out from under the desk, but he's afraid of the light. He's afraid of being exposed. You don't do anything to threaten him. You wait. It's hard. You want to grab him by the arm and shove him toward the door leading to the main part of the station, but you know he's too fragile. You have to wait for him to find his own strength.

Eventually, he stands. His knees shake and he doesn't like the ceiling tiles, but he's upright.

"Go," you say, nodding toward the door. "Go help her."

Nash nods, getting stronger by the second. He starts toward the door, and then stops. "It's in the Geology lab," he says. He looks at the door marked "HALVES."

You know what he is talking about. "Okay," you say.

"But you can't go that way," he says. "You have to go through Atmospherics, and . . ." A shudder runs through his frame. He looks at the other door. "If you go through that door, they'll— they're waiting for you."

"Who is?" you ask.

"Copper and Palmer and—and the others."

"And that's the only way to Geology?"

He nods. "They're waiting."

"I know," you say. "It's okay." You wave him toward the other door. "Go find the doc," you say. "Be safe."

He's already left the room, and he doesn't hear your parting words. Not that it would make any difference.

NOTE: AS FOOLISH AS YOUR INTENTIONS ARE, YOU STILL GET CREDIT FOR SAVING A MEMBER OF THE ENDOLUVION CREW. YOU WILL BE RECOGNIZED FOR THIS AT THE END OF THIS EXERCISE.

Go through the door marked "HALVES."
Go to 233.

Go through the door marked "QUARTERS."
Go to 236.

214

You enter the three-digit code you learned earlier. The keypad beeps when you press ENTER, and you hear a loud *CLACK* from within the locker. The door pops open.

There's an impressive array of chemicals on the shelves of the storage locker. Now all you need a bolt of lightning and you can turn yourself into a superhero.

No? That's now how chemistry works? Rats. Well, it would be nice to concoct something useful here, but let's be honest, you weren't all that enterprising a student, were you? No, you had other plans, and then—you know—things happened, and now you're working for the Night Office, which didn't really care about that dodgy set of science credits on your university transcript, so . . .

It's probably best to leave this stuff here and get on with the mission.
Go to 195.

Come on now. You paid attention during a semester or two of labs. That's enough to make you dangerous.
Go to 229.

215

The idea of making some coffee is really overpowering, isn't it? It's been a day, after all. A nice demitasse would hit the spot.

A light turns green on the espresso machine, and you fumble around in the drawer for the stainless steel portafilter. Oh, very nice. Professional grade, with two spouts.

(All of this banging around, by the way, covers the sound made by something behind you as it grabs the heavy computer monitor off the desk.)

The Hesslaugh MCA800X has a built-in grinder, and you find tiny instructions printed on a label. Ah, yes. Press once for auto. You press the portafilter against the rubberized backing, and the espresso machine starts grinding beans.

(Again, all this noise masks the grunting noise the thing makes as it lifts the monitor over its head.)

Once the grinder stops, you tamp the coffee into a hard puck with the built-in onyx tamper, and then you try to figure out the orientation on the portafilter. Does it go like *this*, or is it more of a lift, *twist*, and . . .

THE MONSTROSITY DROPS THE COMPUTER MONITOR ON YOUR HEAD. YOU FORGET ABOUT THE PORTAFILTER AS YOUR SPINE COMPRESSES IN AN UNNATURAL WAY. YOU CAN'T FEEL ANYTHING BUT A DISTANT TUGGING AS THE BEAST OPENS YOU UP AND FIDDLES WITH YOUR INTERNAL ORGANS.

THE NIGHT OFFICE IS SOMEWHAT APPALLED BY YOUR FAILURE TO PAY ATTENTION TO YOUR SURROUNDINGS.

MAPS SCORE: 14

216

You get closer to the person under the desk. Definitely alive. Their overalls are dirty and stained, but there are no visible injuries. When you try communicating, you get no response.

They also don't leap out and attack you, so that's good news. They haven't been mind-devoured, at least.

Not much else you can do at the moment, so you go back to the espresso machine. You steam some milk, and as you are about to pour the silky foamed milk over your velvety rich espresso, you think that maybe some espresso could bring this person back from their non-responsive state.

Espresso is magic, after all.

You get a second cup and split the shots between the two cups. You add a little steamed milk—enough to color it, but not so much as to turn it into a latte. You put the cup on the desk. Close to the edge, but not too close.

You stand back and lean against the counter, sipping your own freshly made beverage. It's hot and good, and the caffeine wipes away the fatigue that has been hounding you.

Slowly, a hand reaches out from under the desk. It fumbles around, nearly knocking the coffee cup over, but the questing fingers finally find the cup. Cup and hand disappear under the desk.

You wait a bit. "I'm with the second team," you say. "I need to finish what we came here to do."

The person under the desk doesn't answer.

"This isn't going to end well for anyone if I don't do my job," you say.

Slowly, a tousled head pokes out from under the desk. "Go away," the person mutters.

"I can't," you say. "Not until I get some answers."

The head retreats, and a few moments later, a figure slowly emerges from under the desk.

This is progress. Now you just have to not spook them with your questions.

Ask about Argot and Brinkmann.
Go to 220.

Ask about the obelisk.
Go to 223.

217

You don't like the odds of the monster surviving outside the station, but what are the odds you're going to find it outside?

Nearly zero, the Old Man offers.

Or the odds that the weather will kill you?

About a hundred percent, the Old Man says.

Those odds are much worse, aren't they?

As you stand there, debating the futility of trying to catch the monster, something slams into the side of the station. A head that looks like a lion, a giraffe, and a shark all melted together shoves through the hole. The monster is back! And it's caught itself on the ragged edges of the hole that it made when it left the station. What luck! Now you can—

A long tongue unravels from the monster's mouth and wraps around your waist. It's covered with nasty barbs, and they tear through your clothes. You beat at the tongue with your discipline stick, and the monster howls at the touch of the fire on your stick, but it doesn't let go.

You start fumbling through your pockets, looking for something sharp, as the monster shoves more of itself into the station. Blood splashes on the floor from its wounds.

How is it bigger? the Old Man asks. *If it made the hole going out, shouldn't it fit coming back in?*

You find the knife in a pocket where it shouldn't be. You don't have time to think about how it got there. Nor do you have time to think about the Old Man's questions. You flick the blade open and hack at the monster's tongue.

The monster thrashes its head from side to side, yanking you off-balance. You slam into a grow table, and the knife slips out of your grip. As you desperately try to grab it, the monster shakes you again.

Your outstretched hand knocks the knife off the table. You have no idea where it has gone. Nor do you have time to look for it.

Back to your pockets. Surely there's something else in here that will help. A straight razor, perhaps? A box knife? A fat screwdriver? Something . . .

IT'S NICE THAT YOUR COAT HAS SO MANY POCKETS, BUT YOU REALLY NEED A BETTER MANAGEMENT SYSTEM FOR TRACKING WHAT YOU'RE CARRYIHNG. THIS BEASTIE ISN'T GOING TO WAIT FOR YOU TO CHECK EVERY POCKET.

MAPS SCORE: 55

218

You make a quick tour of the lab benches, and they're pretty much what you'd expect in a chemistry lab: test tubes, burners, microscopes, and other machines with lots of buttons and dials. There are notebooks at every station, and you flip through several. They're all neat and tidy, but none of them have anything useful. All kinds of science going on here, but all that's being written down is raw data. No one is drawing helpful pie charts or bar graphs.

At the back of the room is a large chemical storage locker. It is closed, and there's a keypad lock on it.

Ignore the locker, and get on with the mission.
Go to 195.

Examine the locker more closely.
Go to 197.

219

After listening to the wind chortle and laugh for a minute, you decide the odds of you dying outside are really high (*ninety-four percent*, the Old Man suggests). As much as you don't like the idea of that beast running around outside the station, you still have the rest of the station to deal with. *Priorties*, you tell the Old Man, and he doesn't argue.

It takes a little while to draw sigils on all the broken edges of the hole, and your fingers feel like they are going to fall off from the cold by the time you finish. Once the hole has been blessed, you perform a lesser sealing, pulling the wall back together. Then, with the wind howling its frustration through the tiny gaps still in the wall, you prick your finger with your ceremonial dagger and fling droplets of blood at the wall. In your head, you perform Hy'echzets's Refusal—solidifying the Ward you've woven into the fabric of the wall. The wind rises in pitch and then falls silent as the Ward actives.

The wall is Closed. That beast isn't coming back in this way.

You investigate the rest of the room, clearing the stringy remainders of the noxious fog the monster had been slumbering in. You find more dark streaks and splashes on the floor and tables, as well as torn clothing stiff with blood, but there aren't any bodies.

Time to move on to the back half of the research station.
Go to 195.

220

"I need to find my team," you ask. "Do you know them? Argot? Sagalico?"

The person squints at you. "Are they—were the mean ones?"

"The assholes?" You nod. "Yeah, that's probably them. Do you know where they are?"

The lurker hesitates before shaking their head.

"Where did you see them?"

"Saw 'em in the lab."

"What were they doing?"

The lurker glances around nervously. "Arguing," they say.

"What were they arguing about?" you ask.

The person retreats under the desk again. You crouch down and try to look nice and pleasant. Not like you are trying to lure them out with candy. "I need to find them," you say. "It's important."

"Engineering," they mutter. "They're in engineering."

"All right," you say. "Thank you."

Ask about the obelisk.
Go to 223.

Ask about Sagalico.
Go to 230.

221

You look in the little drawer of the Hesslaugh MCA800X for some guidance on how to clean the machine. Maybe that brush thingie? Or maybe that plastic device that looks like a cigar cutter? Doesn't look like there is an instruction manual either.

You peer over the top of the machine. Maybe there's a port in the back or . . . ?

Something strikes you in the back of the head and your forehead bounces off the espresso machine. Your legs get wobbly, and you fall down. There's blood on your forehead. It's streaming into your eye. What the hell just happened?

As you wipe away the blood, you catch sight of a deranged looking person standing over you. Their eyes are wild and bloodshot. They are wearing one of the MacReady Station jackets, so you know they belong here, but . . .

"You got blood on it," this person shrieks. "You got blood on the Precious!"

"No, wait—" you start. "This is all an accident."

They don't want to hear it. As you try to sit up, they shove you back down and then start stomping on you. First your stomach, and then your chest, and then . . .

NEVER TOUCH ANOTHER PERSON'S ESPRESSO MACHINE. WE WOULD HAVE THOUGHT THIS WAS SELF-EVIDENT.

MAPS SCORE: 22

222

You say some nice things about the decor, and that doesn't elicit any response. You make noises like you're trying to get a small dog to come out from under a couch, and that doesn't work either. You yell at the person, which really doesn't work.

Finally, you give up and go back to the espresso machine. It's waiting for you to push the button that makes the espresso. You push that button, and after a moment of gurgling, rich brown espresso starts dribbling out of the twin nozzles of the porta-filter. The room fills with the wonderful aroma of fresh coffee, and . . .

You hear a noise, and when you look behind you, you see a frightened face peering at you from under the desk.

The flow of coffee into the cup slows to a trickle and stops. You bring the cup over to the desk—but not *too* close—and put it on the floor. "Go ahead," you say, indicating the cup of velvety rich freshly brewed espresso.

The person under the desk shakes their head.

"It hot and fresh," you say.

They shake their head again.

"Okay," you say. You kneel down to pick up the cup, and the person under the desk swarms out like an angry beetle. You back away as they snap at you and grab the cup. You keep your distance as they carefully sip the espresso. They're watching you warily.

After the second sip, the person lets out a little sigh. Their shoulders relax and they quickly finish off the rest of the espresso. They hold the cup out in that universal sign for "More, please."

You shake your head. "I have some questions," you say.

They thrust the cup at you again.

"No more coffee until we talk," you say.

They wilt and retreat under the desk. You can wait them out. The caffeine hit will crest in a bit.

After a few minutes, you clear your throat. "Oh, damn. I think there's something stuck in—"

The person comes bounding out from under the desk. "Don't you dare—" they start, but when they realize they've been tricked, their anger deflates. They stand there, looking dejected and haggard, the coffee cup dangling from their slack fingers.

"I have questions," you say.

Their shoulders slump. "Fine," they say.

Ask about the crew of the station.
Go to 205.

Ask about your team.
Go to 224.

223

You want to ask about the obelisk, but you hesitate. The person who had been hiding under the desk is fragile. If you start there, you might not get any answers. You're going to have to ease into that conversation.

"What's your name?" you ask.

"Mac—Nash," the desk lurker says. "Hamish Nash."

"Hello, Hamish, you say, putting a cheery note in your voice. "Are you the one who likes coffee?"

He nods slowly.

"I thought so," you say. "Those are some really good beans. And that Petroi jar. That's some high end stuff."

"It keeps them fresh," he mumbles. "I like them fresh."

"Me too," you say.

Neither of you say anything for a moment. Nash scratches at the carpet with a dirty finger.

"Do you know where the others are?" You keep it general.

Nash shakes his head. "

What about—" You try to remember the name of one of other scientists on staff. You can't think of anyone who isn't already dead. Except . . . "What about the doctor?"

"Jo—?"

"Sure. Jo. What about Jo? Is she all right?"

Nash chews on a ragged fingernail. His eyes are wide, and they can't stop moving. Maybe you shouldn't have given him all that coffee.

Too late now, the Old Man observes.

If you helped the doctor in the briefing room, **go to 213**.

Otherwise, **go to 226**.

224

"What happened to my team?" you ask the crazy person who has been hiding under the desk.

"Your—your . . . What? Your team?"

"I showed up with two others," you say. "And we were the second team on site. We can in response to a distress signal."

That sets them off, and they laugh long and hard. "A distress signal?" they finally manage.

This reaction neatly encapsulates what you and your team thought of the message coming out of the Antarctic. "It wasn't a distress signal," you say.

The person shakes their head. "No, it wasn't," they say. "We were calling them. We were giving them directions."

You sign and pinch the bridge of your nose. Of course they were. This is how it always ends up. "Who?" you ask. "Who was coming?"

"The mind speakers."

"And what—what did they want?"

"To speak in our minds."

You sort of asked for that one. "What did they call themselves?" you ask.

"The Voerdamnikenari."

"That's a pleasant name," you say.

The nut job shakes their head. "It's a terrible name."

"Terrible, as in frightening?"

They nod solemnly.

"What is it frightening?" you ask.

"Do you know what it means?"

"No, I do not," you admit. "Could you tell me?"

"No." They shrink back under the desk until one side of their face is showing. "I can't do that."

"Why not?"

"They will hear me." They look around wildly. "They can hear us right now."

"Right now?"

The person disappears under the desk, and you have to crouch down to look at them. They are pressed into the corner, and their eyes are going all ping-pong.

"Hey," you say, trying to get their attention. "There's no one here but you and I. They can't hear us."

"They're listening," the desk hugger whispers. "They're always listening."

You can see how this conversation is going to go in circles. Perhaps you ought to try a different topic.

Ask about Argot and Sagalico.
Go to 220.

Ask about the obelisk.
Got to 225.

225

"I need some answers," you say. "Tell me about the obelisk." You can feel it, lurking in your head like an angry splinter. You want to get to the bottom of this before this thing digs any deeper into your mind.

The person shrieks at your question and tries to scramble farther away from you. You try to calm them down, but they're totally freaked out now. When you try to console them, they start kicking.

You back off. Whatever information they had is lost now.

There are two doors out of this room. You might as well press on.

Your head is starting to ache.

Time is running out.

Go to the door marked "HALVES."
Go to 233.

Go to the door marked "QUARTERS."
Go to 236.

226

You consider lying to the kid, but given his agitated state, it might be best to be honest.

Weird, the Old Man observes.

Shut up, you tell him. You take a deep breath and give it a try.

"I need your help," you say, trying to build a bond between the two of you.

His gaze is flat when he looks at you. It's not great, but at least he's making eye contact.

"I need to stop whatever is coming," you say.

"You can't."

"I need to try."

His expression doesn't change.

"It's my job," you try, which sounds terribly hollow, but hey, it's all you have. It's all you have ever had. The job is everything.

"Your friends—" He stops for a moment, and his throat works around the words caught in his chest.

"They aren't my friends," you say. "I just work with them."

His lip curls. This is the first emotional response you've seen from him. You take it as a good sign.

"They aren't good people," he says.

"I know," you say.

"There should be some kind of . . ." He flaps a hand helplessly. "They were my friends," he finishes. "And your people—"

You have a good idea what he's trying to say.

"Yeah," you tell him. "There should be an accounting. It's not okay."

"Are you . . . are you going to do it?"

"Yeah," you say. You're not entirely sure what "*it*," but hey, if agreeing to do something for this kid gets you answers, then it doesn't really matter, does it?

He points at the door marked "HALVES." "They're in Engineering," he says.

There you go.

You hesitate for a second, trying to gauge his state of mind. Can you get a little more out of him?

Ask about the obelisk.
Go to 225.

Ask about Sagalico.
Go to 230.

Ask about the Endoluvion staff.
Go to 231.

227

You open the chemical locker. It contains a half-dozen shelves, and on each of the shelves are various white bottles. They're labeled with various warning stickers, and most of the chemical names have a lots of syllables in them.

However, on a lower shelf, there's one bottle that isn't like the others. It's a quart mason jar with a piece of masking tape on it. Written on the tape is "CS48.04-c," and inside the jar is a murky liquid that is sloshing around.

Since you're standing on stable ground, there shouldn't be any "sloshing" going on, which means whatever is in that jar is . . .

You bend over and take a closer look at the jar. Wow, they managed to get a space jelly in a jar. How did they accomplish that?

You tap on the jar, and the space jelly surges against the glass. The jar rocks on the shelf and you instinctively reach out and catch it. As soon as your hand touches the glass, you realize your mistake.

The jelly lunges again. You don't hear the glass break, but you feel a flare of pain as glass pierces your skin. You snatch your hand away, and there's a line of multi-colored goo stuck to your palm. The jar slides off the shelf and shatters on the floor.

You don't care about the glass on the floor; you've got space jelly stuck to your hand. You're bleeding too, which means it has a way into your bloodstream.

You try to scrape the jelly off with the edge of the locker door, and you get some of it. But not all of it. Your hand twitches, which isn't a nervous response that you asked for. Something twists inside your arm . . .

This isn't good.

YOU COULD CUT OFF YOUR ARM, BUT THE OPPORTUNITY TO DO SO PASSED WHILE YOU WERE READING THIS SENTENCE. THAT JELLY IS IN YOU NOW. IT'S ON ITS WAY TO YOUR BRAIN, AND WHEN IT GETS THERE . . .

MAPS SCORE: 62

228

You duck under the rope. The wind happily grabs your arm and escorts you away from the security of the rope path. You stumble through loose snow, and the darkness in front of you starts to solidify. Your heart beats faster, which is good because—*holy shit!*—it is cold out here.

The wind tries tug you in a different direction. You ignore it, because you know it is flowing around the structure in front of you. You actually want to get to that building. You keep moving forward, your hands outstretched.

But—hold on! You stop yourself before you actually touch the building. If it is metal, you're going to stick to it and that's not going to be good.

The wind drops to a growl, and you can hear your breathing now. Your breath is a heavy cloud in front of your face. You trail along the edge of the structure for a moment and nearly brain yourself on the edge of the satellite dish. You've found it!

Now you need to find the access panel. Let's hope there is some kind of windbreak around it. Otherwise . . .

It's a little late to be worrying about that, the Old Man snaps. *Keep moving You don't have much time left.*

You stagger around the satellit dish without touching it. You sense a textural change in the darkness and you slow down. There's something blocky about the dish right here. You think you've found the access point.

There's no windbreak, unfortunately, so you'll have to work quickly, even as your blood starts freezing solid in your veins.

You tug your sleeves down to cover your fingers, and using this makeshift mitten, you tug at the latch on the hatch. For a moment, you fear it is frozen shut and that you've just wasted your life, but with a snap, it pops open. You haul the hatch up.

Inside is a narrow bay; at the back, there is a small viewscreen and a narrow keyboard. You paw the keyboard, and the viewscreen lights up. The system takes an interminable amount of time to register your input, but it eventually puts up a cursor.

You struggle to recall the emergency codes. Everything is starting to slow down. The cloud of warm air you exhale hangs heavily in front of you, and you feel like you need to paw through it in order to see the screen.

Your fingers are so heavy. It takes a lot of effort to move them across the keyboard. You're not even sure if you are writing the correct codes.

Something groans overhead, and you fall to your knees as the heavy satellite dish sweeps past. You've done something right!

You lean against the box, and you can feel the cold bite of the metal through the too-thin fabric of your clothing.

Focus, the Old Man urges. *One more line.*

The wind creaks and moans against the dish. You hear something that isn't the wind.

You're not alone out here.

Quickly, the Old Man snaps, pulling you out of the daze you had fallen into. *Finish sending the code!*

You make your fingers move.

Your shoulder is stuck to the edge of the box. You're going to lose skin when you pull away. *It's just a flesh wound,* you think, trying to force your fingers to finish typing. *Keep working . . .*

The viewscreen blinks and goes dark. You stare dumbly at it. What happened? Did the cold kill the system? Did your message get out?

It doesn't matter now, the Old Man says.

You nod. He's right. You're going to freeze to death before any response arrives. And . . .

You hear something that is definitely not the wind.

You find enough strength to smile. *Come on,* you think. *Come on . . .*

IT'S A MIXTURE OF BAD NEWS, GOOD NEWS, AND SAD NEWS.

THE BAD: THERE IS SOMETHING OUT HERE WITH YOU, AND YES, IT IS GOING TO GNAW ON YOUR FROZEN CORPSE. BITS OF YOU WILL TAKE A WHILE TO THAW BEFORE ACTUALLY BEING DIGESTED.

THE GOOD: YOUR MESSAGE DID GET OUT. WHILE YOU ARE BEING THAWED AND DIGESTED, HEAVY BATTERY IS GOING TO BRING THE THUNDER AND BURN THE ENTIRE SITE.

THE SAD: YOU'RE GOING TO MISS THE FIREWORKS, BUT AT LEAST IT'S A SPECTACULAR SEND-OFF.

THE NIGHT OFFICE APPRECIATES YOUR SACRIFICE.

MAPS SCORE: 74

229

The chemical locker is filled with a number of industrial compounds. Each one is labeled neatly, and they all have lots of warning labels. You root around in the locker, trying to recall some of the things you heard about during your rebellious days at the university. Most of the recipes require a still or take several hours to mix properly. You don't have the time or the equipment, so you'll have to settle for something that is prepackaged.

You find a bottle of strong acid. You find some test tubes with strong stoppers. It takes a minute or two to find a funnel that won't melt when you pour the acid. When you are finished, you have four flasks of acid. You wrap some tape around the stoppers—just in case—and put them in the inner right front pocket of your coat.

Don't forget they are there.

Actually, you have an idea where this acid might be handy.
Go to 191.

Otherwise, if you're just acquiring useful tools and don't have an immediate plan for the acid, return to the mission. It'll come in handy later, right?
Go to 195.

230

"I need to ask about one more person," you say. "There was another one who came with me. He wasn't like the mean guy. He was quieter. Probably muttered a lot. His name is Sagalico. Do you remember him?"

The desk lurker mutters to themselves for awhile. You try not to figure. You need to know, don't you?

"Yeah, yeah." Their voice finally perks up a little. "Yeah. I remember that one. He had the—the *eyes*. Like he saw through things."

"That's the one," you say.

The lurker waves you closer, and even though you're not sure it's a good idea, you crouch and lean under the desk.

"Let me tell you a story," the lurker says.

It takes a while, because this poor bastard's brain has been scrambled pretty well by trauma and caffeine and who knows what else. But the story does come out.

This guy's name is Nash, and he works in the Geology division. He doesn't know why Endoluvion bought the site, but he and a guy named Talmach were plucked from sweet jobs in the Boston branch to manage the core sampling program at MacReady Station. Talmach had a degree in climatological modeling or something like that. The pair were looking for climate and geological anomalies in the core samples.

It was a lot of drilling and sample gathering and data analysis. Pretty boring stuff. For the first few months, Talmach kept up a constant stream of bitching about how the job position was a career-killer. Nash didn't mind, and you figure he was getting away from some situation in Boston. As a result, he paid more attention to the work than Talmach, who was constantly writing emails to management back home.

Six weeks ago, they pulled a core sample that wasn't like the others—it wasn't like anything either of them had seen before, in fact. Nash wanted to file a preliminary report right away, but Talmach talked him out of it. *We don't even know what we've found,* he told Nash. *Shouldn't we do a field analysis first before we tell management? Because if it's nothing, then we're going to look like real idiots.*

He had a point, but Nash suspected that Talmach was secretly planning on selling the data to some other party. This was going to be his way of telling Endoluvion off for posting him here as well as landing himself a better deal somewhere else.

They argued. A lot. Elkhorn locked them both out of their workstations in an effort to get them to cool off. And then Talmach disappeared.

"What do you mean?" you ask.

Nash fumbles with his fingers. "He was just gone, man," he whines. "Like he went out for a beer and didn't come back."

No one goes out for a beer down here on the Antarctic Plateau, but you don't press the point. You suspect Nash knows this too.

In fact, you suspect Nash might had done something terrible to Talmach. The interesting question is: Why? What pushed this guy over the edge?

What indeed? the Old Man sighs. He's heard stories like this before. *Someone's been whispering to him.*

"When did you start hearing . . . when did the voices start?" you ask.

Nash flinches. He tries to get away from you, but there's nowhere he can go. "I didn't do nothing," he whines. "He had the knife. He tried—"

"Who had the knife?" you ask.

Nash starts to thrash and you back out from under the desk. Nash growls and hisses; his face contorts and drool flecks his lips. He buries his head in his heads, and his feet go *scrape-scrape-scrape* against the floor. After a moment, they stop their frantic movement, and Nash visibly relaxes.

When he looks at you again, his eyes are a different color.

The lurker under the desk giggles. "I stabbed the cunt," he slurs. He has an accent now, and his face is different. His jaw is shoved forward, and there's a furrowed line across his forehead. "'E wanted me data. I tole him to fook off, and when 'e dinna—" The lurker makes a stabbing motion.

You take a wild guess. "Talmach?"

"Aye, whodja tink?"

You shake your head. "It doesn't matter," you say.

The lurker spasms again, banging their head against the bottom of the desk. You back up another step. The person who looks up at you isn't either of the two men you've been talking to. This face is rounder. The eyes are wide and alert.

"We're on the verge," Sagalico says. "Between indexes. One choice will tip us either way."

"What—what is happening?"

"There's no time," your Guide whispers. "You have to make the right choice. Don't—" His face contorts, and for a second, his jaw lurches forward and a storm crosses his forehead. "Don't listen to them," Sagalico moans. "Don't listen to the ones in your head either. The Voer own them all. Stay away from the rabbits. Stay—"

He jerks back under the desk, where he starts another bout of convulsions. Keeping your distnace, you peer under the desk. Sagalico, Nash, Talmach—whoever the fuck this is—is having a physio-temporal seizure. Their face stretches and contorts, as the personalities fight for control. You're not sure who is winning.

Talmach surfaces—gaining control—and he arches his back. His hands dig under his raised body, and when he lurches back down, he's got a knife in his hand. Your heart skips for a second when you realize he could have stabbed you at any time.

Talmach's eyes are crazy. He can't keep his mouth from grinning. "Got you, you bastard," he snarls. He plunges the knife into his stomach. "Got you, you fookin'—"

Nash surfaces for a second, wrestles control of the knife and stabs Talmach in the throat. "No more," he gurgles. "Shut your mouth."

Talmach comes back and—

You step away from the desk. You hear the sound of a struggle for a few moments and then it stops. Someone—whichever personality had control last—exhales one last time, and then the room is quiet.

"Damn it," you mutter.

For once, the Old Man keeps his mouth shut.

There's a door marked "HALVES."
Go to 233.

There's a door marked "QUARTERS."
Go to 236.

231

"So, what about the others?" you prompt, trying to keep Nash talking. "The rest of your crew?"

"Elkhorn's gone," Nash says. "So are Norris and Clark, because—" Nash's eyes get big. "You're a monster," he whispers.

"What about—" You struggle to recall another name. Something to get him past what happened to Norris and Clark. "What about Bennington?" you ask.

"Who?" Nash screws up his face. "You mean Bennings?"

"Yes, Bennings. What happened to Bennings?"

"She took over for Morgan. Monitoring the radio. She should be—" Nash doesn't want to think about what might have happened to Bennings. Or maybe he feels something for her. You're not sure.

"Where's Morgan?" you ask.

"I don't know," Nash says.

"This place isn't that big," you say. "How can someone disappear?"

Nash hugs himself and says something quiet. You're not sure what he said. You ask him to repeat it.

"Crew," Nash says.

"What about crew?"

"Don't go there."

"Where?"

"Quarters," Nash says.

You figure it out. He's talking about the crew quarters. You glance at the two doors that lead out of this area. "QUARTERS" and "HALVES."

"That one?" You gesture at one of the doors.

"Yeah," Nash says.

"Why shouldn't I go there?" you ask.

He looks at you with the sort of look you used to get when you were caught not paying attention to one of those interminable monologues that the young revolutionaries would give in the kitchen during a house party.

"Okay," you say. "What about the other door?"

He shakes his head violently.

"Okay. If I can't go *that* way or *that* way, should I just go back the way I came?"

"It won't make any difference," he whispers.

And now you understand why he is hiding under the desk. There's nowhere to go.

"I need to finish this," you say.

Go to the door "HALVES."
Go to 233.

Go to the door marked "QUARTERS."
Go to 236.

232

"Morgan knows more than I do," you say to your Therapeutic Personality Construct as he appears.

You've had a few head injuries, the Old Man points out.

"You're a manifestation of my head injuries," you retort. Which isn't entirely fair, because the voice in your head is a projection of a real person. He was the only one who believed in you when you were first hired by the Night Office. He was the one who kept your secrets, and who listened when you had to tell someone about the terrible things you had done. *Your heart is in the right place, kiddo,* he said to you once when you had come back from a particularly bloody mission. *It's right there in your chest.* Which is more than space jellies can claim.

I'm not right for this, you said at that time. *I can't keep doing this.*

None of us can, he said. *We're all going to die in service of some desperate—but ultimately futile—hope that we can save the world. That has to be enough, right?*

It's not. It wasn't then, and it isn't now. You want something more. You want something real, but damnit, that's asking a lot of a world that is filled with psychopaths and monsters and unbelievable atrocities that are waiting to be unleashed upon the innocent.

"What is this manuscript?" you ask the Old Man. "Was Morgan one of ours?"

I can't tell you what you don't already know, the Old Man says. *I'm just a psychic projection.*

"I think you're lying to me."

His response is to show you his teeth, which is how all animals react when they are threatened.

Whatever secrets there are in this place aren't to be found in someone's secret manuscript. You should get back to the mission.

Go to 165.

Keep reading. You're almost at the end.
Go to 252.

233

You leave the admin room and find yourself in a hall that splits almost immediately. The hallway to your left is short and terminates in a door marked "ATMOSPHERICS." The other hall is longer, and it ends in a door marked "MECHANICAL & ENGINEERING."

Go to Mechanical.
Go to 235.

Go to Atmospherics.
Go to 237.

You know . . . where in the world is the Geology lab?
Go to 239.

234

You head back through the admin area and through the door marked "QUARTERS." You find yourself in another hall, though this one has a lot more doors. You walk down the hall, noting names of the station crew: "Norris," "Blair," "Copper," "Windows," and so on. At the end of the hall, you find two doors marked with the universal male and female icons. These are the station's locker rooms.

Still no sign of a door to the Geology lab.

What are you missing?

You lean against the wall, holding your hands against your head. There's an ache in the back of your skull. It's moving into the center of your brain, and it feels like it is starting to pulse.

This is it, the Old Man sighs. *This is where they make your brain explode.*

My brain is not going to explode, you insist.
Go to 238.

He might be right.
Go to 242.

235

You go to the room marked "MECHANICAL" where the lighting is very moody. At first, you think the Endoluvion crew has a sense of humor about their work environment, but then you realize the mood stems from a variety of fungal spreads and blooms that are obscuring the lights.

It's very humid in here too. Like hothouse sort of humid. Like *What might be growing in the shadows?* sort of humid.

Tucked near a stack of sulking machinery are a pair of gelatinous sacks. They're as tall as you, but they're ovoid rather than lean and eternally stressed out. They give off a slight luminescence—a sickly yellow glow that makes your throat hurt. You peer through the semi-translucent membrane of one of the eggs. There's definitely something inside.

You let out an involuntary curse as a pale shape swims into view. It presses against the membrane and you realize it's a face. The eyes sockets are filled with a pulpy swelling and the nose is nothing more than a ragged hole.

You stagger away. Is that—that *thing* a replication of Argot? Or is actually Argot? You're not sure, and wow, you'd rather not think about it too much. You lurch over to the other sack, and soon enough, a face surfaces in it as well. You don't recognize it, but you suspect it is probably Brinkmann.

What the fuck are these things? Are the Openers being dissolved? Or is whatever alien intelligence Endoluvion summoned making new versions of these men? Like pod people. And if it is the latter—*gross and frightening*—where are the human bodies? Because they're certainly not in this room.

You examine the dizzying confusion of vines and branches contorting along the walls behind the machines. Are these feeder tubes of some kind? Your brain rebels at the thought.

If they're making replicas, they could infiltrate the Night Office, the Old Man says. You can feel him recoiling from the sacks.

They're never perfect replicas, you argue. *Space jellies can't focus long enough to pass for human.*

Nor are they smart enough to make something like this, he points out.

Crap. You're going to have to open one of these sacks. It's the only way to find out.

Actually, you're okay with not knowing. Besides, if you survive, Heavy Battery is going to burn the whole station. Surely these will be torched along with everything else. Right?

Go to 250.

Fine. You'll cut open one of the sacks. *Argot's*, you decide. It's the least you can do for him.

Go to 264.

236

You find yourself in a long corridor with lots of doors. They are all marked with names belonging to the Endoluvion crew. At the far end of the hall, you find a door that presumably leads to the common locker room area.

You don't have time to check every single crew room. You're going to have to be clever about this.

If you talked to the survivor in the admin room, **go to 240.**

If you know who died first, **go to 244.**

How about the guy who was supposedly in charge? the Old Man suggests. That means the door marked "Elkhorn."
Go to 245.

Decide to not decide. Check out the locker room.
Go to 247.

There's a door marked "Childe." Wasn't there a reason you were interested in this person?
Go to 248.

What about Palmer's room? Wasn't he chief scientist or something?
Go to 253.

237

When you enter the Atmospherics lab, you immediately realize you're in the presence of something alien. The room contains a couple of desks and computer workstations, along with a trio of white boards. Like you'd expect in a normal scientific lab. Except everything is translucent. Beneath, behind, inside of—whatever—all the furnishings of the room, there is a boiling sea. Floating above the surface is something with wings. It sort of looks like a deranged butterfly with lots of tentacles, as well as long proboscis ends in a tiny sucking mouth.

It isn't *here*, but it also *is*. It's flickering in and out of this index. You can feel it tickling your mind.

Beyond the tentacled space butterfly, there are clouds that roil and boil with endless gyrations. More of these things are in those clouds. They want to come out, but they can't. Not until the Way is properly aligned. Not until the indexes merge once more.

You know these things, because this floater—a Voerdamnikenari, you realize—is putting ideas in your head. It doesn't have a voice, but that doesn't mean it can't communicate with you. You're having emotional reactions to non-existent stimuli.

This is it, you think. *I've found it.*

The Voerdamnikenari wishes for you to die of a decided lack of physical pleasure, which is an odd thing to wish on anyone. Though to be fair, it's not unlike the last six months of trying to meet someone, so . . .

They're still trying to understand the human psyche, the Old Man whispers. He's standing as far away from the butterfly creature as he possible can. The only thing preventing him from leaving the room entirely is the fact that he can't leave your skull.

I'm not running, you tell him. *And neither are you.*

As a Therapeutic Personality Construct, he's a reflection of your own fears and apprehensions, and so when you tell him to get his shit together and stand his ground, you're also telling yourself.

I'm not running.

You should envelope a spiky fruit rind with the narrow breathing tube in your spindly flesh sack and let it perforate your fluid pump, the Voerdamnikenari suggests.

I'll do the stabbing, you think. You have the knife, after all. **Go to 267.**

Whatever, Mothra, you think.
Mothra isn't a butter—
"Shut up," you tell the Old Man.
Go to 281.

238

What was that mantra they taught you in that self-defense class? Something like "Watch-Wait-Wonder"? Or was it "Wonder-Wait-Watch?"

Does it really matter?

No, it probably doesn't. The trick is to have a strong level of self-confidence and a sterling sense of what's up and what's good. They—whoever they are!—can't hurt you if you can resist panicking about if gravity is going to disappear, or if radio waves are baking your brain, or if all of our political leaders are mouse-eating lizards.

Wait. What's this?

Your nose is bleeding.

This is— you think. *This is how it happens—*

And then everything goes away.

FOR THE RECORD, YOUR BRAIN HAS BEEN UNDER CONSTANT ASSAULT FOR MORE THAN TWENTY-FOUR HOURS. IT'S AMAZING YOU MADE IT THIS FAR.

MAPS SCORE: 70

239

You remember a map posted near the front of the research substation. There was a note about an area reserved for geological science. It had a little icon shaped like . . .

Why is it so hard to remember things?

Something happened before. Something that put you in that bed in the infirmary. It wasn't just the physical attack. There was something else. Something that damaged your . . .

You find yourself fumbling for the right word.

They're in your head, the Old Man whispers.

He's in your head too, but as your Therapeutic Personality Construct—a voice you invented to help you stay sane—he's supposed to be there. You know you can ignore him when necessary, but . . . what if he's right?

And if that's the case, then . . .

During Orientation and Inoculation, you are warned about psychic suggestion, mental coercion, and brain domination. There's even a weekend seminar called "Building Your Psychic Defenses," which isn't requierd, but everyone in your intake group all showed up for it, didn't they? And there was that mission out by Lake Erie where a space jelly tried to tickle your cortex.

Which is to say that, yes, you would know if something was devouring your brain.

And yet . . .

The Old Man whispers once again: *They're in your head.*

Focus. Ask the question. Find the answer.

Where's the Geology lab?

Maybe you have to go through the crew area.

Go to 234.

Don't get distracted. Keep on toward Mechanical.
Go to 235.

What if they—the ones in your head—are trying to keep you from seeing what is right in front of you?
Go to 241.

240

You go into Nash's room. It's exactly the sort of haphazard disaster you'd expect from a scientist who is more excited about rocks than people. The books on the shelves look like they'll provide an answer to any question you might have about rocks, dirt, and geological strata.

On the desk is a picture of a young woman wearing one of the MacReady Station jackets. You're usually pretty good with faces, and the fact that you know you know her but can't remember her name bothers you.

It's not that you don't remember her name, the Old Man says, *it's that you can't recognize faces anymore.*

That's a puzzling observation. *Why can't I recognize faces?*

The Old Man gives you a *It's about as obvious as the nose on your face* sort of look.

"It's my short-term memory, isn't it?" you say. "It's part of what's been taken from me."

That's part of it, the Old Man says.

"And the other part?"

Oh, it's probably best to not worry about that too much, he says.

Well, now you're going to do nothing *but* worry about it.

As you're leaving Nash's room, the name of the woman in the picture comes to you. "That's Dr. Nakamura," you say proudly, delighted that this little detail has come back to you. Your brain isn't totally broken.

Check out another crew room.
Go to 236.

Visit the locker room.
Go to 247.

241

How can you see without using your eyes?

Oooh! I love rhetorical riddles, the Old Man chortles.

You ignore him. How are you going to remember something that an intelligence lurking in your brain doesn't want you to find. You can't trick yourself. You can't accidentally stumble upon something you're being nudged away from.

"Maybe I should close my eyes and tap my heels together three times," you mutter. "'There's no place like home. There's no place like home.'"

Good luck with that, the Old Man says. *You're nearly 14,000 kilometers from Kansas.*

It's a ritual, you coot, you think. A visualization technique. Something to focus your mind without appearing to be focused.

Maybe a mirror would help?
Go to 243.

Ah, rituals. Now you're talking old school stuff.
Go to 249.

242

The trouble with mind devourers is that they don't have to be in physical contact with you in order to get their snack on. You can keep them out with a psychic shield, but if they've got a tap on your mind, your only recourse is to find their physical body.

You found it once before, the Old Man reminds you. *That's when you were attacked. That's when everyone died. You know where it is. You just don't want to remember because you don't want to deal with what you did.*

I didn't do anything, you protest.

Are you sure? the Old Man asks.

You're not.

You wander around for a bit and find yourself in the section of the station with the crew quarters. *One of these rooms,* you think. *There must be a clue.*

What doesn't belong? the Old Man suggests.

You close one eye and squint. Nothing *seems* any different.

How about the one marked "Blair"?
Go to 244.

Try the one marked "Elkhorn."
Go to 245.

Or maybe it's the one marked "Palmer"?
Go to 253.

243

Where are you going to find a mirror in this place?

Where do people like to look at themselves? The Old Man asks.

Their own rooms, you think.

You head over to the section of the station where the crew quarters are. You hesitate when you find the hall full of doors. There are a lot of them, and while any one of them will probably do if all you are looking for is a mirror, you wait for the Old Man to offer some suggestion.

He's suddenly absent from your head. You're on your own for the moment.

What about a locker room? The station probably has some kind of shared bathroom space.

Go to 247.

How about the room marked "Childe"?

Go to 248.

Or this one over here. Palmer's room.

Go to 253.

244

The door to Blair's room is locked.

If you were an Opener, this wouldn't be a problem, but since you aren't, you'll have to do something a little trickier.

The door has a keycard reader. What was that spell for confounding electronics? You root around in your pockets for a moment—ah, yes, here we go: a Sharpie and a restaurant pack of yellow mustard. You draw a sigil on the reader's screen with the Sharpie and activate it with a smear of mustard (the preservatives alone are some very strange science, after all). This'll turn the reader inside out.

Sure enough, after a moment, the reader emits a dismal beep and the light turns green.

You carefully crack the door a little. Enough for a tendril or a stench to slither out. And *whoof!* That's a foul smell. Your stomach rises in your throat, and you slam the door shut forcefully.

A second later, the door shakes in its frame as something inside the room lurches against it.

You lick your thumb and smear the mustard sigil on the reader. The keycard reader wakes from its daze, and the status light turns red. The door lock engages with a clunk.

The door shudders a second time. The lock won't hold.

You write a quick Ward of Closure along the doorframe. While that takes, you find the sachet of dried herbs and a disposable lighter in your coat pockets. You say the ritual words as you flick the lighter and summon a flame. The cheesecloth baggie takes the flame, and as the herbs start to smoke, you slam the whole flaming sack of aromatic herbs against the door.

The Ward flashes, and on the other side of the door, something howls. It hammers at the door, but your work is solid.

The door remains Closed.

It would have been nice to get a look inside Blair's room, but not with the rotting corpse blighter in there. By the time they smell that bad, there's nothing left of the human they once were. All you can do is lock up in an airtight container and let them husk themselves.

You look at the other crew doors. How many of them are going to contain reanimated corpses?

Too many, you think. Check out the locker room instead.
Go to 247.

Who isn't accounted for?
Go to 248.

245

The door to Elkhorn's room has been Closed. You can feel Peele's signature in the vibration of the metal. Whatever is inside this room is meant to stay there, and you don't see any reason to doubt Peele's intent.

What scared Peele so badly that they went as far away as they could get in the station after Closing this door?

That's a thought you don't want to dwell on. Better keep moving.

Enough with the crew rooms. Go find the mechanical area. That's where the bad things are.

Go to 233.

No, there's something here. You know it. You need to find one more clue.

Go to 236.

246

He shows you his teeth. They're stained black, and you can't imagine how they got that way.

Well, okay. Yes, you can imagine.

He springs off the bed, but you weren't kidding about being ready. As he comes through the door, you smack him right across the face with your discipline stick. Blood gushes. He tries to grab you, but you crack him on the knuckles with a back-handed swing.

He hisses and moans as you shove him back into the room and slam the door. Before he react, you knock three times on the panel with your stick and tell the whispering spirit who answers your call they need to seal this door. There is a whistling noise—like air escaping into a vacuum—and then it stops.

As you watch, the outline of the door starts to vanish. In a few seconds, all that remains of the door to Childe's room is a fading shadow.

Well, that was somewhat satisfying, the Old Man says.

A little, you concede.

It would have been nice to get some information—

Don't push it, you warn him.

All the crew rooms might be like this. Check out the maintenance area instead.

Go to 233.

So much for that room. How about another one?

Go to 236.

Check out the locker room.

Go to 247.

247

You enter the locker room area of MacReady Station. There are a row of metal lockers on your left. In the back are individual shower stalls, as well as several toilets stalls. It's utilitarian and functional.

You wander over to a nearby sink and check the water. The cold is really cold, and the hot water takes a few seconds to warm up. You look at the reflection in the mirror. Considering how harrowing the last few days have been, you don't look too bad.

You take a moment to clean your hands and check the bandage on your arm. It's not bleeding, which is a good sign. The pain is manageable too. All in all, it could be a lot worse.

Check the stalls.
Go to 251.

Check the other mirrors. Something might be lurking on an orthogonal vector. Out of sight, but still in this index.
Go to 254.

248

Childe's room is like the other rooms: there's a bed, a desk, a dresser, and a bookcase. Though, in this room, there's someone sitting on the end of the bed.

He doesn't look up, but you know he's aware of you.

You stay in the hall. Your discipline stick is ready.

Slowly, his head comes up, revealing that his eyes have been gouged out of his head. He sniffs noticeably, tracking the stick in your hand. "I can smell you," he whispers. His voice sounds like he has been gargling antifreeze and ice shards. "I've tasted you already, haven't I?"

"I suppose I am." You try not to touch the bandage on your arm.

"You were tasty," he says. He moves his head from side to side, like a snake. One of the sleeves of his uniform is dark with dried blood, and there's a bloody track down his front as well. "What's your name?" you ask, even though his name is on the door.

(Who do you think he is?)

"You're bright," he says. "You're one of those lights they said were coming."

"Who said?"

He inclines his head like he is listening to something. Not you. Something else.

"Are you ready?" he asks.

"I was born ready," you say.
Go to 246.

"Well, I do have a few questions," you say.
Go to 257.

249

There is a ritual for driving out alien influences, but it's not easy. It also requires a knife. And, well, you know how you are about knives. You try not to have them around. Too many mistakes happen with knives.

I'll be careful this time, you think as you look for a blade in your coat pockets.

You stop yourself. You don't have a knife in your coat. What were you thinking?

Your hand closes around something unexpected in your right front pocket. *Is this . . . ?*

Take the object out of your pocket. You know you want to.
Go to 144.

Leave it, you think. *This isn't the way. Not now. Keep moving.*

These thoughts don't stop your hand from caressing the object in your pocket.

It's there, you think. *Just in case . . .*

You know what is happening. You can be ready for this. You took the classes. You know what to do.
Go to 235.

250

Whatever this fungal material is, it isn't going to burn easier. It's too—you try to keep your gorge down—it's too *moist*.

Still, you must have something in your coat that will take care of these sacks.

If you made a concoction in the Organic Chemistry lab, **go to 263.**

Otherwise, **go to 266.**

251

You check the toilet stalls first. Two of them are empty. There's some graffiti in the first one. It's about as sophomoric as you'd expect. Some things never change.

The third stall is locked.

Ignore it and check on the shower stalls.
Go to 255.

Now, why would a toilet stall be locked?
Go to 260.

252

You turn to the last page of manuscript. There's nothing there but an ASCII image of an eye with tentacle stalks floating off it.

You hurl the manuscript away with a curse. You quickly recite Hogart's Litany Against Villainy three times, hoping to get ahead of the evil eye's influence. The fingers of your left hand cramp, and you feel the muscles in your neck pulse unnaturally. But—slowly, eventually—your fingers uncurl and your pulse stops threading like your blood is turning into quicksand.

"This whole mission's a trap," you rail at the Old Man. "Whatever this thing is, it's been here for decades. Influencing people. Plotting. Prying its way into this existence."

You have to stop it, the Old Man says. *You have to do the right thing. Not like—*

"Not like what?"

Your predecessors.

"The other team?"

He inclines his head, as if to say that you aren't entirely wrong, but you are still missing something.

"The other version of me," you say. You look at the bandage on your arm. "I made the wrong choice before, didn't I?"

No one ever gets a second chance in this job, he notes. *Don't waste it.*

If you need to take that chance, **return to the WHITE ROOM.**

If you are confident that you're on the right path, **go to 165.**

253

You step into Palmer's room. Its aesthetic screams "I am a very important scientist." You rifle through his underwear drawer and discover that, like most academic assholes, he's cheap under that shiny facade. The bookcase is devoted to books he's written, and your brain ties itself into a knot as you parse the titles of a few of the books.

You find is a scientific notebook in the drawer of his desk. It's the same type of notebook as ones you've seen elsewhere in the station, but this one isn't marked like the others. Palmer has been using it for something he doesn't want to share with the other kids.

It's always like this, isn't it? Some egghead gets tempted by sexy whispers from outside of time and space. He's something special, isn't it? He's the *One*, and the One has a special mission. Something orthogonal to what everyone else is doing. *I'll show them*, he thinks. *I'm going to change the world!*.

You remember the time in New Jersey where the "mad" scientist actually wrote his maniacal laughter out in his journal. *Mwuhahahahahaha! I will rule the world.* What an idiot.

Anway, Palmer's not *that* much of an asshole. Opinionated, sure, but what PhD isn't?

Blair, for example. "He's like the farmyard dog that can't see, can barely walk, and pisses itself more often than not," Palmer writes. "But everyone has fond memories of the ole dog, and so out of kindness and a glazed nostalgia, they don't put the fucking animal out of its misery."

Palmer's a real peach, isn't he?

Palmer is coy about specifics, but you've read enough crazy toad-licking cult journals to read between the lines. They found something in the ice and Palmer exposed Blair to it. While everyone else was wringing their hands and wondering what the hell happened, Palmer was taking notes.

They're not Shoggoths, the Old Man notes. You feel like he is reading over your shoulder. *This is too . . .*

"Subtle," you murmur.

Obviously, Palmer was already a narcissistic donkey's ass, so he didn't need much of a push, but whatever is doing the pushing has a light touch.

Garry was next, but according to Palmer's notes, the electrical engineer wasn't as much of a push-over as Blair. Garry needed to be *convinced*, in Palmer's words.

You reach for your discipline stick, thinking you'd be happy to share some *convincing* with Palmer.

You flip to the back of the journal, hoping to get a preview of how this horror show ends. Oh, look. Palmer has second thoughts. The last page is a rambling apology where Palmer, frantically tries to warn anyone who might find his journal. "I have done something terrible," he writes. "I may have encouraged the end of humanity as we know it."

Encouraged. What a word.

"They will try to hold me accountable for what I have done, but it was not me."

Here it comes, you think.

"I was under the influence of another," Palmer continues. "An intelligence that does not care about morality or ethics. I thought I was doing good work. That I was bettering humanity, but I was wrong. I was a fool. Forgive me."

Boo hoo. It's not my fault. I wasn't smart enough to know how stupid I was being.

You check under the bed, wondering if he crawled under there and cried himself to death.

No such luck.

Anyway, you'll take the journal with you. It'll go in your report. Just another example of the hubris of self-absorbed academics who think they've discovered a real secret of the universe.

They're all so late to the party.

As you start to leave the room, the Old Man clears his throat. *Aren't you forgetting something?*

"What is it this time?"

What do you know? the Old Man asks. *Forget everything else What do you* truly *know?*

"I—I've been here before," you say. "Time is elastic, in some fashion. Or it loops. I don't know." You look at Palmer's journal, thinking about his hubris. About your own. "But, what I do know is that I've likely done something terrible."

But you can't remember what it is, he says.

"I can't," you say.

Because if you do remember, you'll . . . what will you do?

It's a simple question, and surprisingly, it gives you pause. You already suspect the worst, but if it has already happened, then why are you still wandering around? Why do you feel like you've got a second chance?

That's a harder question to answer, isn't it? the Old Man notes.

"They're not free yet," you realize. Whatever is lurking in the station can't get out. There's something . . . *unfinished.* That's why you can't remember what happened. They don't want you to know, because if you did, you might do something different.

They're hiding in your brain, the Old Man says. *Waiting. They don't control you—not yet. But they can influence you. They can nudge you toward their solution.*

You sit back down and page through Palmer's journal again. What was it you had said? *Subtle.* Yes, that's it. Little pushes here and there. It takes you a few minutes, but you finally notice the way Palmer hides his true revelations within his notes.

I can only see them when I'm not looking at them, Palmer writes. *At first, I thought they were an occlusion in my eye, but when I use a mirror, I can see past the haze. I can see what is manipulating me. You can't look directly at them.*

A mirror, you think. *Where can you find a mirror?*

One of the other crew rooms, perhaps?
Go to 236.

Maybe in the locker room.
Go to 247.

254

There are three vanity sinks in the locker area at MacReady station, and above each sink is a mirror. You stand in front of the leftmost mirror and see yourself head-on, and in the other mirrors, you see yourself in profile.

You move over to the center mirror and look again. Yep. Still one face looking at you and an image on either side, each in profile. The one on the left looks more haggard, but who's keeping track.

You step over the third mirror. One image staring at you. One on the left, in partial profile. And on the right . . . oh, what's this? There's an odd shimmer around the figure in the mirror.

The angle isn't quite right, and it takes a few tries to see the break in reality. *Yes*, you think, *there we go.*

At an oblique angle, you can see two toilet stalls in the right-most mirror. In the other mirrors, there are three stalls.

One of them isn't entirely in this index.

You walk over to the three stalls. The one that isn't in the righthand mirror is locked.

Of course it is, you think.

Kick it down.
Go to 258.

Look. Understandably, you've got a bit of pent-up aggression, but show a little more finesse, would you?
Go to 260.

255

You check the shower stalls in the locker area. There are strange stains around the drain in one of them.

Cautiously, you peer at the stains, hoping that something isn't going to come boiling out of the pipe.

Nothing jumps out at you.

There's a reddish tinge to the stain. Not quite like blood. But definitely some kind of foreign material.

Leave it alone. It could be spagetti sauce, for all you know. Or vomit.

Check out the mechanical rooms.

Go to 233.

It's nothing. Just some residual hard water stain or something. You should check out the crew rooms.

Go to 236.

If you concocted something useful in the chemistry locker—something that'll clear a pipe—**go to 259.**

256

You flip back to the start of the manuscript and discover the page is blank. You check the other pages. They're all blank. "There is no manuscript," you say. "This is all in my head."

Well, Morgan did imagine themselves a bit of a writer, but they never got past the prologue, the Old Man says.

"So, what? I just invented all of this?"

No, you remembered it, the Old Man said. *This is a confluence of indexes. Peele and Sagalico tangled the Way. There are too many possibilities open right now. Too many versions of what might happen. They're all waiting.*

"Waiting for what?"

Waiting for you to
(Find the rabbits)
touch the obelisk.

"But I'm not supposed to touch it," you say. You look at the floating figure of the Old Man. "If I touch it, I complete the ritual. I let them in. That's why I'm—"

He limps away, staying out of reach. *That's not allowed,* he says.

"You're my Therapeutic Personality Construct," you remind him. "I'm the one who makes the rules."

No, he says. *There are other rules. Rules you need to follow. You have an important task to do yet. You have to*
(Use the knife)
Close the link.

"You're lying to me," you say.

I can't lie to you, he argues. *I'm your subconscious.*

"I lie to myself all the time," you point out. "We all do. That's how we survive this job."

That confuses him and he hesitates.

It's all you need.

You grab at his elbow, and as your fingers brush the fabric of his suit, he dissolves into a fog of stars.

You wave the manuscript to clear the air of this infected version of your Therapeutic Personality Construct. When he is gone, all that remains is a single line of text on the top page of the sheath of papers you have in your hand.

I was murdered.

THIS IS UNSETTLING AND UNEXPECTED. YOU SHOULD KEEP THIS REVELATION TO YOURSELF.

FINISH THIS MISSION. YOU HAVE TO MAKE IT BACK. SOMEONE HAS TO SAVE THE NIGHT OFFICE FROM ITSELF.

Go to 165.

257

Childe starts to get off the bed, but you cluck your tongue and jab your discipline stick in his direction. He pulls back his lips, showing his teeth. It's a very feral expression—one you don't see on a human face all that often.

"We're going to talk a bit more first," you say.

Childe hisses and clicks, talking in a language you don't know.

"English," you say. You snap your fingers near the end of your stick, and Childe recoils from the psychic sparks that come off your stick.

"That will not save you," Childe says.

"It's not the only trick I know," you say.

He pouts, but he makes no further attempt to get up.

"What happened to Gull?" you ask.

"That one saw us," he says. "That one tried to tell the others. We could not allow that."

"And me? Is that why you tried to kill me?"

"You are bright. You are tasty." He smacks his lips. "We are very hungry."

"Where are the others?"

"The others? There are no others? There is only us."

"What do you want?"

Childe laughs. You don't blame him. It wasn't a very clever question. What does any alien intelligence that take over a human mind and posses a human body want?

"How you do roast a chicken?" you ask.

Childe frowns. The creature inhabiting his mind doesn't understand the non-sequitor.

You aren't interested in talking about home cooking anyway. As Childe is distracted, you jab the end of your discipline stick at his face. You're already activating stick's liminal declaration.

The iron shavings spark and burn. Childe shrieks when the stick touches his possessed flesh. You turn the jab into one of the simpler strike forms—head, shoulder, head, arm, kneecap.

Childe flails around on the bed. The sleeve of his shirt is on fire, and as he thrashes about, the fire spreads. He starts shrieking—a sound you'd like to forget, but probably never will. You retreat to the door of the room.

Whatever is inhabiting Childe forces itself itself forward, taking control of the body's motor functions. Childe rises to a kneeling position. The bed's on fire. He's on fire. The scene looks like something from a late-night cable horror film.

The sprinkler system engages, and the room is suddenly full of smoke and shrieking.

That's your cue to leave. You shut the door behind you, and start writing Wards along the edge of frame. Steam is curling off the panel as you finish, and you press the hot end of your discipline stick against the metal. Your Wards engage as you say the activation word, and your writing crackles with mystic energy.

One more down.

Check out another room.
Go to 236.

Head for the lockers at the end of the hall. See if you can wash some of this stink off.
Go to 247.

258

You've do have a lot of pent-up aggression. *I can't imagine why,* the Old Man whispers.

"Shut up, you bastard," you snarl as you haul off and kick the toilet stall door as hard as you can. You're imagining that someone is sitting inside, aren't you? Not necessarily the Old Man, though he certainly left rather unexpectedly. No, you're thinking of someone else. Your father? Maybe, but it's been a really long time and summoning anger for him is just exhausting anymore, honestly. Some other figure in your life, then. Whoever it is, you imagine them on the toilet, their pants down around their ankles, their face pushed forward as they wonder what all the fuss is about. The stall door is going to smack this person hard in the face, and wow, you're going to enjoy that moment, aren't you?

The locking mechanism breaks off with a sharp *ping!* The door flies inward. For a moment, you think you see something there, squatting on top of the closed toilet, their face alight with horrible glee, but they vanish—along the toilet—as the back of the toilet is torn away by a vast, sucking vortex of emptiness.

Oh, fuck. It's the Abyss.

Don't look at it! the Old Man shouts.

You're not! You know better.
Go to 262.

Is it? Or is this another Voerdamnikenari trick?
Go to 265.

259

You take out one of the stoppered test tubes from the inner pocket of your coat. You pry off the tape and open the test tube. Keeping as far away from the drain as possible, you pour the acid out of the tube. It sizzles as it swirls around the drain, and you swear some of the stain on the floor twitches and tries to get away from the acid. But no, it's merely dissolving and sliding down the drain.

You wait for a minute, watching a curl of acrid smoke rise from the drain. When the smoke stops, you reach over and turn on the hot water and let it run for while. When you shut the water off, you hear a distant crackling, like someone is popping packing material.

There's a right way and a wrong way to dispose of necrotic and diseased flesh, the Old Man says.

"Amen," you say.

This is why it's always better to call the Night Office than to try to dispose of space fungi by yourself.

You do another sweep of the locker room and don't find any other sign of intrusion. You leave, making sure the door is Closed behind you. Just in case.

Backtrack to the admin room and check out the mechanical rooms.
Go to 233.

Investigate the crew quarters.
Go to 236.

260

You step into the stall next to the locked stall. You climb onto the toilet tank so that nothing can reach under the wall and grab your foot. Balancing there, you fumble through your pockets for some kind of noisemaker. You find one of those wind-up monkeys with tiny cymbals.

You wind the monkey up and toss it over the stall wall. It starts bashing away at the cymbals, making an annoying racket. You expect it to hit something—the toilet, a tentacled monstrosity perched on the toilet—but the monkey falls to the floor without impediment. It spins sideways, its racket slowing down, and then finally, its tiny motor gives out with a sad little "zzzzzt."

And then it's all quiet in the locker room.

You tell the Old Man to count to thirty in your head, and he obliges. He resorts to his fingers for the last six as he's busy refilling his highball glass with Scotch and apparently can't count out loud and pour booze at the same time. He gives you a thumbs-up as he raises the glass to his lips.

You stand up and peer over the wall. The stall is empty. There are attachments and a hole in the floor where you'd expect a toilet to go, but there's no actual toilet.

What there is, however, is a large hole in the wall.

The air coming out of the hole is cold, and there's a rime of frost at the edges of the opening. It's not a dark hole. In fact, the hole is filled with white nothingness.

Like a snowstorm.

Or the curtain surrounding an infirmary bed.

Or an empty conference room.

Or the hole in your memory.

You climb over the wall and drop into the locked stall. When you crouch down and look into the hole, you see that it isn't very deep. There's a larger space not too far back. It's even whiter than the light coming out of the hole.

Are you going to go into the hole?

Yes. Unfortunately.
Go to 268.

Fuck no.
Go to 269.

261

A short access hall connects Mechanical with Engineering, and the lights flicker ominously as you reach the door to Engineering. You go through the door without hesitation, because there's nothing behind you but foul smoke and melting fungal growths, after all).

You find yourself in a spartan industrial chamber. There are a trio of hulking generators, a wealth of pipes and conduits, and a pair of bodies.

You recognize both of them, and when you inspect them more closely, you realize one of them is still alive.

Sagalico groans as you move him over to the wall. The lower half of his left arm is gone, and a leather belt is cinched tight around the stump. You slap him lightly, trying to bring him back to consciousness. Eventually, his eyelids flutter.

His eyes don't focus right away, but he does come back eventually. He looks at you with a look of eternal despair. "You," he whispers.

"Yeah, it's me."

"Have you come to gloat?" he asks.

"What would I have to gloat about?"

"You fooled all of us," he says. "You knew what was here."

"But I didn't," you protest. "I still don't. I don't know anything."

Sagalico shakes his head and the movement gives him pain. "I looked too far," he says. "I saw what Gull saw. What they did. I—I tried to shift it, but it couldn't be fixed. All I could do was make indexes." He sighes. "So many indexes. So many choices. And all of them . . ."

You don't know what he is talking about, but then again, no one knows what Guides are talking about most of the time. That's what happens when they get lost in the Way.

He coughs wetly, and there is fresh blood on his lips. "All but one," he whispers. "They all end badly. All but one."

You lean forward. "Tell me. Tell me how to make it right."

It hurts when he laughs, and his chuckle dissolves into a groan. "That's what you always say," he says.

"And I always mean it," you tell him. "I can make it right."

He puts his head back and stares up at the piping that crawls across the ceiling. For a moment, you think his gaze has become fixed, but he swallows, letting you know he is still alive.

"Here," he says. He doesn't look down as he fumbles for something in his coat pocket. A rectangular shape falls out of his hand as he loses the strength to lift it.

It's a switchblade, like the one you used to have.

"I can't," you say. "It's too risky."

You stopped carrying a blade like this a long time ago. It was too dangerous a tool to have.

"There's always a risk," Sagalico says. "That's what the Way requires of us."

Not the knife, you think. You'll find another way.
Go to 270.

You're stronger now. You won't make the same mistake again. Take the knife.
Go to 273.

262

You turn your head away before the Abyss can make see itself in your gaze. Out of the corner of your eye, you see a reflection in one of the mirrors over the sink and you realize even a reflection is enough for the Abyss to look into you. You only have a moment.

You squeeze your eyes shut. *There's no place like home*, you think fiercely. *There's no place like home.*

Do you really think that's going to work? the Old Man asks.

"Shut up," you snarl. *There's no place like home. There's no place like—*

The Abyss roars. The toilet stall shakes around you. Your grip starts to slip.

There's no place like—

A pressure wave shudders over you. You feel like you are falling. You reach for—

Go to the WHITE ROOM.

263

You retrieve one of the test tubes from a coat pocket. You tear off the tape and thumb out the stopper. Standing back, you fling the contents of the tube at the sack containing Argot's body. As the membrane of the sack crackles and bubbles, an effluvium of rotten eggs, burned human hair, and diseased festive gourds fills the room. When the acid breaches the interior, a fountain of pale green goo spurts out. The smell gets worse.

You going to watch it all night? the Old Man asks.

You shake yourself out of the stupor you've fallen into—you're not inhaling that gas, are you? Unstoppering another tube, you flick acid onto the other sack. It bubbles and smokes and gorps like the first.

The air is definitely getting thick in here. You retreat to the door.

An arm flops out of the sack containing Argot. The flesh bubbles and blisters. Whatever it is, it doesn't like the air in this room.

You've seen enough. You don't need to watch these fungal growth dissolve. They aren't going to survive.

You're about to leave when you notice a door on the far side of the room. That must lead to Engineering. However, you're going to need to hold your breath if you make a run for it.

You're not going to risk it. Head to Atmospherics instead.
Go to 237.

You'll take that chance.
Go to 261.

264

You need something sharp to pierce the skin of that fungal sack. You rummage around in your pockets and don't find a knife.

(Where's the knife?)

Which is odd because you are pretty sure you packed one. What sort of Closer doesn't carry a knife as part of their standard gear?

No matter. You'll find something else. Like . . . ah, here we go: a screwdriver.

You jam the screwdriver into the sack containing the thing that might be Argot. A thick sap oozes when you yank the screwdriver out, and a nasty smell rises from the wound. You hold your breath and stab three more times. The third time the screwdriver sticks in something and you can't pull it out.

That'll have to do, you think.

Pale green ichor oozes from the puncture wounds. Something squirms inside the sack, and the handle of the screwdriver wiggles. You realize what the screwdriver is stuck in.

Oh, for a flamethrower, you think as you back away from the twitching and bulging sack.

You hear a wet, tearing noise. On your left, the other sack has breached. A slurry of the pale goo is all over the floor, and something slick and pink and grey is floundering in the muck. It raises its head and lets makes an almost human noise.

You telescope your discipline stick and take a swing at the slippery figure. You connect with the side of the figure's head, and the stick sinks into the tender flesh-fruit of the monster. You try to pull your stick free, but the flesh-fruit is sticky. It oozes around your stick, slithering up toward your hand. You let go before it can reach your fingers.

The sack with the screwdriver in it ruptures.

Time to go, you think.

You head for the door, bur before you can take more than two steps, something grabs the back of your calf. You stumble and fall to your hands and knees. Something hot and sticky wraps around your calf, working its way up toward your thigh.

The sack monster with your stick in its head is crawling toward you. You try to scramble away, but you can't feel your leg. The screwdriver sack monster grabs your other foot.

Oh, this isn't going to end well . . .

THEY'RE GOING TO SMOTHER YOU AND THEN DIGEST YOU. IT WILL BE SLOW AND PAINFUL. IF YOU'RE LUCKY, YOU'LL SUFFOCATE BEFORE THE WORST OF IT.

MAPS SCORE: 73

265

The Abyss inhales. You grab frantically at the toilet stall, but the walls are slick. The Abyss inhales again, and your grip slips. You are sucked into the endless void of despair that awaits everyone.

YOU ARE GOING TO BE SUCKED INTO THE ENDLESS VOID OF DESPAIR THAT AWAITS EVERYONE. THE ABYSS IS ETERNAL. THE ABYSS IS FOREVER. THE ABYSS WILL NOT BE DENIED.

MAPS SCORE: 57

266

In one of your pockets, you find an old tear gas canister. It expired four years ago, but it'll do. The efficacy of these things is much longer than the manufacturer's recommendation.

You back up to the door before you break the seal on the canister. You lob the smoking canister across the room, and it rolls between the fungal sacks.

The sacks don't like the smoke. They start quivering as the tear gas fills the room. One of the sacks bursts with a noise like a melon hitting the pavement after being dropped from the roof of a three-story building.

You bow out of the room. You don't need to see anything else.

You write a stern message on the outer door for anyone else that might come along. *Warning: Contents are Highly Toxic and Extremely Agitated.* Then, using a wedge of sealing wax, you craft one of Ghyst the Elder's Sealing Wards.

Check out the crew quarters.
Go to 236.

Time to visit Atmospherics.
Go to 237.

If you feel like you've cleared the station, **go to 277.**

267

Who are you going to stab with that knife? The Old Man asks. He's not keen on being close to the Voerdamnikenari, even though it isn't completely in this index.

"Who haven't I stabbed?" you ask.

The Old Man is silent for a minute and when you nudge him, he waves you off. *I'm still counting,* he says.

"It's not that many," you argue.

It's more than you want to admit, he says.

"It's a useful tool," you say. The knife is a comfortable fit in your hand.

On the other side of the room, the Voerdamnikenari flutters its wings, and you imagine tides changing somewhere, in some other time.

You look up and see a mirage. It's a duotone replay of some other time. You and Argot, in one of the labs. You can't hear what he's saying, but he's waving his arms and getting in your face.

(Do you remember this?)

Your hand tightens on the knife.

The voice in your head is coming from the butterfly. It's been there awhile, hasn't it? And it's been trying to convince you. Trying to get you to believe these things are true. That they are real memories.

"It didn't happen," you say.

(Are you sure?)

In the mirage, you wave Argot closer. He can't see what's in your hand.

(You know what is in your hand.)

"No," you say. "That's not what happened. You're putting things in my head."

As mirage-you stabs Argot, real-you darts forward, slashing with the knife. The duotone image separates, vanishing in a wisp of confusion and doubt. You keep slashing. The butterfly flaps. Its tentacles writhe and slap.

The knife cuts something. You feel the blade tug as it slices.

"This is what happens," you say.

You slash again and again. Tentacles come at you, and you stab them. You grab the knife with both hands and drag it through murky flesh that oozes black sap.

(Do you know what you are killing?)

Don't lose yourself, the Old Man warns. *Not now.*

You ignore both of them. The indexes have lined up. You can reach *there* from *here.* The Way will shift soon. You don't have much time.

(You're only hurting yourself.)

You ignore the voice in your head. You ignore all the voices. You know what you must do. Even when the pain starts, you keep cutting.

"You shall not pass," you tell the Voerdamnikenari. "This world is not for you."

It's right in front of you. Its tentacles are limp. Its wings are broken. Sap is oozing for many cuts. It's almost dead. You just have to cut its heart out.

- — - - - — —, the Old Man says.

"It doesn't matter," you tell him. "I am the Omega. I am the Closer. This is the end."

You stab the knife into the trunk of the butterfly monster. A terrible keening noise issues from its snout.

You let go of the knife and stumble away from the dying monster. Your mind rebels at the insubstantiality of the world around you. The lab at MacReady Station is nearly gone. It's a ghostly mirage that slips farther away the more you look at it. The thick storm behind the Voerdamnikenari is pocked with black stars that are growing larger by the second. There's nothing beyond the cloud and the mirage. Nothing but the Abyss.

I am the Closer, you think. *I am the End.*
You sit down. Or you float. Or it doesn't really matter.
You wonder how long you'll have to wait . . .

THE NIGHT OFFICE PREFERS THAT ITS FIELD OPERATIVES FIND THEIR WAY HOME AGAIN, BUT WE ALSO ADMIRE THOSE FIELD OPERATIVES WHO CAN MAKE THE HARD CHOICES.

MAPS SCORE: 88

268

You find yourself in a white room.

There's nothing here except the obelisk, which is whiter than the light it emits. It fills your head with noise and nothingness, in equal parts. When you try to look at it, you can't see it. When you don't look at it, it draws your attention. It's both emptiness and everything.

It demands obedience. It requires worship.

(blood blood blood)

It isn't very tall, but it also exists in a space that is infinite in at least one direction. It comes to a point that is so fine—so sharp—that it would pierce an angel's foot if it tried to dance on the tip.

(give it to us!)

You remember a story your aunt told you about a young girl who pricked her finger on the spindle of a spinning wheel, and thereby saved everyone in her village.

No, that's not how the story goes.

Yes, she did. She gave of herself, and everyone got to live. That's all it took. That's all it ever takes. Just a little self-sacrifice. Why do you deny your gift? Why do you not offer yourself?

WHAT IS WRONG WITH YOU, YOU LITTLE BITCH?

That—that is— "No," you whisper. "That wasn't my fault."

Your aunt knew it wasn't your fault, even as she raised the quirt and whipped you again. And again. And—

The tip of the obelisk is shining.

(Just a tiny sacrifice. That is all we require. Just a tiny prick.)

The blood ran down your back. You remember how it felt. It freed you, didn't it? The pain freed you. *Never again*, you promised yourself that night. You made a blood pact. *Never again.*

(Save everyone.)

Touch the obelisk. Feel that point of infinite nothingness. Let it pierce your finger. Give it a drop of blood.

Go to 274.

Never again, you think.

Everyone is going to die, the Old Man says. *Horribly.*

I'm not giving it anything, you insist. *I will not be broken.*

Go to 282.

269

You resist the pull of the white room. It is a hard choice, but you make it.

As you turn away from the sweet lure of nothingness, your foot twists on the plastic monkey you threw into the toilet stall. You lose your balance. Even though you throw out your hands to stop yourself, you hit your head on the floor.

Everything goes black, and then white.

It's a hard whiteness. Not at all like the other one. It hurts for a moment, but that pain means you're still alive.

Go to the other WHITE ROOM.

270

You shake your head. "I'm not taking the knife," you tell Sagalico. "I have too many memories of bad things I have done with knives."

"We all do bad things," Sagalico says. "That's our job."

"I can't," you say. "If I do bad things, I'll be susceptible to coercion. I have to remain strong."

"You aren't strong," he snaps. "You screwed up. You're the reason everyone is dead. You're the reason I'm—"

You stare at him. "You're lying to me," you say.

He doesn't respond. You lean back and stare at him.

He still doesn't say anything.

You blink and step back. You draw in a long breath.

He doesn't move.

You step forward and yell in his face.

He doesn't flinch.

He continues to stare—not at you, but at some point in the near distance.

"God damn it," you mutter.

Sagalico is dead. He's been dead for awhile. This entire conversation wasn't real.

How many other conversations haven't been real? the Old Man asks.

All of them, you admit. *This whole thing has been one long fever dream.*
Go to 271.

No. The Voerdamnikenari are twisting everything. They want you to be so confused you don't know what's true.
Go to 272.

271

You want to kick something, don't you? You want to scream and wail and generally lose your temper. Go ahead. No one here will mind.

"It won't change anything," you tell yourself. It won't change what has been done. Or what hasn't been done. Oh God, this is the whole problem, isn't it? You don't know what is real and what isn't. How long have the Voerdamnikenari been in your head?

Since you got here, the Old Man says. *They've been in all of your heads.*

You think back about how your team acted. About the others—Gull and Peele. *Peele knew*, you realize. She knew what was happening. That's why she did what she did.

And Gull?

Gull knew, and she still opened the Way.

Why? you wonder. *How could she not see what was coming?*

Maybe she did, the Old Man suggests. *Maybe they both did. Her and Sagalico.*

You look at the corpse of your Guide. "You poor bastard," you say. "You knew you were going to die."

They all do, the Old Man said. *It's part of the job. Closers are the only ones who labor under the illusion that you might make it.*

"It's what makes us special," you say bitterly. "It's what makes us loved."

No one loves you, the Old Man says. *That's why you were perfect for us.*

"Yeah," you say quietly. "I am perfect."

You glance at Sagalico and the knife.

You can still do it, the Old Man whispers. *You can still cut your way out of this.*

Fine, you think. *If that's the way they want to play, I'll play.*
Go to 273.

"No," you say. "Not the knife."
Go to 275.

272

You lean against the wall near the corpses and slide down until you are sitting on the ground. You stare at Sagalico, and eventually you start talking. He's a decent listener when he's dead. Maybe you go all the way back to Hughie Daryrimple—who knows—but Sagalico never interrupts you. He lets you get it all out. All the terrible things you did before you came to the Night Office. All the even worse things you've done since you've become a Closer. He never judges.

Finally, you run out of words.

The Old Man stirs in your head. *You done?* he asks.

"Fuck you," you tell him.

He raises his glass. *You still need to save the world*, he says.

"Again," you say.

Again, he says.

"Fine." You push yourself up from the floor. "Where is this fucking thing? I'm doing chasing it."

You swear Sagalico's body twitches, but it's just a trick of the light.

Light? Where's that light coming from?

There's an opening in the wall that wasn't there a few minutes ago. Or maybe it always was, and the dread influence on your brain has kept you from seeing it.

"This is it," you whisper.

Approach the white light.
Go to 268.

Resist the lure of the light. Whatever this thing is, it likes the shadows. Stick with the shadows.
Go to 276.

273

You pry the knife out of Sagalico's stiff fingers. It's a switchblade, and it looks a lot like the one you used to have.

(Of course it does.)

You flick the button and watch the blade pop out. You push the blade back, and flick the button again.

You look down at Sagalico. He's watching you.

"I know what to do with this," you say.

You hear a door creak open, and you look back at the way you came. That door is closed.

No, not that door. The other door. The one in the back of the room. You don't know how you missed it earlier. Regardless, it's open now. It seems like the only way out of Engineering without going back through the toxic atmosphere in Mechanical.

When you go through that door, something shivers around you. *The indexes*, you think, recalling what Sagalico warned you about. *I'm in the Way. There's a nexus ahead.*

There are no lights in this hall, and you feel your way along.

You've got the knife. You're ready to use it. You're ready for—yes, you are definitely ready.

Go to 144.

You don't need the knife, but you have it. Just in case.
Go to 237.

This has been one long test of faith. Are you ready?
Go to 268.

274

You touch the obelisk.

Nothing happens.

You look at the dot of blood on your finger. It's very red. It's the only red thing in this room. Everything else is white. Everything else . . .

You hear them coming. You don't know from what direction, but you can hear them. A growling, roaring noise of a hundred—a thousand, a million!—rapacious minds and mouths.

The Way is open. They are coming. They are coming to devour the world.

You offered them blood, and they have accepted your offer. The compact is complete. The Calls have been Answered.

This world is theirs.

THE NIGHT OFFICE EXPECTS EVERYONE WILL BE DEAD OR ENSLAVED WITHIN THE NEXT SEVENTY-TWO HOURS, AND SO THERE IS NO REASON TO WASTE A LOT OF EFFORT ADMONISHING YOU ON YOUR CHOICE.

IF THE ELDRITCH HORRORS THAT ARE ABOUT TO BURST THROUGH THE VEILS OF REALITY DON'T EAT YOU, WE SUSPECT YOU'LL BE SHOT ON SIGHT IF YOU MAKE IT BACK TO THE MAINLAND.

MAPS SCORE: - 10

275

Engineering is a dead end, physically and metaphysically. You have to find a way back, but the atmosphere in Mechanical is toxic. You look around the room and discover a toolkit in the corner. It has a lightweight breathing mask in it. It won't protect you long, but it should be good enough for you to make a dash across the toxic atmosphere in Mechanical.

But where are you going after that? You still have to find the Voerdamnikenari.

Or do you? What about the obelisk?

You put the mask on and head back through Mechanical. You can feel the rubber straps of the mask sizzling and melting as you run through the toxic haze of the room. When you get back into the hall near the break room, you rip the mask off and throw it aside. It twists in on itself as you watch.

Atmospherics, you realize, spotting the sign on the nearby door. *That's where they're hiding.*

Go to 237.

The obelisk, you decide. *That's the key of the whole thing. I have to find the obelisk.*

But where is it?

Somewhere in the crew area, you think. You've checked everywhere else.

Go to 247.

276

You stagger out of Engineering, but when you get back to the mechanical room, the fumes are terrible. They make your eyes water and your throat burns. You're not sure you can make it across the room before succumbing to the noxious atmosphere.

You can't go this way. You've got to find another route.
Go to 278.

Chance it anyway. You've got to get out of here.
Go to 279.

277

You stagger back through the station, feeling like you've accomplished something. The job is done. You've taken care of the—whatever it was. Sure, a lot of the Endoluvion crew is dead, but they were dead before you showed up so that can't be laid on you.

You pass through the Umbilical and wander up the West Corridor to Ops. The door is still Closed. Peele hasn't come out.

You tap the all-clear code on the door. You wait. Peele doesn't answer. You tap it out again. Still no answer.

"What the hell . . . ?" You bang on the door, eschewing any sort of coded knock. "Come on, Peele," you shout. "I know you're in there. I've cleared the station. It's safe. We're all safe."

You rest your head against the door. You find yourself whispering the last sentence over and over again. *We're all safe.*

Peele finally knocks. You listen carefully, translating her raps and taps into Morse code.

N - O, she sends. Y - O - U - M - I - S - S - E - D - O - N - E.

"Oh come on," you shout. "Who? Who did I miss?"

Peele knocks one letter.

U.

She's not going to open the door.

You sink to the floor and lean against the wall. *Whatever,* you think. You can wait. The Night Office will send a follow-up team as soon as the weather clears. It won't be more than . . . a couple of weeks. You should be able to convince Peele by then. Or figure out a way to get inside Ops and kill her.

There can only be one report filed about this mission, after all, and it needs to be written by you. That's all that matters.

Indeed, the Old Man agrees. His face slips a bit, but he gets it back in place before he raises a glass in your honor.

You don't say anything about his "accidental" reveal. It's not surprising, really. It is the only explanation that makes sense . . .

YOUR MIND IS NOT YOUR OWN.

YOU CAN ALMOST CONVINCE YOURSELF OTHERWISE, BUT ALL OF YOUR DENIAL AND PRIVATE OBFUSCATION CAN ONLY BE SUSTAINED FOR SO LONG. EVENTUALLY, THE TRUTH WILL MAKE ITSELF KNOWN . . .

MAPS SCORE: 63

278

You retreat to Engineering.

After you're done coughing, ou investigate the rest of the room, looking for a way out. You don't find one. You've trapped yourself.

However, the knife is still in Sagalico's hand. Waiting for you to take it.

Fine. Take the knife. It's the only way out.
Go to 273.

Never. You're not giving up. There has to be another way.
Go to 280.

279

You move quickly, but each step is harder than the last. You hear strange noises like six badgers wrestling with helium balloons. You glance over, trip, and go sprawling.

You gasp for air, and if you had been standing, that would have been a terrible mistake. As it is, your lungs feel like you've inhaled a firestorm, and you start coughing. You spit something up that isn't a good color.

You have to crawl, but the door is farther away than you'd like. Your coughing gets worse. It feels like your lungs are melting, and they are burning down through your stomach and intestines.

The badger wrestling noise gets louder. There's something in here that isn't affected by the toxic atmosphere, and it is coming for you. You're going to have to crawl faster.

Another coughing attack hits, and you curl up into a fetal position, trying to keep your face as close to the floor as possible. Your body is rebelling. Every chance you get, you try to inhale more air, but it's all poison, and each breath only makes things worse.

Your vision is smeared with stinging tears. You can't make out any real details, but whatever is coming toward you has no real shape. It's a ambulatory stew, and the hissing and clawing noises you hear is the floor melting and twisting under its touch.

IMAGINE WHAT IS GOING TO HAPPEN WHEN IT TOUCHES YOUR FLESH . . .

MAPS SCORE: 56

280

You find a spot where the hard angles and metal surfaces of the industrial equipment aren't uncomfortable against your back. You sit and stare at nothing, much like Sagalico. It gets boring after awhile, but there's not much else to do.

Some time later, a machine clicks and whirs and one of the overhead lights starts to flicker. It feels like it is getting colder, but that's probably because you haven't moved recently.

You keep waiting. Eventually, it occurs to you that you may have inadvertently saved the world. If the Voerdamnikenari needed you to do something to finish opening the gate, then . . .

You laugh, disturbing the corpses.

You didn't Close the gate, but you certainly didn't Open it all the way either. That's a successful mission, right?

Later, the flickering light goes out. It's definitely colder now.

You think about taking a short nap . . .

SOMETIMES THE BEST SOLUTION IS TO REMOVE YOURSELF ENTIRELY FROM THE FIELD. IF THE MIND DEVOURERS CAN'T REACH YOUR MIND, THEN THEY STARVE. THAT'S AN ACCEPTABLE SOLUTION.

MAPS SCORE: 82

281

"So what is it going to be?" you ask the mind-devourer-masquerading-as-a-butterfly. "Are you going to eat my brain like everyone else, or . . ." You wait for it to suggest an alternative.

The butterfly's snout wiggles, and you feel a sensation like locusts chewing on your eyeballs.

"That's pleasant," you say, trying to suppress a shiver. "Is that all?"

The Voerdamnikenari suggests that you turn yourself into a fluffy dog and prepare to have your belly rubbed.

A laugh forces its way out of your chest, and the butterfly flinches at the harsh sound. "You don't know me very well, do you? You think I'm like all the other kids." You laugh again. "Oh, are you in for a surprise."

The Voerdamnikenari tries to touch your fear center and misses. They light up the part of your brain that likes donuts instead. They light it up hard. You try to stifle the yelp of delight, but you don't quite manage.

The Voerdamnikenari misinterprets this noise as a sign of its success. It tweaks your brain again, and this time, all it is saying is "Maple bar. Maple bar. Maple bar."

"You know, there's a reason the Night Office likes to hire maladjusted children who don't fit in," you say.

The butterfly's tentacles writhe. Is it fretting about how much control it has over you?

"You want me to open the gate, don't you?" you say. "That's why you let them broadcast that signal. None of them were strong enough. None of them understood what you needed. All you could convince them to do was send the message. First Pabodie and Lake. Then Starkweather. You were patient. You knew someone strong enough would come eventually."

The Voerdamnikenari's wings flutter. Its tentacles shake and quiver.

"But we got smarter," you continue. "We knew you were waiting, and we stayed away until we were smart enough." Another laugh hiccups out of you. "No, until we were *damaged* enough. That's our secret. The Night Office doesn't hire the best. They hire the worst. They hire the ones who will do what it takes to survive. They make sure we have so many scars that we can't feel anything anymore. The Night Office hires monsters, because that is what humanity needs to fight monsters."

You tear at the bandage on your forearm, showing the Voerdamnikenari the bite marks. "You wanted me to think that one of them did this. You wanted me to be angry with them. You wanted me to be angry with you." You shake your head. "But I'm not, because I know that *I* did this. I bit my own arm, because that was the only way to stop myself from touching the obelisk."

The Voerdamnikenari stops flapping its wings. Its snout is opening and closing like it can't breath, even though you know it doesn't breath through that proboscis.

"I know what you are," you say. "And I've faced worse threats than you. You can't hurt me because I know who I am." You slap your arm, sending spikes of pain rocketing up past your elbow. "I know what I am."

The adrenaline lights up your brain and your blood. You can feel your fingertips tingle. "Not this brain," you tell the trembling mind eater. "Not this world."

The Voerdamnikenari suggests you turn yourself inside out and make love to a house plant.

You say the words you've been waiting to say since you woke up. The ones that will collapse the variant indexes. The ones that will invert the temporal fluctuations. The ones that will Close this breach between *here* and *there*.

The Voerdamnikenari tries to convince you to stop. It tries to entice you with kittens and the entrails of goats. It tries to threaten you with plastic forks and plush dolphins.

The air thickens in the room, and you slowly walk backward towards the door. The Voerdamnikenari starts to fade. The storm behind it slips away. The light dies in the room.

You bump into the wall next to the door, but you don't panic. There's no need. You got this.

The Voerdamnikenari begs. It wants you to pass three kumquats out of your sphincter.

You throw it a wet kiss, a gesture gravid with your contempt and dismissal. Your Wards are ready. They start to whine. The light changes in the room. It gets sharper. You start to see edges again.

And the Voerdamnikenari? You can see through its wings.

You reach for the latch on the door. "I'm a Night Office Closer, you goddamned space butterfly, and you will not pass."

It shrieks at you, but you don't feel it. You've been yelled at before, and it's not even saying hurtful stuff. It's just wailing like a cat with its paw caught in a pair of pliers. That noise will stop eventually. You know it will.

You open the door and leave the room. You don't look back. And when the door shuts, it Closes.

WELL DONE. THE NIGHT OFFICE ADMIRES THOSE WHO EMBRACE WHY THEY HAVE BEEN SELECTED FOR EMPLOYMENT.

MAPS SCORE: 96

282

You back away from the obelisk. Its light gets brighter, and within the core of that intense glow, you see—no, you *feel*—a speck of darkness. The speck becomes a dot, like a single drop of blood on a white canvas that slowly spreads into a blot. This is the drop that tarnishes the purity of the absolute offered by the obelisk. This is the question which has no answer. This is the face which should not be seen.

The stain grows. The light gets brighter. You look away, and there, burned on your retinas, is the black dot.

You hear Argot in your head. *She opened the Way. She dragged everyone in with her!*

Sagalico is there too. *They're coming for the Invocation.*

The Old Man wants in on this conversation, but you can't hear him over your team members. And there are others too, from the other team. Brinkmann, his face pinched and red, is shouting: *Put a fucking bullet in both of them. It doesn't matter. Blow their brains out.*

And you see Gull. Careful, precise Gull. The one who reminded you of a librarian, even though you she was more of a butcher than a reader. *It has to be this way*, she says, leaning in close. *They know Peele's weakness. They're already wearing the faces of her dead children. She can't shut them out.*

Argot: *Ygivennski Bifurcation Paradox! We're in a recursion loop. We have to stop it before it implodes.*

They're going to open the Void Firmament, Sagalico whimpers.

We all do bad things, the Old Man says. Or maybe Sagalico says it. Or maybe you say it. It doesn't matter. It's all true. Every last part of it.

The light is fading now. The stain is spreading. The indexes are separating.

We're on the verge, Sagalico says. *Watch for the rabbits.*

You look away from the obelisk, and still see it in every non-Euclidean corner of the room. You don't see any rabbits. You never saw any rabbits.

The light fades.

You remember something the Old Man said to you some time ago. When he was still alive? No, it was more recent than that. Oh, yes. When you were lying in that hospital bed in the infirmary. He was pretending to be an actual therapist instead of this annoying voice in your head.

It's not that the human brain can't process the enormity of cosmic indifference, he said. *It's that a very tiny part thinks it is a special snowflake. This tiny blip of ego gets worked up when confronted with the rather vast scale of the universe.*

You glance up and notice that it is snowing. You put out your hand and watch as snowflakes flash into water on your dirty and calloused palm. Each one, special and unique. Each one, nothing more than a dot of water that will be lost in whatever ocean it falls.

You stick out your tongue and try to catch one.

We all do bad things, Sagalico says.

Not today, you think.

CONGRATULATIONS. YOU HAVE SURVIVED THIS ADVANCED PSYCHOLOGICAL STRATEGIES ASSESSMENT EXERCISE.

PLEASE SUMMARIZE YOUR EXPERIENCE ON A SINGLE SHEET OF 8.5 X 11 PAPER, WHICH MAY BE MORE DIFFICULT–AND TRAUMATIC–THAN THIS EXPERIENCE.

MAPS SCORE: 99.

APPENDIX: This Advanced Psychological Strategies assessment captures the current mental state of an Asset Resource Management field operative. It is intended to provide an unbiased assessment of a field operative's capacity to function effectively in the field, as well as assess whether their personality index has been co-opted by a variety of extra-terrestrial entities, cosmic fungi, and other non-Euclidean monstrosities.

In the course of this assessment, field operatives received a Mental Acuity and Psychological Stability score that reflects the choices and decisions they made during this assessment exercise. This score may used by Night Office management when determining whether a field operative is sane enough to be placed in field operation roation.

MAPS scores will be noted on a field operative's Life Integrity Existential Schematic. MAPS scores may also be considered during advancement protocols, field operation postings, and other administrative matters as managed by the Human Asset Naturalization Department. MAPS scores may also be taken into consideration during audits by Psychological Investment Notary & Emotional Analysis Legation

NOTE: Field Operatives who have recently under-
gone a Wyxstyx-Charbellion Analysis from Labyrinthian Observation & Byzantine Elucidation
may replace any failing MAPS score from this
assessment with their Wyxstyx-Charbellion Index
score, provided that score is greater than 23.

SCORING: There were several opportunities to receive additional MAPS points. Your final score may be modified with the following options.

Each Endoluvion team member rescued: +10 points.

Each mark in your monster tracker log (SIGIL—66/d): +3 points.

Please refer to the following chart for your final Assessment Score.

- 0 > Dangerous
Field operative is under the influence of eldritch influences. RECOMMENDATION: Immediate quarantine. A Level 6 Exposure Team should immolate all containers and vessels that the field operative has recently been in contact with.

0 - 20 > Fail.
Field operative is mentally unstable and is not cleared for further field operations at this time.

21 - 50 > Fragile.
It is highly recommended that the field operative be restricted to menial office duties for 12 - 36 weeks.

51 - 65 > Serviceable. Field operative has suffered some psychological scarring. Cleared for field operations, but should not be placed in a leadership role.

66 - 80 > Satisfactory.
Field operative has demonstrated sufficient
mental resilience to continue activities at
their current status. It is recommended that
they undergo a different APS assessment following their next field operation.

81 - 96 > Excellent.
Field operative has demonstrated a significant
resilience to mental duress and psychological
assault. A citation of excellence should be
forwarded to Topical Human Utilization Management & Benefits in light of this result.

97 + > Psychotic and/or Overly Enthusiastic.
Field operative is exceptionally capable of
efficient operation in mental peregrinations
that are antithetical, amoral, and highly
unethical. Likely to be unable to function as a
productive member of society outside the Night
Office purview. Keep this one close. The Night
Office needs monsters of its own.